DEATHFLASH

Book 3 in the series,
THE CRIME FILES OF KATY GREEN

by Gene O'Neill

THE CAL WILD CHRONICLES

The Burden of Indigo (2002)
The Confessions of St. Zach (2008)
The Near Future (2015)
The Far Future (2015)

THE CRIME FILES OF KATY GREEN

Book #1: Double Jack (2011)
Book #2: Shadow of the Dark Angel (2009)
Book #3: Deathflash (2010)
Book #4: A Stick of Doublemint (2020)

OTHER NOVELS

White Tribe (2007)
Lost Tribe (2008)
Not Fade Away (2011)

COLLECTIONS

Ghosts, Spirits, Computers & World Machines (2000)
Rockers, Shamans, Manakins & Thanathespians (2001)
The Grand Struggle (2004)
Collected Tales of the Baja Express (2006)
Taste of Tenderloin (2009)
In Dark Corners (2012)
Dance of the Blue Lady (2013)
The Hitchhiking Effect (2015)
Lethal Birds (2016)
Frozen Shadows & Other Chilling Stories (2017)

DEATHFLASH

Book 3 in the series,
THE CRIME FILES OF KATY GREEN

by Gene O'Neill

with illustrations
by Greg Chapman

DARK MOON BOOKS
Los Angeles, California

Interior layout by Eric J. Guignard
Cover design by Eric J. Guignard
www.ericjguignard.com

Front cover illustration by Jelena Mišljenović
www.instagram.com/jelena.misljenovic

Interior illustrations by Greg Chapman
https://darkartiste.wordpress.com

First Dark Moon Books edition published in June, 2019
Library of Congress Control Number: 2018942098

ISBN-13: 978-1-949491-22-7 (hardback)
ISBN-13: 978-0-9988275-9-9 (trade paperback)
ISBN-13: 978-0-9989383-7-0 (e-book)

DARK MOON BOOKS
Los Angeles, California
www.DarkMoonBooks.com

Made in the United States of America

(V030920)

This book is dedicated to:
Mu Chuisle

CHAPTERS

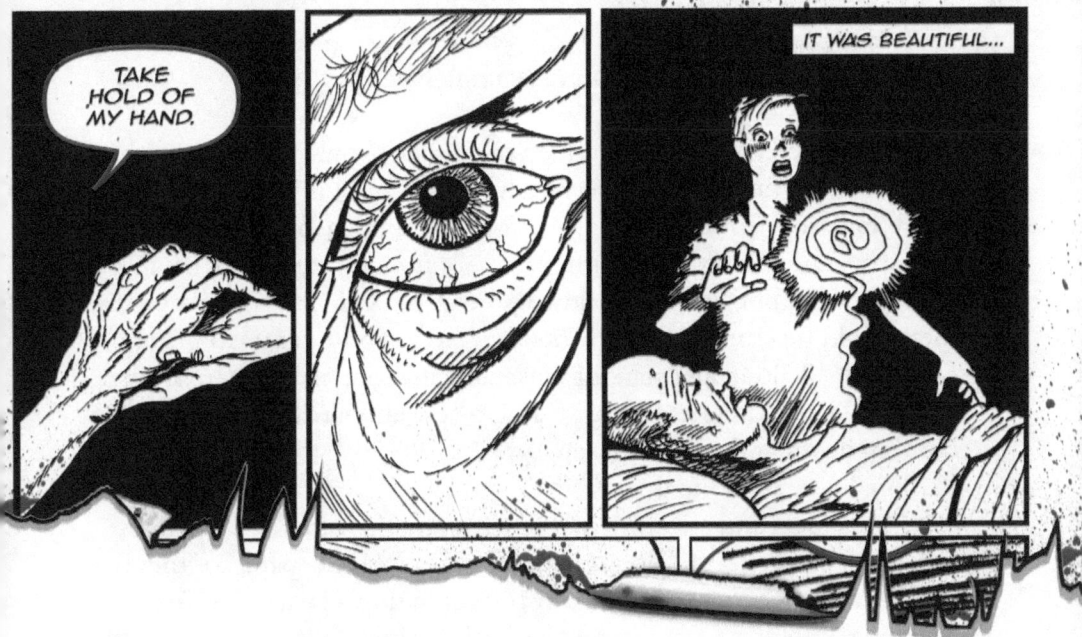

PROLOGUE

Shortly after sunrise, entire families began to assemble for the vigil at the middle of the holler, gathering in front of the white picket fence surrounding the Big House—the home of the Shepherd and the center of the tiny, isolated community. The men stood stiffly in their store-bought dark suits, the women a little more comfortable in hand-sewn black dresses, hugging Bibles to their chests, the children initially too cowed by the solemnity of the occasion to fuss much.

As the morning wore on, the air in the holler grew still, thick, and muggy, announcing a summer thunderstorm building over the surrounding Ouachita Mountains. By midmorning everyone had grown hot, tired, and cranky, the youngest children beginning to squirm and whine. But their elders sternly shushed them quiet and continued the vigil, sweltering stoically in their formal clothes.

About a quarter mile away in a two-room, tarpaper shack nestled at the edge of the great pine forest, a young man—only a little older than a high school boy—waited nervously, dressed in his brand new black suit purchased from a catalogue down at Camden by the Council of Bishops. The young man's throat was extremely dry, and he felt a terrible thirst; but he was afraid to go out back to the spring because they would be coming for him any time now. So he sat uncomfortably on his cot all alone in a state of tense anticipation, his mother, brother, and two sisters dressed in their Sunday best and already taking part in the vigil down at the Big House.

Finally, a rap at the door.

Four elders and a Bishop had finally come for him.

They escorted the young man down the dirt path to the Big House, with over a hundred and fifty people now clustered in front, all watching intently, but standing back respectfully, most a little awestruck, as the procession passed and entered the front gate.

On the way through the yard, the young man heard his younger sister blurt out his name, "Billy!"

He stopped, turned, and smiled sadly at Bet, knowing it was probably the last time he'd hear his boyhood name spoken aloud by anyone in the congregation. He realized that at this very moment his life was taking a significant change. With a deep sigh he left his family and childhood behind and followed the five men on, into the Big House.

In the upstairs main bedroom an old man, completely dressed in a well-worn, navy-blue suit, was lying very still atop his bed. His full, white mane fanned out on the pillow framing stern features. His eyes were closed and the bedding gave off a slightly medicinal smell like eucalyptus leaves after a rain.

For a moment the young man thought he was too late, that the Shepherd had passed on by himself, alone and unguided. But, then, the old man's eyelids fluttered open and two of the elders standing sentinel next to the bed helped him sit partially upright, propping his head and shoulders against the headboard. He stared in silence at the young man for almost a full minute with his steely, penetrating gaze. Then the Shepherd nodded, as if satisfied by what he saw, and ordered, in a deep voice matching his stern appearance, "It is time to bring in the Hand of the Lord God Almighty."

Wide-eyed, the young man looked on as one of the Bishops came back into the bedroom carrying a rosewood box about the size of a half-loaf of bread. He suppressed a shudder as the Head Bishop took out a white leather glove bearing a gleaming razor-sharp talon on its index fingertip. Without any added ceremony or expression, the Bishop carefully slipped the glove over the old man's right hand.

In a surprisingly steady voice, considering the circumstances, the old man said directly to the younger, "I am now ready to pass on to you the Shepherd's Gift of Sight as was passed on to me by the first Shepherd almost sixty-five years ago to the day. Use it and the Hand of God *only* in the performance of the Lord's work as determined by the Council of Bishops." He paused, pointed his left forefinger at the young man, and, in an even sterner tone, warned, "Unauthorized use of the Hand of God and Gift of Sight will bring down on *your* head painful and lasting consequences..." He paused to allow his admonition to sink in, then ordered, "Now, take hold of my bare hand."

Obediently, the young man edged closer to the bed, reached out, and clutched the old man's offered left hand, whose skin was smooth but colder than ice. Clenching his jaws in firm resolution, the Shepherd raked his own bared left arm with the hollow-pointed talon of the glove, leaving a five-inch deep crimson trail on his pale skin. He closed his eyes, his icy grip still clenching tightly around the young man's hand.

For a full minute nothing happened, everyone standing very still, as if posing for a photograph.

Silence.

Suddenly, without a sigh, cry, or word of protest, the old man convulsed violently for ten or so seconds, before finally slumping over onto his side, his darkened gray eyes open and staring dully into eternity. Simultaneous with the seizure, the cold grip relaxed, releasing the young man's hand.

As the old man settled onto his back, the young man instinctively squinted his eyes, just at the moment a blinding burst of light exploded from the dead man's chest.

Awestruck, he held his breath as the brilliant Deathflash hovered over the supine old man like a miniature nova. A sight that only the young man with the newly acquired Gift of Sight could actually experience. A few moments passed quietly, then the young man gasped and sucked in a deep breath, as the multicolored, dazzling display of light seemed to flare up even more in intensity, almost blinding.

Still, he peered at the Deathflash through squinted eyes.

So, so… stunningly beautiful!

After several more minutes of silence, the Head Bishop gently nudged the young man's shoulder.

With an effort, he tore his gaze from the hypnotically glittery ball of light and glanced into the man's face. The Bishop held out the wooden bowl of ashes and nodded ever so slightly toward the front of the house, the subtle gestures obviously intended to respectfully remind the young man of his pressing duties.

Yes, he remembered his prior instruction. The last few days' rehearsals.

He nodded back and sucked in another deep breath of air to ready himself. Then he dipped his left forefinger into the sacred ashes, leaned over the bed, and carefully drew the sign of the Shepherd on the old man's forehead.

"As the Flock's new Shepherd I have experienced the Deathflash, and our past leader's spirit is at this moment hovering, awaiting our holy guidance," the young man announced to those bedside in a gentle but strong voice, indicating his authority as the new leader, possessing the unique Gift of Sight.

After another quick glance at the Head Bishop who nodded ever so slightly, the young man ordered, "It is time for the congregational praying to commence."

One of the other Bishops led them down the stairs and outside.

The gathered congregation bowed their heads, waited, and began to murmur aloud in unison, as the newly ordained young Shepherd stepped out onto the porch of the Big House, and in a confident tone led them in the familiar spirit-guiding prayer of the Flock, "Dear Lord, please accept this soul that we commend to thee…"

ONE

Just about dark, a heavy fog rolls in from the Golden Gate, creeping up from the Embarcadero into the Tenderloin, misty tendrils swirling about your head and shoulders, icy fingers slipping down inside your black windbreaker, raising goose bumps along your neck, arms, and chest. You shiver, but smile to yourself, realizing the cold fog is really an ally, helping conceal your presence as you lurk in the shadows of the doorway. So, you pull up your collar, blow on your fists, wrap your arms around your chest, and shrug off the chilling discomfort, watching the stairs directly across Turk Street leading up to the apartment door of the dealer they call *The Cajun.*

Patience in spite of discomfort, you remind yourself, is indeed a valuable virtue. It is a trait you fortunately possess in abundance, developed in the past when you were a young boy back home, stalking game with an old single-shot .22 rifle in the mountains. The thought reminds you of early spring in the great short-leaf pine forest north of the holler, the fresh, sharp, tangy smell of the trees, the game plentiful again after the long winter. You fondly remember your family those days, usually together for the evening meal, sometimes eating game you'd proudly brought to table—your mother, Sissy, Bet, and J.J. The five of you, your alcoholic father long gone, little more than a bad dream by that time... And, oh yes, all those wonderful Sundays. On Sundays, the family with the Flock, gathered together to pray and sing and listen to the sermon, to share the evening meal. Everyone so close back then. And your family, how proud they all were when you were selected to be the new Shepherd. *You,* a member of a pious family of so modest means—

You blink, jarred out of the reverie. That's all over, you think, silently chastising yourself for dwelling in the past, letting the mist chill the warm memories. You have a new kind of life here in the West, intentionally cut off from your family. Still involved in the Lord's work, but in a different, less formal, way. And daydreaming about the past, your old life, your family, is not constructive in any way. It only stirs regret for decisions made.

You shudder and blow on your hands again.

As you wait, you occupy your mind by attempting to separate and pinpoint the early evening sounds of the city: A far away wail of a squad car, somewhere from the west, probably on busy lower Van Ness; nearby angry Spanish curses from an open window a story above your head, then, *"Puta,"* with a smack, followed by loud silence; the distinctive voice of B.B. King singing "The Thrill is Gone" in a bar a half block downtown, the Delta Blues reminding you of the good time spent in Chicago; the powerful diesel engine acceleration of a double-bus as it begins to gear up from low to second over on Geary Street—you can almost smell the belched fumes. The joyful sound of a small child's laughter is carried on the drifting, thick mist from somewhere from the east, carefree, so full of life. You are lulled—

Suddenly, a figure emerges from the doorway at the top of the stairs across the street. You squint and focus your gaze.

It's *him*, Jaime, wearing a green and gold A's cap turned backward... And he is indeed backsliding into his old habit as you suspected. The guilt is clearly visible on his young face in the furtive way that he looks about, like a kid with hidden candy shoplifted from a convenience store, not wanting to share with his neighborhood buddies. No doubt he's scored some dope—*Mexican tar*—from The Cajun.

After cautiously walking down the stairs, he pauses for a moment on the sidewalk, glancing both ways before heading west on Turk toward Van Ness, leaving you still hidden across the street in the misty shadows of the doorway.

Forcing yourself to wait another five seconds, you eventually follow him, hanging back on your side of the street, trying to maintain at least a quarter block of separation between Jaime and yourself.

A half minute later, after crossing Leavenworth, he darts to your side of Turk without even glancing down the normally busy block for vehicle traffic, and he immediately disappears into an alley.

You speed up to a jog, concerned now that you've lost sight of him.

But at the mouth of the alley, you halt and cautiously peer into the foggy darkness.

A sudden flare of light illuminates Jaime, who is now sitting on a pile of flattened cardboard, with his bare arm already tied off and exposed to your view. So anxious to fix, he hasn't even taken the time to properly conceal himself. Nor does he even glance back toward the street when you appear.

After a moment, you work your way quietly along the shadowed wall, edging closer. Finally stopping only a few feet away... Still, he is not aware of your presence. Or perhaps he just ignores it.

Laid out picnic-fashion on a wrinkled brown paper bag on the boy's lap are an empty yellow balloon, syringe, water bottle, and cotton ball, the waning flame from the matchbook held under a blackened spoon. After the flame finally dies out, he flips away the worthless matchbook, places the cotton ball in the cooked tar, carefully inserts the syringe into the makeshift filter, and sucks up the dark fluid. Then, with a steady and practiced hand, he hits a raised vein inside his elbow, and leaves the needle dangling in his arm as he releases the narrow rubber hose he's used as a tourniquet.

Fascinated, you see a string of crimson backwash into the slender instrument, as you ease a step closer, carefully slipping on the glove in your windbreaker pocket, avoiding the hazardous razor-sharp point of the index finger talon. The backslider is still unaware of your stealthy approach, so completely absorbed in the ritual-like nature of his drug use. As you watch, his back stiffens briefly; then, with a loud moan, he slumps back onto a short stack of tied-up, old newspaper bundles, and his body goes completely limp.

A disturbing sight to be sure.

You shake your head with dismay at the cavalier risk, knowing that tar heroin is an extremely strong opiate, a high-powered sedative, and each fix, because of poor quality control, is a potentially fatal overdose that can shut down the heart and respiration. The OD'd user, after uttering a characteristic, deep-throated cough-grunt, slips into an unconscious state and may never wake up without immediate intervention, his neglected soul left to wander aimlessly in the eternal night.

No way that is happening here now.

Moving next to Jaime's side, you see his eyes are closed, his facial expression completely relaxed, almost a look of... *of what?*

Contentment. He looks as if he were completely at peace, not a care in the world. You stare down at his clothes, threadbare and wrinkled, his dirty hands, and his emaciated build—

Ridiculous!

You barely suppress an outcry of righteous indignation at this self-indulgent stupidity by sucking in a deep jolt of icy air; then, closing your eyes while struggling for self-control, you gather yourself together. You blink, almost composed now. It's time to end this stupid backslider's meaningless existence, you tell yourself, time for you to execute your self-assigned duty, save his soul in spite of himself. He has relapsed for the last time. Burned his last bridge.

"Oh, yes," you murmur under your breath, as if punctuating your resolve.

Kneeling, you withdraw your gloved hand and, with the talon on the Hand of God, you carefully scratch deeply the boy's exposed arm, just below the dangling syringe.

His eyelids flicker and try to focus as he slurs a feeble protest, "Hey, man, who—? Get the fuck away from me."

In slow motion he reaches across with his right hand, and flicks his fingers back and forth over his arm, as if he were feebly shooing away a pesky mosquito. A half-hearted gesture at best. But his hand drops back to his side. You're only a phantom in his twilight zone of semiconsciousness.

You wait and watch intently.

A minute later and the poison begins to take effect, making Jaime abruptly sit up straight and moan loudly. "Ohhh."

He stares at you wide-eyed with pinned pupils, without any apparent recognition, and gasps for breath; then his body convulses violently for several seconds, as if hit by a lethal jolt of high voltage current. Finally, he sags back down on the cardboard, collapsing limply in on himself, his eyes still wide open, but glazed over, forever unseeing.

Backsliding over—

At that moment bright light explodes from his chest.

The Deathflash!

Unable to even twitch, you stand frozen in place, consumed by the anticipated phenomenon, peering at the nebula of tiny dots glowing like a million distant stars in the sky on a wintry night—a fortune of twinkling rubies, emeralds, turquoises, opals, diamonds. So compellingly lovely.

You close your eyes, savoring the effect on your other senses: the richly luxurious clinging *warmth* of it, like being bathed in moist subtropical sunshine; the *smell*, the mixed perfume of a thousand exotic fresh blossoms; and the tinkling exotic *sound* of alien music, a soothing full symphony from heaven.

All of it so elegantly blended and wonderful.

For a brief period of time you remain motionless, actually holding your breath as you surrender yourself completely to the powerful euphoria of the unique experience, so settling, so calming… But you're unable to suppress a loud groan of pleasure, which causes you to gasp loudly for breath, disturbing the entranced state.

You blink, still dazed by the experience, look about, gradually becoming fully aware of the filthy, littered nature of the alley around yourself and the shimmering Deathflash. A dismal background for such a grand moment. Only then are you able to regain a measure of your previous self-control, just as the individual dots of light seem to coalesce into one large brilliant critical mass:

Flaring,

Hovering,

Waiting.

Ah, yes, waiting…

You remind yourself of your remaining responsibilities.

"Of course," you whisper into the drab darkness of the alley with renewed conviction, stirring yourself to action.

Quickly, you strip off the Hand of God and slip it into your windbreaker pocket, avoiding any accidents with the tip of the talon. You open an old snuffbox, dip your finger into the sacred ashes carried from the holler in the mountains, and, bending over, you scrawl the Shepherd's sign on the boy's forehead. Then, after another deep sigh, you bow your head, close your eyes, drop to one knee, and commence the prayer that will guide the hovering spirit into the hereafter to meet its maker, "Dear Lord, please accept this soul that I commend to thee…"

Rising to your feet a few seconds after the disappearance into eternity of the Deathflash and conclusion of your prayer, you feel the familiar flush building around your eyes, followed by the tunneling of vision and the faintly medicinal smell of eucalyptus. All this just moments before the sliver of white-hot agony plunges into the sinuses above your eyes. And in your head, you again hear the old man's admonition from so long ago: *Unauthorized use of the Hand of God and Gift of Sight will bring down on your head painful consequences.*

Painful, oh, so painful.

He was right.

Yes, he was.

You groan as you momentarily lose grasp of consciousness…

2

A little later you find yourself back at your apartment on Eddy Street at the corner of Polk, only a few blocks away from where you left the backslider's empty husk in the cluttered alley, the short walk home through the fog only a hazy memory. Your last vivid memory is the explosion of pain in your head and the Shepherd's voice, followed almost immediately by the now familiar blackout. Excruciating pain, devastating.

You step into the bathroom and wash your face with cold water, consumed with guilt; all the old nagging questions surface again.

Are you being punished for the self-assigned work, unauthorized by the Council of Bishops, like the old Shepherd implied years ago?

Are the debilitating headaches a kind of retribution?

Or more like a warning?

But from whom?

Or are you really just going mad?

For some time you have feared the latter.

You pause a moment, staring at your reflection in the mirror, pondering…

And just like all the past moments of soul-searching—*No answers appear to the questions*. No guidance.

You do not know what is really happening to you or why.

You dry your face.

All you know for sure is the headaches are becoming more intense, more debilitating, coming sooner after the departure of the Deathflash, and the blackouts lasting longer, rendering you vulnerable at the scene. An intolerable, dangerous situation. A terrible risk for you and the work. But what can you do?

After another moment, you shrug, forcing the lingering questions and guilt to the back of your mind.

You should now be studying your Bible, but you're too drained, the whole experience of the Deathflash still too fresh in your memory. In fact, you remind yourself with a sense of regret that you rarely study scripture anymore, your thoughts usually too preoccupied with plans to experience the guidance of another needy soul, the time between Deathflashes growing shorter and shorter—only a few days now—your need growing ever stronger and more demanding.

For a sobering second or two you experience a new surge of remorse, realizing that you are now focusing on *your* need over any consideration of the needs of the straying flock. But it's only a fleeting twinge that you quickly turn away from and shift focus, gazing out your second-story front window, absently noting the surreal fuzzy orbs of fog-shrouded streetlights disappearing up Polk Street: One, two, three, four, five… and all the others out of sight. So much responsibility, so many wayward spirits in this modern-day version of the Biblical Sodom and Gomorrah, so many lost sheep requiring your special assistance.

You sigh to yourself, feeling exhausted and wrung out, bearing the weight of it all. It is indeed a cumbersome burden, the accompanying headaches taking a truly debilitating toll on your energies. But, you are willing to pay the price, because you have to.

You have no choice: It is your duty.

GREEN HORNET AND CATO, AGAIN

S unlight streams down warmly on the panhandle of Golden Gate Park where Haight Street dead-ends into Stanyon Street. One of the two sites for this year's San Francisco Recreation and Parks District, 3-on-3 Women's Summer Basketball Tournament. The site has drawn a fairly big crowd for a Saturday morning, most of the spectators packed into the three sets of portable bleachers lining the north side of the hoop areas. Games are in simultaneous progress on all three Panhandle courts on this second day of the single elimination tournament.

On Court 3, Katy Green dribbles to the top of the key, considers a bounce pass to CeCe, who is flashing across from the right corner; but instead of making the obvious move to her open teammate, Katy pushes a lob over the other team just above the rim that a leaping Sidney anticipates perfectly, catches on her fingertips, and guides through the metal-stringed basket for the winning hoop.

20-14.

Katy grins to herself, thoroughly satisfied with the performance of *Little Women*—one of her childhood favorite books, and an obviously ironic team nickname. At a lanky 6' she is the smallest member of the team. CeCe Reyes is a husky 6'-1" and Sidney Williams 6'-3". A physically striking trio of women.

The Court 3 spectators are all hooting and clapping now, some black dude in the crowd shouting loudly over the applause in a falsetto ghetto voice, "*Ooh-whee*, that sista gotta be name' Swoop, y'all."

"Why's that, bro?" a companion asks, playing the straight man.

"Cuz she jus' *swoop* down on tha' basket like a big-ass bird, man!"

Of course that draws a laugh or at least a chuckle from most everyone rising to leave from that area of the stands.

Katy's team shakes hands with the other team, waves at the departing crowd, then goes over to a south courtside bench and their gym bags.

"Katy, that last pass was so sweet the ball actually felt sticky," Sidney jokes, her dark face shiny with perspiration.

All three women towel off and gulp down a drink of water.

Holding her bottle of Crystal Geyser in hand, Katy realizes that Little Women could actually make the quarterfinals tomorrow, *if* they win today's afternoon game, which means they have a chance of making the semifinals next Saturday. She glances at her two teammates, feeling a growing tingle of excitement in the pit of her stomach. If everything breaks right they may even be playing for the city championship on the Marina courts next Sunday afternoon. Oh, yeah—

Whoa, girl, Katy says to herself, reining in her enthusiasm. Get a grip on yourself, kiddo. One game at a time. And remember, girl, this is only a summer recreation basketball tournament, for crissake, not March Madness. She smiles wryly, recalling their team goal a few days ago: *Just be competitive with most of the other teams, think of the games as good workouts.*

Yeah, right!

Katy had hooked up with Sidney Williams earlier that spring, both spectators at the famed Oakland Recreation Tournament. But they'd only recently found the perfect third member for Little Women, after CeCe Reyes had graduated from Sacramento State—Katy's old college team—and moved to San Francisco. Katy had worked out a number of times with CeCe four years ago at American River Community College in Sacramento, the summer after the younger woman graduated from Natomas High School, and later Katy watched CeCe star at power forward for a year with ARC before moving on to play three years at Sac State.

At that moment in her reverie, Katy spots Johnny Cato coming across the court from the nearly empty section of the stands, and waves.

"Terrific game, ladies," he says, giving Sid and CeCe a high five and Katy a smack on the cheek. "That last was some kinda pass, kiddo."

After a brief post-game audit, CeCe and Sid excuse themselves to go check out their afternoon opponent, still competing on Court 1.

"We play again at 2:30," Katy explains to Johnny. "Probably be the team from USF, those three on Court 1 dressed in green. They're tough and young." She shrugs dismissively, as if saying, *Oh, well.*

Katy will soon be thirty-four and though she'd never admit it to Johnny or her teammates, she is indeed feeling the physical and emotional strain of the three games already played in the first two days of the tournament. She's tired, an irritating twinge in her lower back, and her legs feeling heavy.

"Yeah, but you guys are bigger, experienced, and shoot better," Johnny says, ignoring Katy's look. "Lotta people courtside are talking up Little Women as the favorite to win the Panhandle semifinals."

Katy shrugs, trying to be more nonchalant than she feels, and takes another long drink of water, grinning inwardly. With his broken nose and scar tissue around both eyebrows, Johnny's ruggedly handsome face looks like it belongs in boxing headgear in a gym, working on the big bag as he waits to spar in the ring, certainly *not* on a basketball court, critiquing her team in a women's summer tournament. And, indeed, he had been an undefeated collegiate light-heavyweight years ago before she met him, when Sacramento State College still had a boxing team. Even at forty-three he's remained in excellent shape, working out regularly at the Harrison Street Gym downtown, occasionally sparring with one of its more illustrious club fighters, Pat Lawler, who once actually upset Roberto Duran in a middleweight match.

"You want to maybe catch some lunch?" he asks, an innocently casual expression on his face. "I'm springing."

She recognizes the look. Oh, oh. "What's going on, big spender?" she asks, making a *c'mon-and-give-it-to-me* gesture with the fingers of her right hand.

He grins a little sheepishly. "Well, I just think we have a case you might be interested in hearing about, that's all. No big deal."

"Me? I'm a writer, pal, not a private investigator. That's your bag."

"Yeah, I know. But this friend of mine, Richie O'Brien, believes there's a dangerous *nut* running loose in the city, and this psycho murdered his younger brother, Jaime, last week."

Katy has heard Johnny speak of Richie O'Brien a number of times, always with respect. O'Brien is a recovering addict—once a longtime heroin user—who's been clean for over eight years and works at Walden House, one of the City's renowned drug rehabilitation programs. He's also the secretary at Johnny's NA meeting, and apparently a straight-up type of guy. This is the first time she's heard about a brother or a murder.

"How come he doesn't go to the law?" Katy asks, slipping on her well-worn, green and gold, Sac State Hornets sweatsuit.

"He did, but homicide isn't interested," Johnny replies with a shrug. "They don't think his brother's death is a homicide, only a routine dope OD."

"So?"

"Richie doesn't buy the OD cause of death. He thinks someone killed his brother, and maybe *two* other junkies the week before Jaime."

"Why would someone want to kill three dope addicts?"

"He doesn't know, although he has a theory. But he wants us to help him check it out. Heard about our Green Hornet and Cato rep."

"Our reputation?" Katy smiles wryly. "Uh-huh, who told him, I wonder?"

Katy Green and John Cato haven't worked together professionally for some time, not since moving to San Francisco from Sacramento, where they'd been nicknamed the Green Hornet and Cato by the *Bee* and local TV stations. They'd partnered together effectively as Sacramento PD homicide detectives for over five years, catching several notorious criminals, including the 400-pound murder-rapist Double Jack, and the equally infamous Red Chief, the completely hairless psycho giant, who had killed and scalped three women before they finally stopped him. But Katy has been a full-time writer now for three years—two published novels and recently some engaging nonfiction features for the *San Francisco Bay Guardian*, including an interview with her science fiction writer friend, Kim Stanley Robinson. And Johnny has been retired from the Sacramento PD for almost two years, recently going into the P.I. business with his old friend, Hap Sullivan, a retired San Francisco detective.

But, with the exception of movies, PIs rarely get involved in homicide investigations, Katy reminds herself, curious despite her professed lack of interest.

"Anyhow, I was hoping you would come to my NA meeting tonight and at least meet Richie."

"What do you really think about his suspicions?"

"Despite SF Homicide's response, I think Richie deserves to at least be heard," Johnny says. "And if he *is* on to something like he thinks—three linked murders of young junkies—it might indeed be some kind of psycho killer operating with impunity, and right up your alley, kiddo."

Katy was the homicide detective partner with an intuitive, almost supernatural, knack for getting into the heads of psychotic or sociopathic serial murderers, her fascination dating back to Abnormal Psychology courses at Sac State. And in fact, both her published novels—*The Burden of Indigo* and *The Crimson Man*—although marketed as science fiction, actually were really psychological studies of convicted criminals, only both books set in the future with some intriguing background.

Of course she agrees to attend the NA meeting after she nails Johnny for a super lunch of their favorite tapas at the nearby *Cha Cha Cha*, half a block east from where Haight dead ends into Stanyon.

2

Little Women win the 2:30 game against the younger but less experienced USF team, Katy getting into that special zone, swishing seven of eight long jumpers. She calls it the Eddie Felson zone or touch, after the slick, pool-shooting character played by Paul Newman in the movie, *The Hustler,* who poetically describes to Piper Laurie exactly what it feels like when he's on in straight pool, his arm directly in synch with his brain, everything dropping *plunk, plunk, plunk.* And he's absolutely convinced the ball is going down before it even nears the pocket.

Little Women will play the quarterfinal game tomorrow at 1:00 on Panhandle Court 1 against the *Purple Gators,* a good team made up of stars from San Francisco State's recent teams, and, if they manage to win, move onto the semifinals next Saturday at the Panhandle courts.

She's stoked.

3

At 7:30 p.m. Katy is at the Capp Street Meeting at the Community Center in the heart of the Mission, listening to a disabled addict tell his story.

It's a big room filled with half a dozen rows of folding chairs. She's sitting in the last row, an unused stage with closed curtains at her back, the air around her thick with blue smoke and charged with a kind of nervous energy generated by the large crowd, who are mostly quiet now, except for their vibrations. Many of the people are wound pretty tight, some probably tweaked, and a few obviously loaded—Johnny says every addict comes to his first meeting loaded. Of course there are a number just getting their *book* signed, ordered by some judicial authority to attend so many meetings. Katy had been to a few meetings in Sacramento, both NA and AA, with Johnny—he'd had a drinking and cocaine problem after going through a long, nasty divorce when they first teamed up in homicide eight years ago. But she's never attended a Capp Street meeting since moving to the city.

A different experience, indeed.

This Mission crowd is a pretty rough-looking bunch, she thinks, glancing around, suppressing an impulse to get up and move closer to Johnny at the front table. The men, a mix of mostly Latino and White, many bearing heavily tattooed arms, necks, and even faces, the quality and monotonous blueness of the tattoos giving away their prison origins; the women a broader ethnic mix, including more Blacks and Asians, many dressed up in gay colors, wearing dangling earrings and bright bracelets, the heavy makeup not quite hiding the hardened features and ancient eyes that have seen it all, some of them also displaying tattoos. But their tattoos are a little more subtle than the male subject matter, like a flowered anklet, or butterfly bracelet, or a Janis Joplin heart on an exposed breast. A crowd with *colorful* backgrounds, to say the least.

Before the speaker was introduced, there was a lot of mixing, flirting, loud signifying between the men and women—doing the thirteenth step, as Johnny calls it. Of course it's considered poor form at a meeting to really hit seriously on someone or do anything else of a personal nature, like using a meeting contact to get a job and so forth; but here in the Mission, meetings are apparently conducted a little more loosely than up at Sacramento. Different clientele for sure.

So, this one-legged dude is running his story, and Katy finds it really kind of interesting.

He's rode the whole circuit: Alienated all his family and friends, been in jail numerous times, even a three year stretch in San Quentin, been through several structured rehabilitation programs, exploited numerous women, and personally witnessed four fatal overdoses. But nothing really affects him; he always goes back on dope—he's "… hardcore, man." He's standing there on one leg with crutches as he tells all this, having taken off his prosthetic leg at the knee. As he winds down, it's obvious he's done it for a reason.

"So, what got me here, right?" he rhetorically asks the crowd, balancing on one leg, holding his crutches in one hand and bending over to rub his stump with his free hand. "*This* finally did it," he continues in a low, sad voice, pointing at his missing limb. "Nothing impressed me until I lost my leg, and then…" He paused a long time for dramatic effect, before smiling thinly, shaking his head sadly, and finally admitting in a barely audible, hoarse voice, "It suddenly hit me, man: doing shit is fucking *dangerous,* you hear what I'm tellin' you."

The crowd cracks up, releasing a lot of pent-up energy, all the noise not necessarily humorous laughter, because there are many here who have been using long enough to have experienced junkie ulcers just like the speaker did on his leg, the abscesses caused by infections from dirty needles. Or, in his case, not being able to hit a vein because legs and arms were too scarred and ropey, and he'd impatiently muscled the injection, the leg becoming infected with a deep, long-term, non-healing abscess that turned to gangrene.

Katy just watches this guy grin shyly, kind of embarrassed by the applause—apparently his first NA talk. He sounds like he must be somewhere in his late thirties, maybe early forties, but he's skinny and stooped, his hawkish features heavily-lined, and of course, he's got a cigarette in hand, even smoking during his story, occasionally pausing and coughing. *Jesus*, she thinks after looking hard and reflecting for a moment, this guy is really a used-up, frail husk, an *old man*, the years on dope devouring his youth. She shudders.

People are standing up now, moving restlessly, heading for coffee, or outside to smoke, or to the restrooms located across the patio in another building, or just leaving—anywhere to just be moving. Katy notices that there's one noticeable difference between the AA and NA groups—NA people seem a bit more hyperactive.

She stands and lets the crowd thin out more, before moving up front to where Johnny and Richie sit at a folding cafeteria table, one corner stacked with NA literature, surrounded by a dozen people extending their paperwork. As the meeting's official secretary, Richie has to sign the various 12-Step or other recovery books to validate for some court or P.O. or social worker, that the bearer actually attended this Capp Street meeting on this date.

The last book is finally signed, and Katy steps next to the table.

"Katy Green, this is Richard O'Brien," Johnny says, formally introducing the guy who'd read the NA traditions at the opening of the meeting. He's tall and thin, wearing worn Levis and a faded black Joe Cocker T-shirt; his hair cut short and face freshly shaven. Angular, heavily lined features. Up close she sees he's older than he looked from a distance... At least thirty-five. And yet, attractive, handsome even, resembling a scuffed-up version of a young Clint Eastwood.

Richie leans across the table and offers his hand. "Hello, Katy, I've heard lots of good things about you," he says warmly, his soft, gentle voice contrasting with his hard features. "Actually, if you can believe it about me, I've even read one of your sci-fi books, *The Burden of Indigo*. It was really interesting and moving, especially the redemption scene with the rainbow man at the conclusion. The whole thing pretty heavy stuff, probably makes readers pause and think about outcasts in our own society. I just got a copy of *The Crimson Man* from Johnny and look forward to reading it, too."

Katy smiles broadly, thinking, *I like this guy already.*

"Why don't we get some coffee and find a place outside to talk?" Johnny suggests.

They cross the room to a table with a pair of coffee urns, several plates of cookies, napkins, a carton of milk, a bowl of sugar packets, and three stacks of paper cups.

Johnny introduces Katy to a young guy—late twenties, early thirties—in a blue-and white-checked western shirt standing kind of slumped behind the table. "Katy, this is Jackson Williams, who has the job to come early and make our coffee, set up the refreshment table. The quality of the coffee has definitely improved in the two weeks he's been coming to Capp Street."

Katy shakes his hand, knowing that taking on different meeting commitments and giving back is part of the NA recovery plan. Johnny is presently taking care of all the group's literature, hauling it back and forth from their apartment.

"My pleasure, ma'am," Jackson says politely with a slight but distinct country drawl. "Care to try an outstanding peanut butter cookie, homemade by Donna C?" He pushes the plate forward.

"Thank you," Katy replies, putting a cookie on a napkin and noticing that Jackson has really unusual eyes—Paul Newman blue—with an alert, keen gaze. Despite his country bumpkin dress and speech, Katy decides, he's probably a sharp guy, a real *Cool Hand Luke*.

She takes a bite of her cookie. "Hmm, good."

Cool Hand makes an *I-told-you-so* face and nods.

"See you later, Jackson," Johnny says, taking Katy's arm and leading her and Richie outside. The three of them find a place to sit on the far side of the patio, away from the clusters of people smoking, visiting, and talking loudly.

"Tell Katy what you told me about Jaime and your suspicions, Richie," Johnny suggests after they get comfortable, taking a sip from his coffee cup.

"Well, last week, my brother died in an alley in the Tenderloin, after recently going back out—"

"Going back out?" Katy interrupts, suspecting but not really positive what the expression means.

"Using dope again… relapsing," Richie explains.

Katy nods, finishes her cookie, and quietly stares back at him.

"Cops think he OD'd. And two friends, too, all in the last two and a half weeks. I don't think any of them really died from an OD."

"Why not?" Katy asks, her tone brisk, businesslike now.

He combs his fingers through his short hair, and then looks Katy square in the eye. "I know this probably sounds a little bit thin, and actually, it's really just a kinda street sense, a gut feeling, if you know what I mean. OD's usually come in bunches when there's high-grade or a bad batch of dope on the street. But there's been no bad dope out there lately… And, there are several other small, but significant things. To begin with, Jaime'd been living the last two weeks at Brother Timothy's but was turned away the very night he was wasted. You know the private homeless shelter in the Tenderloin on Jones?"

"No, but go on," Katy says, taking a drink of her coffee.

"Well, coincidentally, his two friends—Joey Bartkowski and D.L. Mathews—they were wasted the same night they were turned away from Brother Timothy's…" He pauses, looking at her intently.

Katy doesn't say anything, just sips her coffee.

Richie continues, "And all three had been in Walden House's 815 program, but were recent splitees—"

"What's a splitee and the 815 program?" Katy interrupts again.

"Walden House's two adult rehab program locations are at 815 Buena Vista West and 890 Hayes Street, known simply as 815 and 890. A *splitee* is someone who leaves before completing the entire program. If he's thrown out he's *spotted*; if he can't ever come back to the program he's *banned*. Walden House argot, you know."

"I get it," Katy says, impressed more by Richie's appropriate use of the word 'argot' than anything else said so far.

"Anyhow, even though they were splitees, they were all three still attending meetings right here at Capp Street until just recently."

Katy frowns. "Yeah, okay, I understand what you're driving at now. *Same* rehab program, *same* NA meeting, and *same* homeless shelter. Then they go out and they all get whacked? Sorry, but that doesn't seem like much of a pattern indicating murder to me. How many others follow a similar path and nothing happens or they do actually OD? You got anything else to support your belief?"

Richie nods. "Yeah, one other thing. I think the dude left his *mark*, at least on Jaime."

"Like how?" Johnny asks, obviously hearing this for the first time.

"With the capital letter, *J*," Richie answers. "I ID'd Jaime at the morgue, and I saw what appeared to be a smudged *J* signed with something like a charcoal stick on his forehead. Didn't even mention it to the cops at the time. Wasn't thinking murder at that point. I don't know for a fact about the other two, but I bet he marked them, too..." He pauses for a second and lifts up his hands in a defensive posture toward Katy. "Yeah, okay, I'll admit that from the cops' point of view they all look a lot like everyday OD's. And my suspicion is poorly backed up. But I just ain't buying it, okay? It doesn't shake down right." His expression now is determined, stubborn, resigned.

Silence for a few seconds.

Katy asks, "Assuming you're right about your suspicion, how do you think this guy killed Jaime and the other two?"

"Well, this is the really slick part," Richie explains, "that makes Jaime's murder definitely appear like a routine OD. No signs of violence... except for this funny scrape, more like a deep scratch, inside his arm near his new tracks, like a pissed-off chick might make with a long fingernail. But Jaime hasn't had any time for women, not lately, anyhow." He looks away, shaking his head sadly, his eyes distant, a kind of hurt expression on his face, softening his angular, hard features. After a long moment, he blinks, clears his throat, and focuses a slightly moist gaze directly on Katy again. "I know this might sound farfetched, too, but I think the dude actually poisoned Jaime somehow with that scratch, and probably the others in a similar way, too."

"*Poison?*" Katy repeats in disbelief, momentarily surprised by Richie's suggestion. She knows that in the Tenderloin or Haight or in the Mission, anyplace in the city where street people are found murdered, they're usually killed with an obvious weapon of some kind—bludgeoned with a piece of pipe, stabbed with a knife, or shot with a gun. But poisoning is extremely rare in *all* homicides nationwide, less than a percent or so. She remembers only one case in Sacramento, just before she transferred into Homicide, the old lady... What was her name? Ah, Dorothea Puentes. She supposedly poisoned nine male boarders for their Social Security checks. And the forensic people never actually found traces of poison in any of the nine victims in that case, just assumed it.

Her attention shifts back to O'Brien's lined face, the pain he represses.

"Hey, Richie, I'm really sorry about your brother," she says in a less aggressive tone, shrugging sympathetically. Johnny had mentioned earlier that Richie actually tried to raise Jaime the last six or so years, their parents dead. And she can identify with that. Her parents were killed in an automobile wreck on the freeway in San Diego when she was ten. She'd bounced around foster homes kind of lost, until Gerri Robinson, a black cop and her PAL basketball coach became her big sister role model, gave her direction, actually got her to go to Sac State. "It must be hard talking about him like this in the past tense?"

He nods back. "Yeah, it is." He shrugs, his eyes dry now. "It's gotta be done though."

"Okay, so you know *when*, you know *how*," Katy continues, pushing her empathy to the back of her consciousness. "But *who* would kill Jaime and the others? A dealer, another user, someone like that? And *why*—?"

"Nah, I don't think it was a user or dealer. Jaime didn't rip off anyone for dope, nothing like that—he still had a few dollars left when he died, from working as a cook while at 815. He'd only been using again a few days. Actually, I think he was hit because he had gone out again. Same with the others. Could be someone from here at this meeting, or Brother Timothy's, maybe Walden House; someone who knew that they were back on the street, knew they were using, and then punished them—"

"Wait a minute!" Katy cuts him off again. "You mean to tell me that you *think* your brother and the other two were all poisoned for using again, relapsing on their recovery?"

"Yeah, exactly," Richie replies, looking one hundred percent convinced. "Could be he's whacked out others, too, others we just don't know about. The invisible underclass that society pays little attention to: junkies, whores, winos, and the homeless. Dude's on a crusade. Maybe that's why he's signing the victims he's punishing with a *J*, some kind of religious significance in the letter, standing for Jesus or Job or maybe Jehovah—the moral hand of righteous indignation striking out, you know?"

Katy nods, infected slightly now by Richie's intensity and imagination, knowing that in addition to a sexual element that often serial murders do indeed have a religious aspect. Like Red Chief in Sacramento. "Okay," she says, "okay, I think that all makes sense."

"Of course, I'm not exactly flush right now, but I can probably get a loan, or maybe scrape something together right here from a few friends, to help pay at least part of your retainer up front—"

"Hey, man, that isn't the problem at the moment," Johnny says, rubbing his broken nose, something he does when pissed, unsettled, nervous, or considering a tough problem. "First, Katy and I need to convince ourselves that Jaime and the others were actually murdered, you know. Then… Hell, maybe I can take you on as a kind of *pro bono* project, knock it off our income taxes like the big-shot law firms do."

"Well, I've got a better idea for a sort of barter payment plan," Katy suggests thoughtfully. "For some time I've been thinking about doing an in-depth feature piece for the *Guardian* on the whole local heroin bit. You know, who's actually an addict, where it's bought, the health hazards of sharing needles including getting AIDS and hepatitis, the difficulty of withdrawal, and of course something about programs like Walden House and the NA twelve steps. You know, everything significant. Not a medical diatribe, like that, something more personal from the street. But I could use a knowledgeable guide and resource person. An insider. What about you, Richie? Interested in an exchange of expertise?"

"There you go, that sounds like a great idea," Johnny adds, smiling at Katy.

"Yeah, right on," Richie agrees immediately, tasting his coffee for the first time and making a face. "Cold." He dumps the contents of the cup into a planter box, then crumples the container and tosses it in the nearby trash barrel. "Time someone did a good in-depth newspaper article, anyhow. Like the documentary on HBO last Wednesday night at 10:00, 'The Dark End of the Street,' by Steven Okazaki. Did either of you see it?"

Johnny and Katy shake their heads.

"Too bad. It would've been helpful for your project, Katy. Okazaki followed five San Francisco addicts for… two years, I think, showing it all. These were young, bright people in the beginning. The film focuses on the nightmare downslide of addiction, perhaps implying a little too hopeless of a conclusion. But it should've opened a lot of viewer's eyes, especially young people. Maybe I can get a copy of it through Walden House."

"Great," Katy says, nodding. "But, before we get too excited, let's do a little preliminary checking like Johnny said, see if we can really be of any help," she cautions Richie. "Then, *if* we take it on, you and I will talk some more about the guided tour—you making installment payments?"

They all rise and shake hands.

Richie goes back inside.

Katy and Johnny leave the Capp Street Meeting, headed for the Marina and their apartment.

"SEE THAT GIRL, KATY, CALL HER SWOOP? SHE IS PLAYIN TO WIN, WIN IT ALL!"

LITTLE WOMEN VS. THE PURPLE GATORS

S unday at 1:00, Katy, Sid, and CeCe play the team of young ex-stars from San Francisco State on Court 1 of the Panhandle courts.

Both teams are apparently a little too tight, missing their first couple of shots, the boisterous crowd of two hundred or so spilling over out of the bleachers, sitting and standing along courtside, joking, cheering, and being loudly supportive of their favorite players. Sidney's newest fan, the black dude with the falsetto voice, back again, and easily heard over the hubbub, "Yeah, yeah, Swoop, y'all got game, girl!"

On their third possession Katy drives past her defender, then pulls up suddenly and nets a ten-footer to break the scoring ice.

2-0.

Winner's outs.

Little Women pass the ball around, in and out, all three touching it; but CeCe misses a long set, and the Gators rebound, take it out, and score.

2-2.

They follow that with a long jumper off a screen.

2-4.

Nevertheless, it soon becomes apparent that the smaller Gators are indeed at a serious disadvantage. Katy's team is allowing only one opportunity, effectively boxing out—screening away their man so the basket is circled by Little Women after each missed shot by their opponents—and snagging every defensive rebound. And nothing goes inside on Sidney, all Gator drives rejected emphatically. The game is soon out of hand, after those two initial Gators' scores.

After a continuous run of eight straight baskets by Little Women, Katy hits another ten-foot jumper and it's over.

20-4.

A surprising rout for a quarterfinal game.

Little Women will be in the semifinals next Saturday, and they have picked up quite a few fans, who shake their hands, pound their backs, shout encouragement, including Sidney's number one fan, "Yeah, yeah, Swoop and Lil Women, solid, man, big-ass bird, solid!"

As the immediate after-game excitement dies down, Katy, Sid, and CeCe all give each other congratulatory hugs, laughing, doing their own post mortem on their performance.

"Those screens were bone rattling, CeCe," Katy says.

"Yeah, and your outside shooting was awesome, girl," CeCe responds, grinning and giving Katy a high five.

But Sidney halts their little after-game celebration with an uncharacteristic pessimistic warning. "Hey, that team from CerTek is gonna be rough next weekend," she says, referring to the biotech company entry from the peninsula, who had easily won earlier and will be their Saturday opponent. "Those two from last year's San Jose State team are good ball handlers and excellent shooters, and I played against Jamie Worley when she was at the University of Arizona. She made all Pac 10 in her junior year when I was a senior at UCLA. She's a smart player, rugged rebounder, top defender, and ferocious competitor, playing much bigger than 6-foot."

"You can handle her, girl," CeCe says in her upbeat, cocky manner, as she picks up her sports bag. "Heard *you* made all Pac 10 three years straight, and AP All-American first team your last year, uh-huh. In fact, I think we all match up pretty well with them scientific girls, 'specially if Katy gets her ya-ya goin' from the outside early. What's she call it— her Eddie… Fuller thing? Yeah the Fuller Brush man deal."

"Eddie *Felson*," Katy says, correcting her teammate, and chuckling.

"Whatever," CeCe says, shrugging dismissively, then shaking a threatening finger at Katy. "Just bring your A-game, you hear me, girl!"

"How about a short practice night this week?" Sidney suggests, still looking a little concerned despite CeCe's enthusiasm about the matchups.

"Sounds good to me," Katy agrees.

CeCe nods her acceptance.

They agree to meet Wednesday evening at 5:00 at the court in the park across the street from Sidney's apartment in Pacific Heights, for a short practice session and to plan their strategy for the semifinal game against CerTek.

As Katy leaves the Panhandle courts, she remembers their earlier agreed-on modest team goal about just being competitive, getting a little exercise.

Yeah, maybe that was *too* modest, she tells herself, with a chuckle, because it appears that Little Women will indeed be more than a little competitive.

And she's never really settled for just being competitive anyhow. She has always been driven to win, be the best, and prove herself over and over. Like back when she was a kid and first met Gerri Robinson, coach of the PAL team in the San Diego projects, making the team against stiff competition and initial racial discrimination, then even starting for two years, finding her niche as a defensive player and rebounder. Later she went on to play at Sacramento State, becoming a shooter and star in her senior year.

And now, here.

She was just kidding herself when they first formed Little Women, setting goals—and she bet Sidney and CeCe hadn't really bought into that old flippant *just competitive* B.S. Katy smiles and shakes her head.

"Uh, uh," she says aloud. Those two women are players. Shoot, even at those pickup games back at American River College, when CeCe was only a kid out of high school, she was a gamer. And Sidney had been drafted by the Sacramento Monarchs after UCLA—would've been a pro if an Achilles tendon injury hadn't been a lingering problem.

So there is no way that Little Women is entered in the tournament for only exercise. Forget that crap. They're playing to win, win it all— each of the three of them still having something to prove, at least to themselves. She imitates CeCe's cocky tone, *"Got that, girl?"*

HAP SULLIVAN

arly Monday morning Johnny's partner, Hap Sullivan, uses some connections within the SFPD to get a copy of Jaime O'Brien's Incident Data Sheet, dated five days ago, and a copy of D.L. Mathews's IDS dated eleven days ago. Apparently the third IDS for Joey Bartkowski, who died about two and a half weeks ago, is missing or misplaced.

Hap is waiting for Johnny and Katy at the tiny office of *Sullivan, Cato, & Associates*, just off Geary Street near Japantown, to go over both reports.

"Well, good morning," the beefy ex-cop says, looking up from a sheet of paper at them through a thick layer of bluish-gray haze. He sets his cigar in an ashtray next to his coffee cup as they pull up folding chairs around his desk. "Coffee?" he asks, pointing to the pot.

Katy thinks Hap Sullivan is the spitting image of Al Pacino's detective sidekick in *Sea of Love*, John Goodman, including the jovial used-car-salesman nature. Hap's nickname is a respectful reduction from his early patrolman days' street moniker of Harelip, due to a bad upper lip scar slightly resembling the birth deformity.

"IDS confirms a long red scrape found just below the needle still sticking in Jaime's left arm when they discovered him," Hap announces, looking up from the IDS. "Also mentions a mark on his forehead, but does *not* say it looks like anything special including the letter *J*." He hands the page to Johnny.

Putting a heel on the corner of his desk, Hap continues, "And I don't see anything here about a strange scratch or cut anywhere obvious on the other kid... But it does mention a dirty smudge on his forehead, could be something like Jaime's." He looks up and grins. "How 'bout that? Maybe your guy O'Brien is onto something after all, Johnny."

"Yeah," Johnny says thoughtfully, reading over both one-page reports. Then, unable to hide his rising enthusiasm, he declares loudly, "Now, those two similar forehead marks are a coincidence I ain't buying. How about you, kiddo? Richie have something or what?"

Katy agrees, after she reads both reports, not even trying to hide the sharp edge in her tone. "He just might at that."

Then she looks up with a growing frown at Hap and Johnny. "But where do we go from here? We have no forensics at either of the sites or medical reports on the bodies, no support at all... Start with the shelter where they all lived their next-to-last day? Work back from there, the shelter? What's it called?"

"Brother Timothy's," Johnny answers, rubbing his nose. "Yeah. Let's start there. Probably be a good idea to go over to Walden House's 815 facility, too. Look around. And I guess we should check out the Capp Street Meeting, maybe talk to some of the regulars." He pulls at his nose again, stands, and looks down at his still-seated business partner. "Hap, you on board here? Don't think there will be much of a fee for this one."

The big guy shrugs his shoulders, picks up his cigar, and takes a long puff. "Why not?" he says with a John Goodman grin, adding to the layer of haze hanging in the tiny office. "Business is really pretty slow right now. If we catch the dude, maybe it'll be good PR for the agency—a shot in the arm, if you'll forgive the expression."

"You're right," Johnny says, slapping his friend affectionately on the back. "How about checking around some more at SFPD records. See if you can locate that missing IDS report for the other kid, what's-his-name... Bartkowski? Then maybe talk to the three blues who filled them out. See what they remember. You know the drill. Who knows, you might even be able to get Homicide interested enough in the forehead marks to come on board now."

"I don't think so. Street people, especially junkies, ain't real high priority at SFPD right now; but, sure, I'll drop in at Homicide, see what I can do," Hap replies with raised eyebrows and a little grin, his expression suggesting, *Okay, let me check with the sales manager, see about getting you a better deal.*

Katy and Johnny both laugh at the funny facial expression.

"Anyhow, let's all meet here tomorrow night after dinner, including Richie if he can make it—say about 7:00?" Johnny suggests, as they get up to leave.

2

Later Monday afternoon, Katy and Johnny meet with Richie O'Brien in his office at Walden House Administration down on 520 Townsend Street, where he's the MIS Programs Coordinator. They share what they've found so far, their reactions, and discuss strategy. Then Richie makes an appointment with someone at 815 to show all three of them around Tuesday at 10:00 a.m.

After their brief discussion, Richie suggests to Katy, "Want to collect your first installment payment for services, maybe later tonight?"

"Yeah, sure," she answers enthusiastically, but kind of surprised by the prompt nature of the offered barter payment.

"Well," Richie adds thoughtfully, "what do you say we start with *rippin' 'n' runnin'*, how an addict scrounges up his daily nut? How he gets together the bread to support a $500 or $100 or even a $40-a-day jones. Most can't maintain a regular job, and we ain't usually talking about someone with a trust fund or rich relatives. Not many Guggenheims for dope fiends either."

Katy smiles. "Sounds like a good starting point, Richie. Where do I meet you?"

"I'll pick you up around 9:00 tonight?"

"Okay," she agrees, writing down the address of their apartment on Chestnut Street in the Marina and handing it to him.

RIPPIN' 'N' RUNNIN'

*Junkie hustling ain't got time to be no criminal genius. He's like a
dude trying to catch up to a departing Muni, running, running, running,
but never catching up to that bus.*

—Beechnut

R ichie O'Brien picks up Katy at a little after 9:00 that night in
his mustard-colored, beat-up, Volvo station wagon—
obviously a surviving veteran of San Francisco's notorious
Parking Wars—and they head downtown.

Riding along, Richie explains the evening focus. "Every junkie has
to have a hustle of some kind to support his jones. It can be anything,

but they all have at least one element in common: the hustle is *quick*, down and dirty, something that doesn't require a lot of planning or time to execute. You follow a junkie, he's a man on the move from the time he gets up, usually in the afternoon, until he goes to bed—fix, hustle, fix, hustle, and so forth. You see few supporting their habits by sticking up armored cars or anything like that, too much planning and patience required… Though we have a couple of recovering addicts down at the Capp Street meeting who were once bank robbers. They're pretty unusual though. A junkie describes his desperate life as *rippin' 'n' runnin'*, and he means that literally. He leaves behind a wasteland of burned bridges. Which reminds me of a story I saw on TV told by Chuck Negron, the lead singer for Three Dog Night, that demonstrates the desperation in the life of an addict. Late one night he's strung out and needs quick cash for dope, so he signs over a million dollar apartment he owned in New York City to this dealer for something like $35,000— whatever the dude had immediately available. Now that's desperate."

They've crossed Market on 6th Street, and Richie slows the old station wagon to a crawl.

Katy notices a not-so-subtle change in Richie's features—more serious now, like a jock pulling on his game face. And his speech is different, too—shorter sentences, sharper-edged, a little like a detached bus tour guide reeling off a canned spiel, but more hard-boiled, more slang laced with occasional cynical metaphors.

"Along here and around the corner on Mission are the City's main pawn shops. They're real busy right about now and also when they first open up in the morning, people hocking stuff for their morning and evening fixes. See what I mean—"

He double parks the station wagon and points across Katy to a line of people waiting on the street to go into *A-1 Pawn*, a string of neon-green $$$$$$ glowing over the entrance, signaling the promised land. Most of those waiting are men, carrying TVs, VCRs, cameras, binoculars, musical instruments, and other stuff in brown shopping bags. While they wait, some of them are hopping back and forth foot-to-foot nervously; one guy at the end of the line is popping pills openly.

Even at a distance, Katy can sense their distress.

"Beechnut," Richie continues, "an old musician-philosopher-addict I knew years ago, used to say that pawn shop lines of junkies reminded him of film on the depression, desperate people with their deposit books waiting in line anxiously for a failing bank to maybe open its doors—expecting to get at most ten cents on the dollar. Same sense of resigned hopelessness."

They watch silently for a few moments, as the line moves slowly inside the pawnshop.

"Is most of that stuff from their own homes or stolen?" Katy asks, looking over at Richie as he starts the Volvo back up and moves slowly along 6th.

He snorts derisively and shakes his head.

"Well, yeah, at first I guess it does come from home, but a junkie's pad is soon emptier than a roomful of straight-talking politicians. No furniture, no clothes, and eventually no place. They don't pay utilities or rent. Everything goes for dope. So they're out on the street fast. But some of the big stuff—like those TVs, VCRs—probably come from burglaries. Most of the smaller stuff though, is boosted. That's actually the most common street hustle—shoplifting or boosting stuff from parked cars. Rippin' 'n' runnin'. Trouble now days with shoplifting is you can't take stolen stuff back to very many places for a cash refund. The Gap, Orchard Supply, only a few others give customers money instead of credit. Either way, boosted or burglarized, you begin selling stuff on the street, flea markets, or most likely go to a pawnshop and take a *big* discount. Back there at A-1, the Russian looks at your stuff, names a price. You argue, he waves you away and beckons the next person to come up to the window. Dude is tougher than a two-dollar steak."

They continue slowly, Katy actually surprised at the number of pawnshops along the street, all doing a brisk business buying stuff this time of night. She's been by here lots of times of course, but never really paid any attention to the nature of the storefronts. "Don't the pawn shop owners question a guy who comes back every few days with another TV or VCR or camera?"

He laughs, turning right on Mission, but doesn't say anything.

"Dumb question, right?" she asks, remembering her Sacramento PD days—realizing she'd never looked at things from this viewpoint before.

Smiling kind of wryly, Richie says, "You know every junkie sees this time when he's forced to sell his own stuff as a temporary deal, something to look back on as the bad times. I've known homeless, long-term addicts who have a huge handful of pawn tickets saved and kept together with rubber bands, almost all of the tickets outdated, no good—the stuff has been sold by the shops long ago. But they still keep them, because *soon*, they'll be back on their feet, buying some of their stuff back…" He glances over at her, still smiling, but there's no humor in his eyes. "Can't throw any of that shit away. Be like giving up, you know."

They suddenly stop and park.

"C'mon," Richie says, leading Katy across the street to a little place with a brightly lit blue sign, *Tasty Donuts, open 24 hours.* "Sooner or later a guy boosting needs a fence. And here in the city, he learns to specialize in small, packaged, high turnover stuff."

They take a seat at the counter up front, Richie ordering them both a coffee. The place is noisy, busy, people coming and going.

"Okay," Richie whispers after watching the crowd for a few minutes, leaning close to Katy. "Check out the two young dudes in the heavy, dirty jackets… Yeah, the ones slipping into that far booth with the old ladies."

Katy glances surreptitiously over her raised coffee cup past the line at the cash register, back into the corner. Two elderly Mexican women are sitting with their backs against the wall facing the street. The young guys are leaning over talking to them, heads finally bobbing up and down, agreeing to something.

"The dudes are probably slipping something they boosted under the table about now."

"You mean the old ladies are fences?" Katy asks, setting down her coffee cup.

Richie smiles thinly and nods. "You got it. They sit in that spot most of the evening doing business. Buying packaged batteries, film, and other small stuff, anything easy to quickly turn over for a profit. See them slipping something into that shopping bag between them?"

The two young guys get up and hurry out.

A minute or so later, a skinny, nervous woman slips into the booth and talks for a few moments, before she gets up and hurries out.

Katy and Richie finish their coffee and head out themselves.

Back in the station wagon, they take off, turning onto Capp Street off Mission before slowing down again.

As they ease along, past the sleazy hotels and noisy bars, Katy notices a number of prostitutes standing around or cruising the street, often in pairs, dressed inappropriately for the cool night—their work uniforms brightly colored, low-cut, short-sleeved blouses, vinyl miniskirts, dangling earrings, and high heels. A few wear sweaters or vests, but everything about them, including their makeup, is cheap, gaudy, and flashy—they look like whores.

Richie pulls over into a parking spot, and they watch a young, black woman, wearing a bright orange wig, slip away from her white partner and stick her head into a double-parked green Escort two spaces in front of them.

"This is the end of the line in the city, the absolute bargain basement for hookers," Richie explains. "They may ask for $20, but will settle for something less. If you were buried any deeper, you'd need sunlight piped down to you. These women are *all* addicts, either crack or heroin. They're too old-looking, too beat-up, too sick, or sometimes just too out of it to work even over in the Tenderloin, which is a slight step up. What you see here is indeed what Dr. Dean Edell on Channel 7 might medically describe as *high risk behavior.*"

Up the street, the black woman with the cheap wig beckons to her partner, and then opens the double-parked Escort's door, and they both slide in, apparently hooking up with a live one.

"They do their business in cars, alleys, or sometimes in one of the nearby hot sheet hotels with five-dollar-an-hour rates. Few here have a protector. They're often raped, beaten, and ripped-off. You probably read in the *Chronicle* last year about the building contractor who hit a 19-year-old hooker over the head with a pipe, then dumped her in the Bay, only she miraculously survived and fingered him for the cops?"

He glances over at Katy who says, "Yeah, I think I did read that."

"Well that ain't uncommon down here. A large number of the women working this area have had similar accidents in the last few years. And that isn't even mentioning the other risks common to their hustle—AIDS, hepatitis, and now a nasty new strain of TB. Jail or prison are two of the better outcomes. The girls here say, 'Honey, you gotta bring *it* to peddle it.' And that neatly sums it up—they're resigned to risking their asses because of their joneses. Some as high as two-three hundred dollars a day—depending on the number of tricks they can turn."

After she absorbs all that, Katy asks, "Young men sell their bodies for dope here, too?"

"Yeah, but over in another neighborhood off Post, and that's even a more difficult, scarier hustle—risk of AIDS even higher. Yeah, hooking is harder than Chinese arithmetic."

Up the street a pair of cops are pushing two struggling prostitutes into a patrol car, the Latina grabbing the door and shouting loudly in an accented voice, "Help, *po-leese broo-ta-lity!*"

"A woman here on the street lasts a year, maybe two if she's smart and lucky. Then she's too skinny and scuffed-up with junkie sores to make her nut, or too sick and beat up, or just locked up too often. But it's an unskilled hustle that doesn't require much capital outlay, and there is always someone to take your place. It's something every female junkie at least considers doing. When we do the kickin'/rehab installment, remind me to tell you about SAGE—Standing Against Global Exploitation—a good program for ex-hookers that Walden House helps facilitate."

Of course Katy has seen her share of prostitutes in Sacramento—one even a victim in the famed Red Chief case—but nothing quite like here along Capp Street, some of these women barely eighteen in calendar years, but already skinny, strung-out, *old* ladies. She can almost smell the despair hanging heavy in the air along the street.

2

A little later, after showing Katy some young male prostitutes aggressively soliciting cars, Richie is cruising east on Market Street, slowing down as they approach each Muni Station, peering out the window intently as they pass the little clusters of night people, shaking his head with frustration after inspecting three stops. "Shit."

He slows to a crawl at the fourth one—

"*There*," he says, nodding out the window. "See that skinny white dude talking to the Asian guy in the dark suit and red tie?"

Katy looks, and then says, "Yeah, the suit is giving the kid money, and the kid is handing him back... what?"

"Fast pass," Richie explains. "He's selling the guy in the suit a counterfeit fast pass for the bus. It's a great hustle the first couple of days of the month. They sell the phony pass for ten bucks, when a real pass costs thirty-five or more. With all the high-quality new printing technology, a fake fast pass is cheap to make and almost impossible for a driver to spot."

"But what about the muni cops that Mayor Brown says ride the buses?" Katy asks. "It's easy to spot the sales here out in the open at bus stops even from the street."

"Yeah, you're right about that. Kid won't last long doing business at bus stops. Smarter ones, with a little nerve and more moxie, work places door-to-door like the projects in the daytime. Anyplace where lots of people regularly use the bus, you know. But when he needs bread, an addict does what he has to, right? Like Beechnut used to say: 'Being a junkie is like riding a taxi to nowhere, and the meter is always ticking'."

They keep going, Katy watching the clusters of people at each stop for several more blocks… without spotting any more open sales.

Richie glances at his watch, then suggests, "We could hit a few strip joints in the Tenderloin or North Beach. Strippers and lap dancers often support a jones of some kind." He glances over at her. "Or have you had enough for tonight?"

Katy sighs and says that she's tired, ready to head home. She has a lot to think about when she writes up her notes—not so much about what she actually saw, but the nature of it all, the often resigned, almost hopeless desperation of the junkie… probably exactly what Richie intended to reveal when he called this segment, Rippin' 'n' Runnin'.

As Richie turns off Market Street, heading north in the direction of the Marina, Katy asks, "What's the most unusual hustle you ever heard about?"

Richie thinks a minute, and then laughs out loud, his hard expression easing up some. "They talk about this guy at work, I didn't know him or remember his name, he's passed on now. He had a dog he trained to snatch purses, had the dog hooked on used cotton balls—the filters. Anyhow, he gets arrested, and at his trial his P.D. derides the prosecution's contention. Assistant D.A. then brings in the strung-out dog who tries to snag one of the jurors' purses right there in court."

"That's unbelievable."

"Yeah, and the kicker is that the dog was too smart to get hooked again. When the guy finally gets out of the slammer, dog snapped at him when he offered it a cotton ball. *No way, Jose.*"

They both laugh.

Parking in front of her apartment building on Chestnut, Richie adds thoughtfully, "But I guess the slickest scam I ever heard of was this junkie who was a pretty good calligrapher. He probably had this skill before he got strung out. In any event, he checks the obits in the newspaper each morning, then phones up the new widows. He tells them that their husband recently ordered a Bible with the widow's name gold-inscribed just before he died. Can he bring it over? Nine out of ten say, 'Of course.' So he takes over the Bible he just inscribed after the call and picks up the remainder due, usually $50 or $60, the maximum he thinks the old ladies will pay. The Bibles cost him $6 a piece in volume, and the inscription takes five minutes at the most." He grins at her and shakes his head.

"That's ingenious," Katy says with a chuckle, as she opens the car door. "Well, Richie, thanks for the tour. It was great. I have a lot to think about already."

"See you tomorrow morning at 815," he says.

"Goodbye."

Katy slides out and waves as he takes off in his mustard Volvo.

3

Inside their Marina apartment, Johnny is watching the Giants and Dodgers game on Channel 2 and chuckling about something. Robb Nen, the closer, is pitching the last of the ninth, the Giants ahead.

"What's so funny, pal?" she asks, bending over and taking a drink from his Michelob.

He repeats a story that Jon Miller, one of the Giants announcers, told just before she came in. "You know the Dodgers have the largest payroll in the majors, about 100 million dollars. Well, their new general manager, Maloney, after hearing that the Yankees had picked up the hard-throwing Roger Clemens for big bucks from Toronto in the off-season, said that they would indeed need him when the Yanks meet L.A. in the World Series."

Katy laughs, knowing that here at the halfway point of the season, the Dodgers are ten games out in last place in the western division, the Giants in second. She doesn't enjoy it quite as much as Johnny, growing up down in San Diego and kind of excited by the current Padres, who have been in the cellar but are now making a run, winning sixteen in a row, with Tony Gwynn closing in on 3,000 hits.

"You remember I said in the preseason that *USA TODAY*, *The Sporting News*, all of the eastern pundits, were full of it when they predicted the Giants fourth or last in the division, and the Dodgers winning both the division and the pennant," Johnny says, draining his beer. "Same crap every year."

"Hey, pal, what did Yogi Berra say?" she warns.

He glances at her with a slight frown and replies, "Yeah, yeah, I know. It ain't over 'til it's over."

She smiles to herself, knowing how much he loves the game—second only to boxing—really enjoys going out to the Stick. He claims the attraction of taking in a game in person, especially a day game, is like time-traveling back forty years. The pace of life out there slowed down, more relaxed, traditions—like the seventh inning stretch—keenly observed. Everything just like it was in the old days. And she thinks it's probably true, picturing all the business people sitting around them at the Stick last week, playing hooky, suit coats off, ties loosened, laughing, eating a forbidden hot dog, hollering at the umpires, their personal and business concerns forgotten. She grins a silent agreement.

Johnny glances at her. "What's so funny, kiddo?"

Still feeling playful, Katy shakes her head. "You know you're pretty jacked-up tonight, pal. Wonder if there is anything I can do that might relax you?" she teases in a seductive voice, doing her exaggerated imitation of the Groucho Marx ogle, before beginning to unbutton her blouse and heading off nonchalantly for the bedroom.

She glances back over her shoulder, as Johnny quickly clicks off the ballgame and follows her into the bedroom.

SIX

For what is a man profited, if he shall gain the whole world, and lose his soul? Or what shall a man give in exchange for his soul?

—Matthew 16:26

Early Monday evening you are leaning against the corner of the apartment building next door to the entrance to the *Majestic Hotel* in the Tenderloin, watching the street people shuffle by, highlighted by the backdrop of neon glaring to life across the street, up and down the block: *Hyde Corner Grocery, Black Knight Pub, Top Hat Billiards, Homeboy's Liquors, Bangkok Massage.*

Waiting and watching.

As the night noises begin to crank up in volume, the number of women loitering on the street in the vicinity of the hotel increases—a mix of sizes, shapes, and gaudy colors, their faces painted, their dress skimpy. You close your eyes, your nostrils flaring with their layered jezebel scents—cheap cloying perfume and deodorant covering the biting smell of tension and musky she-odor; and underneath it all, the lingering stale-sour smell of sweaty male bodies.

You blink, again scanning the nearby painted faces, with no luck, for it's a special whore you seek among these Tenderloin outcasts.

But no Carla.

Where is she?

You walk uptown a block, searching the crowd, still with no success. Carla is tall, 6'-2", and should stand out, but you don't see her. You know she has gone out again and has to be plying her trade to support her habit, her soul in jeopardy. But she's not here anywhere around her old cruising grounds. Just not here.

Where else could she be? you ask yourself, puzzled.

Capp Street maybe?

No. You don't think so, not yet. Not so fast. She hasn't had time to sink to that lower level yet. She hasn't been out long enough. She's around here someplace.

You turn and impatiently walk back to the *Majestic*, picking out and approaching one of the others, a young woman with a thick mane of fiery orange hair.

"Say, sport, you lookin' to party," the woman asks aggressively. Before you even open your mouth, she's taking you possessively by the arm, steering you away from the Mexican woman chewing gum and looking bored behind her. The redhead's strong, hot scent is overpowering, and for the briefest moment your concentration on the important task at hand is weakened, and you feel a slight stir of sexual attraction, a tightening sensation in your groin.

No, you shout silently, turning away from the momentary weakness of the flesh, a fleeting lapse of concentration. You shake your head emphatically, reinforcing your denial. Poise partially recovered, you say to the woman, "I'm looking for Carla. Can you help me?"

"Carla?" the redhead repeats, frowning and considering. "Hmm… A tall tranny, right?"

"Speaks funny," you add, nodding. Carla is indeed a tall transvestite, a *he*, a Dutch man with a noticeably guttural, foreign accent.

"Hey, whatcha want with that bitch?" the redhead snaps back. "You got all you need right here, fella, the *real* stuff." She pushes her soft breast against your arm, licks her glossy-orange lips suggestively, and winks lewdly.

Finding the Jezebel's cheap come-on crude and even repulsive, you still manage to maintain your polite control and explain calmly, "I really need to see Carla, herself. It's very important. A sort of… ah, private family matter, you know. Have you seen her tonight?"

Obviously disappointed by the rejection and loss of a potential sale, the redhead releases your arm, backs off a step, folds her arms over her breasts, a kind of teenage defiant pout on her face. For a moment you think you've blown it, that the jezebel won't answer at all. But she quickly dismisses her sense of loss and says in a not harsh voice, "Ain't seen her for a long time, man. Think she's out of the life. Heard she went into rehab, may've even got born again, you know what I'm saying." She shrugs dismissively, turns away, and moves back to the side of her Latina friend.

Born again—?

No, you didn't think so.

Not Carla.

But you nod at the now disinterested redhead and whisper politely, "Thank you kindly." She doesn't hear, her and her business associate engaged now in animated conversation with a prospective client in an idling car.

At loose ends, you consider asking around, maybe checking out more of the women, but, after reflection, you suspect that will be only a further waste of time. Carla just is not out here this evening.

Resigned to not finding her tonight, you begin to leave the brightly lit area in front of the *Majestic*, walking only a few steps before stopping abruptly at the mouth of the adjoining alley. An old man, a pretty but unkempt girl, and a half-starved dog are sitting on cardboard, the old man shaking a paper cup, begging, the girl resting her hand on the skinny mongrel's head, an exhausted look in her eyes.

But it isn't the shabby condition or incongruous nature of the trio that holds your attention, it's a feature of the girl when she blinks and looks up into your face. Her eye color is an exact match to your family's distinctive summer-sky blue. And for a fleeting moment you think she may even be your younger sister, Bet.

But no, you tell yourself, deciding this girl is way too old to be your younger sister, perhaps sixteen or so, her expression even older than that. Bet would only be about twelve or... maybe thirteen at the most. This conclusion makes you realize that it's been five, almost six years since you saw Bet last.

My God!

It is difficult to believe she must be a teenager now, your baby sister...

2

It was hot and muggy, the sky dark and overcast when you made your way up the trail to the little tarpaper cabin. The holler deadly quiet at that late hour, even the dogs asleep, only a distant cricket chorus disturbing the complete stillness. And just as you had hoped, Bet was sleeping with her cot pulled out on the porch, where it was a few degrees cooler, your mother, J.J., and Sissy sleeping inside. You tiptoed close, careful not to step on the loose stair next to the porch, and kneeled, just watching your younger sister's chest move up and down rhythmically.

Of them all, you were going to miss her most, such a joyful, happy nature, not always shared by the others. She's too young to remember Daddy and his disgusting sinfulness and the hardship he brought to the family.

Hoo... hoo... hoo.

It was the old gray owl startling you, hunting nearby in the forest.

Bet's eyes popped open at the sound, and she sat up when she realized someone was watching her; but she didn't shout or make any loud noise that might awaken any of the others, recognizing you and the *Be Quiet* sign you made with your finger to your lips. She was always quick, smart, too.

"Billy!" she whispered softly, smiling.

You kissed her forehead, then sat on the foot of the cot, and smiled back.

"What are you doing away from the Big House?"

"I've come to say goodbye, Bet," you explained in a hushed tone, one eye on the door to the shack.

"Goodbye?" she repeated, swinging her bare feet off the bed and scooting herself next to you at the end of the cot.

You nodded. "I need to go someplace where I can do my duty. Use my Gift of Sight and the Hand of the Lord—"

"But that's why you are *our* Shepherd," Bet protested. "The Bishops picked you special to replace the old Shepherd, to take care of the Flock right here."

"That's just it, Bet," you explained quietly. "The congregation is too small, they don't really need me. After the old Shepherd, the Council hasn't designated anyone needing soul guidance in the last year and probably won't for a long time. No one is old enough or sick enough. I can't practice the Gift here for who knows how long."

For a few moments your sister just looked into your face, fighting back the tears that eventually welled up and ran down her cheeks. "Where will you go?" she finally asked, her whisper hoarse and choked.

"St. Louis," you answered a bit too loudly, frowning at the front door.

Then in a lower voice you added, "I'm going to walk to Camden tonight and catch the bus early tomorrow. I've told no one, so it's our *secret*. But I had to come see you before I left, Bet." Then you bent close and kissed her again on the cheek. "I'll really miss you."

She threw her arms around your neck and kissed you back. "Oh, I'll miss you too, Billy."

You smiled and gave her a little present you'd wrapped up. A whizzer you'd made with a large button cut from a seashell you'd found at the Big House and threaded in the middle of a loop of three feet of fresh-waxed, heavy string.

She was delighted with the gift, immediately twirling the toy, and then pulling the twisted string, making the iridescent button whiz and glitter in the moonlight.

You watched her for a few more moments, then turned and left without looking back again at the little cabin, picking up your duffel bag at the beginning of the hill trail, and trudging down to the dirt road leading southeast.

3

You blink, still looking down at the dirty face of the blue-eyed girl, who makes a pitiful attempt at a seductive smile; then you quickly avert your gaze and drop a dollar into the old man's empty cup.

"Thanks, young fella," he says, as you abruptly turn away and head back up the street away from the *Majestic Hotel.*

You walk back to your apartment, disappointed that you were unable to find Carla, knowing that you will have to find her or someone else soon.

Very soon.

4

In your apartment, you sit with the Bible in your lap, opened to Matthew. But you are not really mentally able to track what your eyes glance over, the words almost in code.

No.

Your hands shake, your chest is tight, and you feel slightly nauseous.

Your need is too great, breaking your attempted concentration.

Your need, that simple.

You must find another wayward soul. Backsliding isn't really so important to you now. A sinner... almost any sinner will do.

You must guide another soul to the hereafter, very soon, your well-being depending on it.

You pace the apartment nervously.

5

Later, on an impulse, you go out again, grabbing your black windbreaker, but forgetting the Hand of God, leaving it behind in its rosewood box. You wander about with nothing really in mind, just considering the many prospects at random—the hookers, bums, panhandlers, and the human litter of the Tenderloin. So much work to do, so many derelict sinners. But you need to pinpoint one... and soon.

Who?

Sighing aloud, you stop wandering, across the street from a liquor store, an idea forming in your mind.

As the customers come and go, you wait, shiver in the cold, and watch. Finally you spot him, the *right* one, an arthritic old man shuffling along, bundled up in an overcoat. Yes, he is the one, you decide, forgetting about the cold now. It is written on his wrinkled, gaunt features, his despairing need. His time at hand. Even though a stranger, you sense an invisible bond with this special sinner.

He goes into the store and comes back out a few minutes later. You stalk him down the street half a block, stopping and watching him from the mouth of an alley, as he noisily prepares himself a resting spot on cardboard in front of a dumpster at the dead end of the short alley. All his movements since entering the alley are familiar, part of an obvious routine. This is his place, his home.

You peer about.

There is no one else in the alley!

Your pulse races.

Your hands search the pockets of your windbreaker… empty, only a handkerchief.

Oh, if only you had come prepared to do your duty tonight, you chastise yourself silently. If you had only remembered to bring the Hand of God, the ashes. A golden opportunity.

But no, you think, glancing down at the empty handkerchief in your hand. You're unprepared.

Your spirit sags. But after a moment you buck up, smile thinly, for you realize that you have successfully identified your next target. He will probably go to sleep back there. Maybe you can go home, pick up your things, and return later.

Yes. Your spirit soars now—

"Spare change?" a nearby voice to your left asks, the unexpected sound startling you.

You shake your head and frown at the bundled-up female panhandler, who has decided to stop, empty her shopping cart, and set up camp in the darkened building entry near the alley corner.

You can't return now, not with a nearby witness staked out.

Not tonight.

Disappointed, you decide you will return to this spot, tomorrow, tomorrow night. Yes, you have discovered the next candidate. The thought raises your spirit.

Your step is lighter as you head home.

815

uesday morning, Johnny and Katy arrive a little earlier than 10:00 at the Walden House facility, parking on the SW corner of Central and Waller, one block up from the heart of the Haight. Richie's Volvo isn't there yet.

"We're early," Katy says to Johnny. "I'm going to take a look around. You want to walk a little?"

He shakes his head, his nose buried in the green sheet, the sports section of the *Chronicle*, and an article on the upcoming, much-anticipated, Trinidad and De La Hoya fight.

Katy gets out, crosses the street, looking over the four-story building. She is at the foot of the steps leading up to what is actually the back entrance of the pink and white stucco structure. From this vantage at the cross streets, the building is an odd triangular shape. She leaves Johnny to wait for Richie and walks a block up the steep sidewalk of Central along the western side of the facility, up to Buena

Vista West, and the main entry of 815 at the base of the triangle on the second story of the building. She notes the beautiful stained glass windows along the base side of the old building. Coming around back down Waller, Katy stops again at the rear stairs leading up between four columns to a set of beautiful wooden doors, and she notices the stained-glass window above the doors that is lettered with an announcement:

WALDEN HOUSE
Eternal Change Within

Katy glances over where Johnny is parked on the corner in the quiet neighborhood, not a soul out on either street that she can see— but only a block away from the busy madness of Haight Street. She remembers Richie mentioning that the building is over a hundred years old, originally built as a Franciscan Sisters' convent. Katy turns back, noticing for the first time the small cupola over the top of the triangle, really appreciating the whole structure now. Only the two silver fire escapes, dropping down from the fourth story along each wall, actually mar the century-old spiritual elegance of the oddly shaped cathedral.

At that moment Richie drives up in his mustard station wagon and parks in a vacant spot half way up Central.

Time for business.

2

Inside the elegant entry, Katy's initial impression is of stepping into a dimly-lit Victorian hotel lobby, the sturdy wooden reception desk in front of them, a closed door to its right and long hallway to the left—a triangular-shaped waiting room with dark wood paneling. While Richie inquires at the desk, she looks around more carefully. A young guy is signing a sheet at a little end table to her far right, in the corner near the draped windows looking out on the steep climb along Central; after dropping the pencil, he takes tobacco from a canister on the table, inserts it and paper into a machine, and cranks out a rolled cigarette. He nods at her with a glimpse of delight, as if he'd performed something magical, and disappears back through the doorway and up a stairwell.

To her far left is an antique high-backed chair, and a young woman is sitting on it stiffly, gazing down between her spread legs as if inspecting the pattern of the beautifully maintained hardwood floor.

Richie comes back to Katy and Johnny. "Jeff Walters, who is going to show us around, will be right down."

Katy nods toward the young woman in the chair and whispers, "What's she doing?"

Richie glances to his right and chuckles. "Looks strange, I guess. She's probably new or someone on contract for a discipline breech. Either way she's going over the error of her ways, getting her mind right. May sit there for three, four, or even six hours, depending on her infraction."

"Hello there," a tall man says, hurrying out of the hallway just past the high-backed chair and penitent.

Richie introduces them to the staff member, a young fellow—mid twenties—mixed hip dress, well-worn Levi's with a long-sleeved white shirt and sky-blue tie with large white polka dots.

Katy shakes Walters's hand, noticing his strong grip, pleasant smile, and steady gaze that matches the color of his tie.

Richie explains that Jeff Walters is the orientation counselor, and as the most junior staff member here at 815, he usually catches the escort duties. Then he nods at the young man and says, "So, give us the five dollar tour, Jeff."

Walters speaks in a slow precise way, like an inexperienced T.A. in a university class. "Well, as you may know, Walden House is a TC, a therapeutic community, using behavior modification techniques with clients who have a number of lifestyle issues and problems, including foremost, drug addiction. The program is designed to work on the whole person, not just isolated issues, while staying focused, of course, on the drug addiction."

He pauses, looking around the lobby, his gaze resting momentarily on the woman in the high-backed chair. He frowns, and continues. "This is the rear, downstairs lobby, mostly used by clients going off to work or in and out on pass. They must sign in and out here at this desk. The main public entrance is up on the second story on Buena Vista West. C'mon this way—"

"What's the chalkboard?" Katy interrupts, pointing at a board with dates and names just to the left of the seated penitent:

New Status

29 June	Wilma May Jackson	splitee
29 June	Kenneth Czys	
	& DeRae Robinson	banned
30 June	Delma Cutler	spotted
1 July	Thuy Vhang	splitee
2 July	Wilfredo Hernandes	spotted
2 July	Carl Vanderwaal	splitee
5 July	Cynthia Bryan	splitee
5 July	Eugene Parker	banned
5 July	Bobbi Jean Leiter	spotted

"That's the current status of people recently leaving the program prematurely for whatever reason," Walters explains. "No one in the program can associate on the street with anyone whose name appears on this board."

Katy smiles at Richie, who had explained the exact meaning of the terms the other night at Capp Street. "So everyone here at 815 knows when and why someone leaves the program?"

"That's right," Walters replies. "If they take time to read the board."

They glance over the names, then they move down the hallway.

"And this is where meds are dispensed," the young counselor explains, stopping at a closed Dutch door a few steps down the left hallway. "All a client's needs are met here at Walden House, including therapeutic, legal, and medical..." He turns around and points back across the lobby to the little table and the cigarette-making equipment. "Even tobacco needs. Of course we encourage the clients to eventually quit. But when they come in here most do smoke, and that's usually the least of their problems at the time."

He continues up the hallway and through the doorway. "This is our mess hall. 815 has ninety-six beds at the moment, so we normally feed that many clients here." He points at a sign high on the back wall. "That's the Walden House Creed that everyone memorizes in orientation, and tries to live up to."

W	Who are you?
A	Ask yourself?
L	Learn to listen.
D	Demanding of yourself.
E	Eagerness.
N	Now is your life.
H	Here is how.
O	Owe it to yourself.
U	Union of body and mind.
S	Satisfaction gained.
E	Eternal change within.

"Of course, there is a little more detailed discussion and work involved with each phrase before reaching that final E."

They spend an hour and a half more with the orientation counselor, visiting Harvey Hall on the second floor, named after the late Harvey Milk—the supervisor murdered along with Mayor Mosconi by Dan White—mostly small meeting rooms and offices, where the bulk of the program takes place; and then they climb up to look at various sized bedrooms on the two upper floors—only senior residents sleeping in the two-bed rooms. During the tour Walters explains that the program here at 815 is six months long, the program over at 890 longer, usually twelve months. The first two weeks of orientation is his area of responsibility, the most difficult time for clients—some still physically detoxing, learning rules of conduct including the Walden House Creed, getting back into a normal routine after running the streets, strung out on drugs. During the first several months the client has an in-house maintenance job, usually in the kitchen, mess hall, or on the housekeeping staff, and works on his GED if not a high school graduate but close. The last half of the program involves getting a job in the community, saving money for an apartment, completing the GED, and learning how to readjust to everyday living in the community. During the program, the client gets a heavy dose of various groups, depending on his issues and needs—always under the guidance of a counselor. Until recently, rehabilitation at Walden House has centered on behavior modification by peer counselors—individuals who themselves are recovering addicts. But, Walters explains that the recent emphasis is to encourage peer counselors to obtain academic credentials. He's currently attending San Francisco City College.

Katy wonders, but doesn't ask, what was Jeff Walters's drug of choice? He doesn't look like her picture of an addict… But then again no one here does either, since everyone here is drug-free.

During the tour they meet various staff and spend some time with a group of senior clients, working the phones in a little room with job information bulletin boards, setting up job interviews, or getting other information about employment. All important steps in the rehabilitation process.

Outside, after the tour, Johnny says to Richie, "Anyone could be a suspect in there—clients, staff, even visitors would all be aware of that status board, know exactly when Jaime and the other two left the program."

Richie replies, "Yeah, that's right."

"Why don't you privately contact a few senior members of the staff," Johnny suggests. "See if they noticed anyone, staff or client overly interested when Jaime and the other names were first put up on that board?"

"I'll check it out," Richie replies, nodding.

"Well, let's go uptown, grab some lunch, and take a look at that homeless shelter," Katy suggests to Johnny. "We'll see you tonight at the meeting at the office on Geary," she says to Richie.

"What do you think?" Johnny asks Katy, getting into their car, after Richie has headed back toward Townsend. "See anything interesting?"

"Only that status board out in plain view." Then she shrugs and adds, "An impressive place though. Got a good feeling about what's going on in there." Before Johnny drives away, she glances again at the stained glass over the door, the inspiring last line of the Walden House Creed: *Eternal change within.*

BROTHER TIMOTHY

The homeless shelter is located on Jones just off Eddy, near the heart of the Tenderloin, once a fashionable storefront. Now, its large display window is completely blacked out, with white letters announcing—

BROTHER TIMOTHY'S SHELTER

A handmade sign is hung inside the glass of the front door, backed by dusty and yellowed Venetian blinds that block the view; it reads:

Shelter opens nightly at 7:30 p.m.

RULES OF ENTRY

1. No alcohol
2. No drugs
3. Sobriety required of all residents

After looking over the sign, Johnny says, "That's pretty simple and clear."

Katy glances at her watch: 3:55 p.m. "Hope someone is around." She raps loudly on the glass door, feeling slightly depressed by the poorly maintained, shabby exterior of the place. For a few moments she thinks no one is going to answer her knock, and she wishes they'd called ahead from Chinatown where they'd eaten a leisurely Dim Sum lunch.

Suddenly, the blinds separate just above the sign, and for a second or two they are confronted with a bushy face and a pair of large, bloodshot, faded-denim eyes. Then the blinds snap back into place, and Katy hears the door being unlocked.

"Brother Timothy?" Johnny says to the bearded man who opens the door.

The young man responds in a soft-spoken drawl, "No, I'm Jeremy Featherstone, Brother Timothy's assistant." He's dressed in sandals, faded jeans, and wears a sweatshirt with cut-off arms that reads: *MR. ZOOG'S SEX WAX, The Best For Your Stick*

Katy wonders if the latter-day hippie knows his sweatshirt is an ironic '70s ad for surfboard wax. This guy doesn't look like much of a surfing enthusiast.

"Well," Johnny asks, looking past Jeremy into an empty hallway, "is he in?"

"Yes, of course, follow me," Jeremy answers, opening the door wider. He leads them a few steps into the hallway to another door simply labeled: *PRIVATE*.

After knocking, Jeremy opens the door and announces, "You have some visitors." Finally, he steps aside and gestures for Johnny and Katy to enter.

The private office is brightly lit, wood-paneled and decorated tastefully in fall colors, with a thick-pile, sandy carpet, a far cry from the shabby exterior. Brother Timothy sits behind a huge oaken desk, wearing an expensive three-piece tan suit, his dark hair fashionably styled—a sharp contrast to his scruffy assistant. Both the office and man look as if they've been transplanted from Montgomery Street in the heart of the financial district.

"Yes, I'm Brother Timothy," he says, rising. "How may I help you?" He smiles, apparently amused by the obviously surprised expressions at his appearance.

Johnny flashes his P.I. card and introduces himself and Katy. He pauses, waiting for some kind of reaction, but Brother Timothy just shakes their hands and says, "Please have a seat," indicating the two plush brown leather chairs in front of his desk.

Katy settles in as Johnny begins to explain the purpose of their visit. "We are conducting a private investigation of what may turn out to be a serious crime—"

Brother Timothy brings up one hand like a traffic cop, the amused expression slightly strained on his face. "Please, let's save time and be frank, Mr. Cato. You've talked to Richard O'Brien and are interested in his... ah, rather unusual theory concerning the death of his brother?"

"Well, yes, that's right," Johnny admits, rubbing his battered nose. "But—"

Brother Timothy interrupts again and continues, "O'Brien came to see me the other night with his accusation about his brother and apparently two other former residents, too. We have never had anything like that occur here *in* the shelter. No serious violence of any kind whatsoever. And he suspects someone responsible from here? The idea is completely ridiculous—"

"Oh, really?" Katy says, a little irritated by the man's overstated indignation, his whole dismissive attitude toward the investigation. "Your screening up front appears to be minimal, no mention even of weapons. At any time you might be harboring an ex-convict, maybe even a murderer, perhaps armed for all you know. So, Mr. O'Brien's suggestion that his brother may have been murdered by someone following him to the street from here doesn't seem completely ridiculous to me."

Richie nods agreement.

"Miss Green and Mr. Cato," Brother Timothy begins and sighs, much like a teacher forced to state an obvious conclusion to a pair of slow students. "We have 150 beds, our clientele turns over almost nightly. People come here as a last resort. They are from the lowest rungs of society: alcoholics, drug users, and the mentally ill. Yes, it's true that some may have indeed served time in a correctional facility. But they are, by and large, unsophisticated people, carrying a full load of personal problems. They do not know what tomorrow will bring for themselves, and they are certainly not interested in the problems of others—whether a person is on or off the wagon, so to speak. Sometimes they are indeed violent, but it is usually a spontaneous response. A brief fight, usually ineffective as far as serious physical damage. They do not kill with poison, probably wouldn't know where to obtain something like that. Do either of you really think that anyone here is capable of that type of planning?"

Katy isn't sure if any of the residents are that capable or not, and notices that Brother Timothy excluded mention of members of his staff as possible suspects.

She has more questions in mind…

But, considering Brother Timothy's defensive posture, Katy just shrugs and decides to try another, less direct tack, something she and Johnny had briefly discussed on the way over that morning.

"Okay, we get the point, Brother Timothy."

She shows him her *Guardian* press card and takes a little notebook from her purse. "I'm professionally a freelance writer, only helping Mr. Cato out as a part-time investigator because of a past association. Been considering doing a feature for the *Guardian* on the various resources of the Tenderloin, like your shelter. Now that we are here, how about a few questions about your operation? Would you mind? Who knows, it might help with funding?"

Brother Timothy brushes a piece of invisible lint from the sleeve of his immaculately cleaned and pressed suit coat, smiles broadly, and says, "Of course, Miss Green, always glad to help the press in any way possible."

Katy checks a few earlier notes about Brother Timothy gleaned from a phone call to her editor friend at the *Guardian*, Jessie Warner, who checked the paper's morgue—the data bank of background information. Then she asks, "Speaking of funds, you do not accept any government support whatsoever? That's kinda odd isn't it?"

"We're not associated with any formal church," Brother Timothy explains, "and conduct no religious services here. Until just recently we were not considered a nonprofit corporation by the IRS. So, we did not qualify for the usual government grants in our field, including city, state, or federal."

"That's interesting," Katy says, leaning forward slightly. "Not a church sponsored organization… but you call yourself, Brother. I take it that you are not actually ordained?"

"That is correct," he answers, "I'm a lay brother, which is quite common in a number of denominations, including the Catholic Church."

"Yes, of course," Katy says in a more neutral tone. "I wasn't suggesting otherwise. How long have you operated here in the Tenderloin?"

"I came to San Francisco about two years ago and set up the shelter shortly after that."

"And where did you come from?"

As if annoyed by the personal direction of the questioning, Brother Timothy frowns slightly and answers a little more sharply, "Chicago."

Then, after a moment's awkward silence, he adds in a slightly more congenial tone, "Let me help you cut to the chase, Miss Green. We're non-secular humanists. We help people not to save souls, important as that may be, but as a pragmatic attempt to solve an urban social problem. These men need a place of respite from the street. Society— in the tangible form of business and merchant associations—wants them off the streets, especially at night. These business groups represent our major donors." Abruptly he turns his chair and taps a file cabinet behind him. "Our financial records are available to legitimate inquiry at any time. As I mentioned, the IRS deems us nonprofit, as of this June fifteenth. So that's about it. No big rip-off, nothing shady, as you can see. Everything on the up and up." He turns up the palms of both hands in a gesture of complete exposure.

Katy closes her notebook, thinking, *This guy is just a little* too *defensive about the financial backing of this place.* But, then, she asks herself, could that really have any bearing on Jaime's death? She can't imagine how it would. Jaime wasn't doing an investigative report on the shelter or anything else like that. Brother Timothy probably never even met him. Inwardly she sighs to herself. She's run her line of questioning out.

"You've been very cooperative, Brother Timothy. We appreciate that."

Johnny asks, "Perhaps, we could take a look at the facility before we leave?"

Brother Timothy stands up. "Certainly, follow me." He leads them out into the hallway and pauses in front of a table. "We screen here in the entryway," he says, "before they are allowed in the dorm. In addition to the prohibitions concerning sobriety on the sign outside, we do not accept anyone seriously ill—mentally or physically—but refer them elsewhere. We have no medical staff or capability in that regard. Normally we fill all our beds by 8:15 each night, and we're forced to turn other clients away after that."

"How many on staff?" Johnny asks.

"Six full-time," Brother Timothy replies. "Myself and Jeremy handle most of the day-to-day logistics and administration—with him focusing on direct supervision of the young staff. We have four counselors. Two on duty every night, to do screening, hand out bed linen, keep order, and to sleep over. They're supposed to have everyone up and out each morning by 7:30."

He leads them through an open doorway into the dormitory, a long room with three aisles lined with double bunk racks, each bare mattress displaying an uncovered pillow atop two folded olive-green blankets. It resembles a military barracks in its practical simplicity. At the far end of an aisle, Jeremy is supervising a group of young people, who are mopping and cleaning up. "Of course," Brother Timothy adds, "we count on a large number of volunteers from the community for help in fund-raising or more routine daily requirements, like these five high school seniors you see here, taking a community service internship at Washington High, I believe."

Johnny nods, and then asks, "You don't have a kitchen?"

"We don't serve food," Brother Timothy replies. "That requires a whole different agenda, including permits, licenses, and inspections involving compliance to several different jurisdictions. And there are a number of excellent programs already serving food in the Tenderloin, like St. Anthony's. But we do have a small laundry room. We do our own linen." He leads them to the far right, a Dutch door, and a garage-sized laundry room, where they watch another pair of high school volunteers loading two commercial-size washers with sheets from a hamper. At the far end of the room an unmanned, giant dryer turns, white pillowcases flopping around in its large glass window. Along the entire length of wall are shelves stacked with freshly laundered linen.

"Clean sheets and pillow cases are issued here through the door each night, the dirty linen turned back in the next morning by 7:30," Brother Timothy explains, closing the bottom half of the Dutch door.

Katy watches for a few moments, reminded of the much larger

laundry in the basement of Sutter General Hospital in Sacramento where Red Chief worked. This place is not nearly as loud or as dusty, she thinks.

After another minute, Brother Timothy announces, "Well, that's about the extent of the tour. Nothing much else to see around here at this time of day. Of course it's busier and a lot noisier after the clients begin coming in at 7:30 tonight."

They follow him back into the entryway, but before they can shake hands and offer their thanks, they hear a key in the front door.

Two young men enter, one fair and medium height, the other tall and dark, both clean-cut in appearance.

"Ah," Brother Timothy says, "these are tonight's counselors, Derwood St. James and Waylon Bryant, here early today for a staff meeting, before I leave for the evening." After introducing Katy and Johnny, Brother Timothy says, "Come back again or call if you have any more questions for your article, Miss Green." He begins to take a step toward his office—

"Oh, do you mind if we visit a few minutes with your counselors, ask them a few questions?" Johnny says, holding his hand out to Brother Timothy.

Katy notices a slight tightening of the lines at the corners of the man's eyes, but he smiles and replies, "Of course not. Be my guest. But you will have to excuse me now, I have some pressing paperwork I want to finish before the staff meeting..." He glances at his watch. "Ten minutes, Derwood, Waylon?"

The counselors both nod.

Johnny shakes his hand. "Thank you from both of us for your cooperation."

Katy adds, "I'll be in touch if I need more information, Brother Timothy."

The well-dressed head of the shelter disappears into his office.

Katy and Johnny turn their attention to the young men.

St. James, the tall, dark boy has apparently recognized Katy's name. "Haven't you written some stuff for the *Guardian*?"

She nods and smiles.

"I thought so. The interview with Kim Stanley Robinson, right? He's my favorite writer, the *Orange County* trilogy, the *Mars* trilogy, and the new book, *Antarctica,* all are really cool novels."

The other boy just stands by, quietly watching the exchange.

"I'm glad someone is reading my stuff and Stan's, too," Katy says, smiling a little self-consciously. "Do you think we could ask you two a few questions about the shelter?"

"Sure, why not," St. James says, glancing at his quiet friend. Waylon Bryant just nods his agreement, looking a little embarrassed by the attention.

"We're specifically interested in three recent clients who died unexpectedly after being turned away from the shelter. Jaime O'Brien, Joey Bartkowski, and D.L. Mathews. Do either of you know anything about those residents or their deaths?"

"No," St. James says, "other than hearing about them from Jeremy."

Bryant shakes his head.

"Jeremy told you about them?"

"Yeah, I didn't even really remember the three guys," St. James answers. "Did you, Waylon?"

Bryant replies, "No."

"How come Jeremy remembered?" asks Johnny.

"He kinda takes a… well, a special interest in some of the younger clients here at the shelter, if you know what I mean?" St. James replies, shrugging dismissively.

Katy nods, glancing sideways at her partner.

"So, he mentioned that each of the three had died the night after being turned away from here?" Johnny says.

"Yeah," St. James answers. "All three were OD's, I think he told us."

Katy directs a question at Bryant, "Other than maybe Jeremy and the two on-duty counselors, *who* would know why and when someone was turned away?"

The young man looks taken aback, shrugging his lack of an immediate answer, then finally saying, "I'm not sure, maybe another resident?"

St. James volunteers, "Perhaps another client waiting in line nearby would notice when someone was turned away. But they wouldn't necessarily know why. I don't think anyone else would be interested in a turn down."

"What about Brother Timothy?"

Bryant laughs, adding in a slightly derisive tone, "He's always long gone by that time of night. He'll leave right after he talks at the staff meeting in a few minutes."

At that point, Katy shifts the questioning, "I imagine you two are college students or graduates?"

St. James says, "Not a grad, but I'm going to take two fall courses at San Francisco City College."

Bryant shakes his head. "I just finished taking and passing my GED last month."

"I see," she says. "Where did you get your training as counselors?"

"Actually that title is misleading," St. James answers, looking a little uncomfortable. "Brother Timothy sends all new hires to the Crises Center Workshop, then everyone here calls them counselors."

"That's the one where they train volunteer counselors to man their hotlines?" Johnny asks, looking at Bryant.

The boy answers, "That's right."

"How long does training last?" Katy follows up.

"The orientation is two days," St. James replies. "Then you work phones at the Center and attend seminars for another three days."

"One week's training?" Johnny says, unable to suppress an almost incredulous look on his face.

St. James smiles and nods. "Actually, your first week back here is OJT with the on-duty counselors.

Johnny smiles thinly. "Okay."

Katy says, "May I ask your salaries?"

"We're paid $80 for each twelve-hour-shift, which normally includes eight hours sleep-over time," the tall boy says, "and Kaiser health benefits after six months on the job. I get benefits next month," he adds with a grin.

It hits Katy then, that these two are just part of the huge labor pool of unskilled young people that man the normal unskilled service jobs of the city—including the McDonalds, the Domino Pizzas, the other fast food places. But these two have a little better gig and they're more than happy to get paid while they sleep at night.

After Johnny asks a couple of more routine questions, St. James lets them out the front door.

They pause for a moment on the street, watching a tanned and wrinkled old man talking to the parking meter in front of their car.

"Well?" Johnny says to Katy.

She just shakes her head. "His shelter may not be a rip-off, but Brother Timothy is certainly a mercenary in the war on poverty." As she follows Johnny to the car, she adds, "But in addition to learning that we don't like the boss, what did we learn about the murders?"

Johnny gives the old man some change, then he replies, "Not much, except we need a little more background on our hippie friend, Jeremy Featherstone, don't you think?"

"Oh, yeah," she agrees.

QUESTIONS BUT
NO ANSWERS

J ust after 7:00 p.m., Hap, Richie, Johnny, and Katy meet at the P.I. office. Johnny takes charge of their initial meeting, summarizing results of his and Katy's first day, including Jeremy Featherstone's awareness and interest in the three victims. He then explains his Progress Board, a blackboard with four columns: PERP'S DESCRIPTION; QUESTIONS; ANSWERS; and MISC. DATA.

He leaves the columns blank, setting down the piece of chalk. "We'll make some entries later, especially in the Questions column," he says. "But for now, let's see what progress each of you others have made today. Hap?"

The big man takes his unlit cigar from his mouth, an apologetic, almost sheepish look on his normally cheerful face. "Homicide almost threw me out of their office, today. 'We're not interested in dirty foreheads and scratched arms on dead junkies, for crissake. Come back if you get something solid.'" The characteristic smile creeps back on his pudgy face. "I didn't get a copy of the third kid's IDS, but I sweet-talked an old records clerk friend of mine, and she's going to keep looking, see if she can dig it up. If it's there, Darcy'll find it. And I spoke to one of the blues, actually the guy who found Jaime, wrote up his IDS. After I mentioned it, he agreed that the smudge mark possibly did resemble a letter *J*."

"Okay, Hap," Johnny says. "Good work." He nods at Richie. "You get a chance to talk privately to any staff at 815?"

"I talked to a pair of the older counselors, people I know well and trust. They didn't notice anything unusual when Jaime and the others split. But they're going to nose around, let me know if they dig anything up."

"Okay," Johnny says. "A slow start, but a start. Katy, you want to bring up anything at all?"

"Yeah, how about C.I.s, Hap? You got any left on the street here in the city?"

Before the big guy can take his unlit cigar from his mouth, Richie interrupts with a question, "What's a C.I.?"

Katy smiles and nods. "Sorry, Richie. Cop argot. *Confidential informant.* When something like this goes down, sometimes the perp talks to someone, maybe that someone talks to another someone, so eventually the word slips back out onto the street. It's iffy, but you never know how or when a break will come." She turns back and nods to Hap.

"Yeah, still got a few contacts, you know. I'll check around tomorrow, see what's on the street." He pops his cigar back into his mouth.

"You might ask around, too, Richie," Katy suggests. "Even though you don't call them C.I.s, you must still know some street people who are aware of what's going down?"

Richie smiles. "Yeah, there are lots of people like that out there, especially in the 'loin, the Mission, and the Haight. I still know a few. I'll ask around."

"Katy's thinking about an article in the *Guardian*, alert the community, maybe put a little pressure on SFPD to get more involved, be a little more cooperative," Johnny says, his tone tentative. "What do you guys think? Too early for something like that or what?"

Richie shrugs. "Not my department, not my call."

Hap replies thoughtfully, "Why don't we hold up on that for a day or so, see what I come up with tomorrow, see if my clerk comes up with the other IDS. Give me a chance to talk to the patrolman who made out the other kid's IDS—he may remember more than he wrote, too, especially about that *J* or whatever on the forehead. It will be better for my relationships in the department if Homicide gets on board voluntarily without somebody prodding them in the ass, you know what I'm saying?"

"I understand," Katy says. "I'll just think about a rough draft of the community alert angle for now."

Johnny says, "Tomorrow, there's a noon NA meeting at Capp Street. I think I'll go over and check in with a few acquaintances, see if they know anything. Then run a background check on Mr. Featherstone at the shelter. We'll probably go back and talk to him, but be much better prepared this time. Okay... Anyone got anything else?"

No one adds anything.

Johnny stands. "Let's fill in a few items on the board, mostly questions right now." He writes:

What does the J mean? Is perp using poison?
What does Jeremy Featherstone know? What's the word on the street?

Then he turns and faces the others. "Let's meet again tomorrow about the same time. Okay?"

Everyone nods.

Richie leans over and asks Katy, "Want to pick up your second installment, tonight?"

"Sure, right now?"

He nods and gestures for her to follow him.

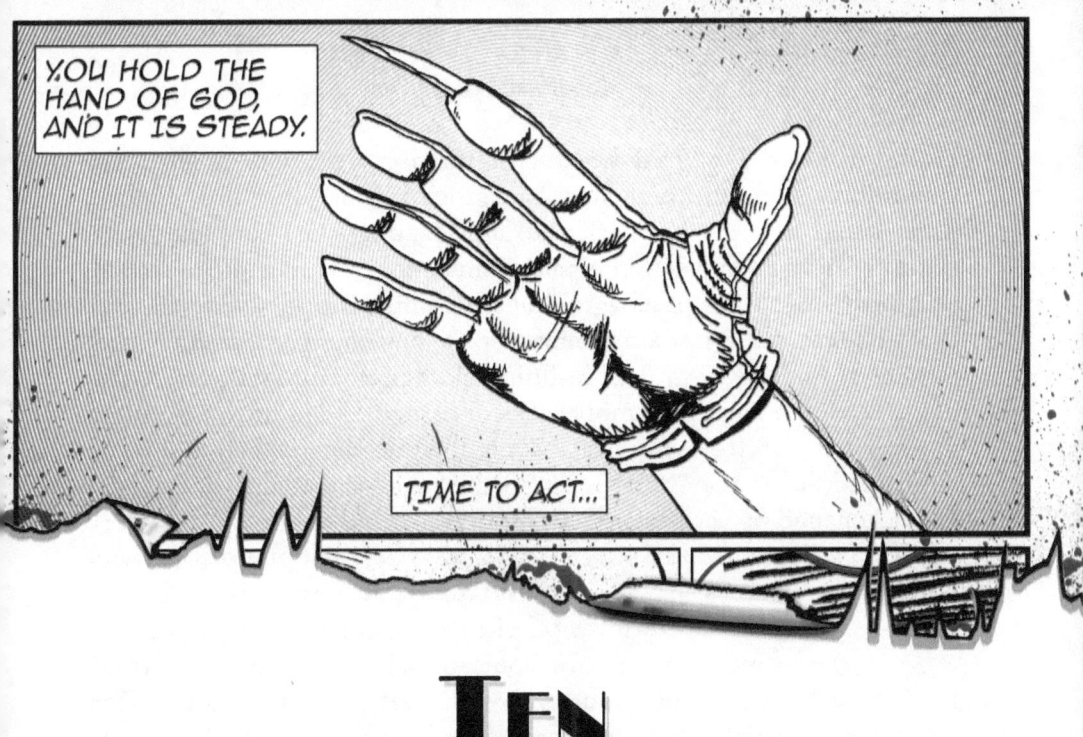

YOU HOLD THE HAND OF GOD, AND IT IS STEADY.

TIME TO ACT...

TEN

Abstain from fleshly lusts, which war against the soul.

1 Peter 2:11

Y ou wait across the street, invisible in the shadowed doorway, ignoring the penetrating dampness of the mist that settles over the neighborhood. Waiting and watching. Most of this block at street level is dark, everything closed at this time of night, storefronts secured by chained heavy metal latticework grills, entryways littered with the nightly accumulation of paper, plastic, and bottles, the drab sleaziness relieved only by the colorful graffiti sprayed here and there—gang symbols, short rants, tagger names, and cartoon-like scenes in bright green, yellow, blue, and red. At mid block across from you, through a heavily barred window, a neon-blue sign blinks:

RAY'S

It provides a blurred beacon in the fog that attracts shadowy apparitions from the darkened background, who only take human form when they finally reach the light fanning out from the open doorway next to the sign, the pale illumination revealing a procession of mostly male faces of all ages, but with similar lined, dissipated, and defeated features. After a moment or two they emerge from the store, pausing to hide away in their ill-fitting clothing the brown bags or the contents of the bags, the empty sacks discarded to end up in the gutter or screened storefront entryways. Only then do their etched, sad faces soften a little, as they hurry off into the night, apparently buoyed by their exchange of hard-earned nickels, dimes, and quarters for a short leg of *Mad Dog*, or a forty-ouncer of *Magnum*, or a half pint of *Wild Irish Rose*. The purchases are the last and probably unsuccessful line of defense against the nightly invasion of demons in this neighborhood.

You try to wait patiently for your special sinner, the one stalked from here last night; but you are a little early, overly anxious, your throat dry and tight with anticipation and need. You stand on your tiptoes, flexing the muscles of your legs, then suck in a long deep breath, trying to settle your nerves. But nothing seems to help much as you cope with your own demon.

At last a shadow catches your attention, something familiar in its stooped appearance and stiffly shuffling gait. The figure stops in the lighted doorway, glancing up and down the block, like a mangy cur at an overturned garbage can, ever wary of its competitors. In that revealing moment you recognize the old man's lined face and your pulse races wildly.

Oh, yes, you have been waiting for *him*, hoping he will make his appearance.

You watch as the old man disappears into the liquor store. Quickly you leave the doorway, turning left and hurrying down the block, hesitating for a brief moment at the mouth of the alley to glance both ways, careful not to attract any attention before you finally duck into the passageway.

At the end of the empty alley you slip in behind the dumpster overflowing with flattened cardboard, select a short piece, drop it at your feet, then kneel down. Concealed from view behind the dumpster now, you suck in a deep breath, the icy air chilling you to the core, making you shiver, but the overwhelming reek of urine suddenly making the breath catch in your throat.

You cough, suppressing a gag.

Then you try to consciously divert your attention from the strong odor, knowing the old man will soon be returning to this spot. You won't be here long, you promise. You busy yourself, slipping the Hand of God from your pocket, tugging the glove carefully onto your right hand and flexing your index finger. A drop of liquid oozes from the hollow metal talon, glistening like a jewel in the dim light. Fascinated, you stare at the lethal gem for a moment, your gaze frozen by the iridescent beauty of the deadly drop. Finally, you break out of the semi-trance and breathe easily through your mouth.

You are ready.

Yes, indeed.

After a few moments your knees begin to stiffen and ache, one sheet of cardboard not nearly enough of a cushion for the hard asphalt surface. You glance at your watch: 8:01 p.m. It won't be long. You have to tough it out now, not daring to rise up and be seen getting more cardboard to help cushion your knees.

It seems like an eternity before the quiet is finally disturbed by heavy footsteps.

You hold your breath, cock your head, and listen intently.

Yes, the slapping sounds are moving in your direction. It's him, the old man.

He finally comes to a stop, so close that you can count each labored breath. Like you did earlier, he pulls a piece of cardboard off the top of the stack, just above your head, and lets it drop to the ground. Then, you hear him sit and you feel him lean back heavily against the dumpster. Just like last night, when you followed and watched from the mouth of the alley. Same place, same routine.

Another moment or two passes, and you hear him drinking his purchase, making greedy gulping sounds. When he's finished, he tosses the empty bottle noisily aside. Still, you remain frozen in place, your aching knees crying out for relief now; but all you can do is grit your teeth and try to quietly shift your weight, leaning forward slightly as the minutes crawl by, nothing easing the ache. Pins and needles of pain.

At last, he is still and quiet, except for his asthmatic breathing.

You rise stiffly, and for a minute you rub life back into your tingling knees with your bare hand. With some normal feeling back, you slip from concealment behind the dumpster, the filthy stench clinging stubbornly to your presence. For a few moments you just stand quietly over the old man, letting the heavy mist cleanse the lingering foul smell from your nostrils. Only then are you able to look down, order your thoughts for the sacred task at hand.

The old man's chest rises and falls in a labored manner, the breath wheezing from his open mouth like air escaping from a partially punctured bellows. He has slumped forward, his head lolling on the chest of his filthy overcoat, exposing his skinny, dirty neck.

Now is the moment.

But you hesitate, paralyzed by a sudden indecisiveness—a last minute attack of what... *conscience?* This old man is not really a backslider like the three recent addicts. You know nothing about him or his history, other than he is a human derelict. He's a stranger picked at random. This time is much different from anything in your past. You are a hunter now, a stalker of other men, complete strangers.

But the key question—Is it right?

Or could it be wrong?

The Hand of God is shaking. A bad sign.

You feel confused, your conviction shaken, unsure of the answer to the double-pronged question.

You close your eyes, and, after a few moments' thought, you recall and mouth a line from Peter over and over like a mantra: *"Abstain from fleshly lusts, which war against the soul."*

The repeated admonition eventually eases your panic. You feel better. After sucking in a deep chilling breath, you force all lingering doubts aside. No question you are doing the Lord's work, you tell yourself, even with this complete stranger. The man is obviously a self-indulgent sinner who has given himself up to lusting after the bottle. A long-suffering, but obviously unrepentant offender of Biblical canon, beyond possible Earthly redemption. You will be setting his soul free, before he passes away alone some night from exposure, disease, malnutrition, or who knows which other horrible malady. It is truly a service in the Lord's name, preventing additional and unnecessary suffering.

Yes, indeed, you are comfortably convinced of your own righteousness, now. All doubt resolved.

The Hand of God is steady. A good sign.

Time to act.

In one smooth motion you squat by his side and caress the old man's dirty neck with the talon, leaving a long, bloody wound opened from his ear to his breast bone. He groans in his sleep, his head slipping off his chest to the cardboard with a loud plop; but surprisingly he does not waken.

You stand and wait.

A minute passes... almost two.

His breathing becomes more labored, rattling in his chest, and his eyelids flicker just before he gasps a weak moan. A tremor rumbles weakly through the old man's upper body, cut off by a last gasp for breath—

At that moment the stunning spectacle explodes from his chest!

Your senses are bombarded, and you are absorbed in the sight, the sound, the touch, and the smell. You even open your mouth and swallow, trying to taste it. Oh, yes. After a moment you begin to relax, a warm glow slowly building in the pit of your stomach, then radiating waves out across every synapse of your nervous system, traveling to the very tips of your fingers and toes, the sensations so strong, so soothing, so calming that your knees grow weak and almost buckle under your weight. You forget yourself, close your eyes, and give yourself up completely to the awesome, orgasmic experience, unable to suppress a loud moan of pleasure.

The joy of it, the utter relief after so long!

Oh, yes...

And after a few minutes, feeling completely drained of all tension, you blink, realizing the dancing gems have been coalesced into a hovering ball of brilliance for some time now. Shimmering in front of you.

Waiting for guidance.

For a few seconds you struggle to concentrate, to pull yourself together, and to regain control. You have a duty to finish performing; you are only partially through your obligations.

"Yes, indeed," you whisper, forcing yourself to look down at the relaxed face of the stranger at your feet. So peaceful in repose, relieved of his wheezing, his alcoholic demons banished forever.

You strip off the Hand of God and carefully slip it into your windbreaker pocket. Then, you drop to a knee by the side of the prostrate old man, dig the tin from your other pocket, dip into the ashes, and with a steady forefinger you calmly trace the sign of the Shepherd on his forehead. Finished with the marking, you replace the container of ashes in your pocket.

Good, almost done.

Then, knowing in your heart that you are showing this unknown suffering sinner the ultimate kindness, you bow your head, and begin to pray aloud, "Dear Lord, please accept this soul that I commend to thee…"

You barely complete your duties before you see the aura of light, feel the hot flush, smell the wet eucalyptus leaves, and hear the old man's voice.

So soon—?

The spike is slammed into your sinus cavity.

My God, the blinding agony of it.

Nauseous, but too stricken to even vomit, you are overcome by the spell of faintness.

Dazed and gasping for breath, you partially regain your senses, then glance at your watch, the figures taking a moment or two to focus and register: 8:18 p.m. You must have actually been struck fully unconscious for at least two minutes, completely vulnerable if someone came along and saw you standing

like a statue beside the empty shell of the old sinner—

Crunch.

A sound from the mouth of the alley.

Startled, you glance up, but only catch a glimpse of a disappearing shadow.

The shadow of a person?

Or an animal?

Yes, only a cat, a dog, you think hopefully.

You stare at the empty entryway, unsure of what you saw… if anything was really there. And the sound, the sound?

You take a step, but your knees give way, and you just catch yourself before falling, reaching out with a steadying hand against the alley wall. You have to get away from here. But you are so weak, this attack the worst, each one seeming to last a little longer, more severe in nature than the last episode. You rest in place a moment longer, sucking in another deep breath of cold air. Glancing again at the alley mouth, you're consumed by another wave of paranoia.

What if the sound *had* been someone there a minute ago? you ask yourself. The thought stiffens you with fear.

At this very moment they may be alerting the authorities of what they have seen take place here. No one will understand what you have really done, the Lord's work. No indeed. "Escape, now!" you whisper hoarsely, trying to take control of your escalating panic.

Despite the real danger of being apprehended you are forced to linger, your shaky legs barely able to support your weight. You close your eyes again, fight for mental and physical control of yourself and wait as your strength gradually begins to return.

Another minute and you blink, feeling a little stronger.

It is time to do something about these debilitating attacks, you tell yourself.

But what?

See a doctor, get medical help?

Yes, maybe there is a drug or therapy that will help to prevent the attacks.

Your spirit spikes.

But your elation is short lived, for you realize the solution is illogical.

Of course you can't see a doctor.

How would you explain what actually triggers the attacks?

Describe using the Hand of God? And the Gift of Sight, the unique ability to see the Deathflash? Explain about the previous Shepherd's admonition concerning unauthorized use... ?

No, you can never tell anyone anything about any of this. They would only laugh, think you insane if you persisted.

It's ridiculous to even consider the idea of outside help.

No doctor, no medicine. Period.

Heal yourself, as the Book says.

You will just have to steel yourself to the attacks, reconcile yourself to the pain. Perhaps you can cut the time spent on doing your duty and get away from the scene *before* the onset of the mind-numbing, crippling pain. Reduce your window of vulnerability.

Maybe that's possible.

Yes, you will try.

Your thoughts return to your present predicament.

Right *now* you must escape from here, this location.

With an effort of will, you push away from the wall and head for home, breathing deeply again, regaining almost complete physical control, forcing the negative memory of the terrible attack from your consciousness and momentarily forgetting about the glimpse of a shadowy presence at the mouth of the alley. Instead, you focus your thoughts on the positive, the glorious moments of being bathed in the hovering Deathflash, and the settling, calming effect of the whole experience.

Something you truly needed.

Yes indeed.

2

A little later, approaching your apartment building, a car turns your way, its lights flashing into a doorway directly across the street from your address, exposing for just a brief moment two people in long raincoats, standing side-by-side on the stairway.

Alarms go off in your head, your breath catches in your throat, and thoughts leap about in your head like startled rabbits.

Why are they there?

What do they want?

Who are they?

The police?

You remember the shadowy glimpse of something at the mouth of the alley. The sound preceding it. Someone must've indeed spotted you as you set the old sinner's spirit free.

Or perhaps saw you, standing stunned and incapacitated in a pain-induced trance next to his empty husk?

Maybe even followed you from the alley?

Or... ?

Your heart thumps rapidly, your pulse races wildly.

At that moment, a man and a woman move into the light and stroll away from you, up the street to a parked van.

You gasp, surprised.

Not the authorities.

Just a couple.

Thank God.

You breathe a loud sigh of relief.

Regaining your composure, you remain in place for a minute, but that first initial image of two people in long coats lurking in the shadows, apparently waiting for you, reminds you vividly of your fortunate escape from St. Louis…

3

Anxious to get started, you had arrived a little early for your job at Quail Ridge Nursing Home on the East side—a full fifteen minutes before midnight. The swing shift custodian, DeWayne Hurd, had stripped, mopped, and waxed the main hallway after traffic had died down around 10:30 p.m. or so. Now, as planned by the two of you the night before, you were making your way slowly down the long hall from the main entrance, buffing the freshly waxed old linoleum to a high gloss. To the left in a gliding slow wide arc with the buffer, then smoothly back right to the opposite wall, the soft whirr of the machine and the monotonous rhythm of the task almost dulling your anticipation.

Almost, but not quite.

You grinned to yourself, and nervously glanced up, as Josie Washington, the young night shift aide, slipped by on your right. She just nodded as she passed, after completing her first round of checking on patients, on her way back to the main desk up front by the reception area.

You made one more pair of half arcs with the buffer, and then looked at the reception desk.

Josie and Mrs. Hrbek, the night nurse, were sitting now, doing paperwork, actually out of your sight. More importantly, you were out of their view. And Mr. Toomey, the graveyard shift security guard, was at this moment starting his nightly outside tour of the grounds, checking windows and doors, making sure all the lawn furniture was locked in the shed.

Everything going as planned, you thought, as you slipped the machine into neutral, the buffer's motor still humming, but the machine resting in place. You glanced at the closed door to your left, 110, the next to last on that side of the main wing, directly across from the janitorial supply closet.

Looking at your watch, you figured on a window of about ten minutes unobserved: 12:25 to 12:35. By then, Mr. Toomey would have completed his outside round, returning inside to the front desk and visiting for a minute with the two women, before making his first inside pass, including this main hallway.

Before 12:35, no one should even glance down the wing. But just in case, you left the buffer running in neutral in the middle of the floor, as you stepped across the hall and opened the supply closet door, leaving it noticeably ajar. Returning to the other side of the hall, you hesitated just a moment before the closed door, 110. Just long enough to have slipped on the Hand of God in your jacket pocket.

Then you cracked open the door, whispering softly into the darkness, "Mr. Jacobson?"

No answer.

Good.

You stepped in, closed the door, and paused, letting your eyes grow accustomed to the darkened room.

Not even a stir from the thin-faced man lying on his back in the bed, an I.V. hooked into the back of his right hand, the only sound in the room the steady breathing of his respirator.

Mr. Jacobson was very old, very sick.

Yes, it was his time.

You approached the bed, withdrawing the Hand from your pocket, and with one motion, you scraped the old man's exposed left forearm with the talon.

Only then did he move, a slight facial tremor.

And, after a few minutes, he frowned ever so slightly, sighed, and died—

The Deathflash exploded from his chest!

You stood frozen, fascinated with the glorious spectacle of the hovering lights, enjoying the experience even more than the first time back in the holler with the old Shepherd, if that were possible.

Awesome.

Breathtaking.

Yes, it was truly a hypnotic, exhilarating experience.

But you were still consciously aware of your duty and the closing window of time. You withdrew the container of ashes you carried from home, drawing the sign of the Shepherd on Mr. Jacobson's forehead, before you kneeled bedside and began the prayer, "Dear Lord, please accept this soul that I commend to thee…"

It was 12:34 when you slipped back out into the hall from 110, back to your buffing job. But, before you finished the hallway, you experienced a strange flushing sensation of your face and a funny tunneling of the light, accompanied by the faint medicinal smell of eucalyptus, followed by a piercing pain above your right eye. At that moment you remembered the warning of the old Shepherd lying on his deathbed back at the Big House, regarding approved use of the Gift and Hand only by the Bishops. His stern words ringing in your head: *Unauthorized use of the Hand of God and Gift of Sight will bring down on your head painful consequences.*

Both pain and admonition had disappeared even before you took two aspirins at the main desk a few minutes later. Of course you dismissed the voice in your head, attributing it to an overly excited imagination; but the sharp pain and the other peculiar sensations had been real enough for sure, leaving you actually drained of all energy.

An hour after giving you the pain relievers, Mrs. Hrbek noticed you dragging around and insisted you take off early, right after you finished the last of your most pressing nightshift custodial tasks.

Later that night, after getting off the bus in the dark at your stop, you walked half a block and stopped short of your apartment building, spotting the two men in long coats standing in your shadowed doorway, recognizing them almost instantly. The two youngest Bishops from back home. Waiting for you, but obviously not expecting you quite so early. Questions whirled in your head.

Why had they come?
What were they going to do?
Take back the Hand of God, the sacred ashes, and the poison?
Try and drag you back to the holler?
Did they suspect anything about tonight?
Maybe they were going to have you arrested?
Maybe the police were right now on their way?
But how could they have known about tonight?
They couldn't… unless they were at the nursing home.
Confused, you weren't sure what was happening. And as you

remained in the shadows out of view you were badly unnerved by your own speculations. You decided that you were too shaken to confront the two Bishops for whatever reason they had in mind.

You turned and fled back up the street into the night.

Downtown, at the Greyhound Bus Station, you looked up at the departure schedule, a confusing blur of unfamiliar town names, the destination, *Chicago*, finally popping out and catching your eye. You stepped to the counter and asked the ticket clerk, "How long before the next bus leaves for Chicago?"

After checking his watch, the bald man answered, "Well, you're in luck, young man, considering that it's Sunday morning and a reduced schedule. There's actually an express leaving in just twelve minutes at 6:00."

"Give me a ticket," you said, feeling happy at first, but also a little sad about leaving St. Louis so soon. You'd only been there about six weeks, just long enough to cash your first full paycheck from your job, yesterday. Fortunately, you still had most of that money in your pocket.

At that moment you remembered the Bishops waiting back at your apartment.

How had they tracked you to St. Louis, to your specific address?

Had Bet revealed your destination?

No, she wouldn't do that, not after you told her it was a secret. Not Bet.

Maybe the Bishops found out your destination down at Camden, at the bus station?

Yes, of course, that was probably how they did it. Then they followed your trail somehow to your apartment building. You had used your own name. And of course they could do that over again, starting here in St. Louis at the Greyhound Station.

No, you weren't going to allow that to happen not if you could prevent it. You would need a different name. But first you had to cover your trail.

"You never saw me if anyone ever asks, okay?" you said, slipping an extra twenty dollars to the bald ticket clerk. A precious share of your slim savings.

He stamped the ticket, counted the fare money, put the twenty in his pocket, and finally replied with a sly grin, "Gate 3, six sharp, Mr. Faceless Man."

Surprisingly for so early on a Sunday morning, the bus, when you got on, was almost full. In the next to last row, you slipped into a window seat next to a middle-aged, heavy-set woman, who looked up from the newspaper she was reading with a no-nonsense expression, and shook her head when you asked if anyone was sitting there.

A little later, the rising sun shining in your face through the window prevented you from dozing off any longer. You straightened up in the seat and looked around.

The woman next to you was still reading the Sunday edition of the *St. Louis Post Dispatch*, but kind of smiling in a cynical way. She shook her head, nodded at the article she was reading in the paper. "Now, don't this beat all," she said, shifting and leaning her heavy bulk your way slightly, holding open the paper so you could see the Sunday Feature Section. "Some people will believe in almost anything if it's in the name of religion."

The article took up most of the page, and there were several grainy black and white photos—

The Big House!

Mama's little cabin!

You were stunned, just able to scan the headline before the woman leaned back in her seat:

NEW SHEPHERD ABANDONS FLOCK
by Ann Jones and J.T. Warner

After a moment you cleared your throat and asked hoarsely, "May I read that article when you are finished, ma'am?"

She glanced your way again with her stern expression, then, after looking you over carefully, her features softened slightly, and she nodded. "Sure you can, son. I'm finished with this part anyhow." She slipped out the Feature Section from the rest of the *Post* and handed it over to you.

"Thank you, ma'am," you said gratefully, and opened the pages to the article and pictures.

You read slowly.

It was an article by a pair of reporters, who had apparently visited the holler three weeks after you'd left. The sidebar said the full-time reporter, Warner, taught a Journalism class at Washington University and first heard about the Flock from a student, Ann Jones, a young woman from a family who lived in the forest near the holler. Someone in the student's family had written to her about your sudden disappearance.

The reporters described the Flock, never mentioning any specific names or the exact location of the holler, but wrote that the group was "an isolated off-beat religious cult located deep in the Ouachita Mountains of Arkansas." The details seemed fairly accurate and presented in a straight-forward manner, except there was a real sense of skepticism concerning some of the specific beliefs, like the transfer by touch of the Gift of Sight from the old Shepherd to you when he died. The last of the article detailed the distress of the Flock over your disappearance, and the search for you by the elders. They longed for their new Shepherd to come home to the holler and minister to his Flock. That explained the Bishops showing up at your apartment back in St. Louis.

You looked over the photos carefully, especially the cabin, hoping for a glimpse of Bet or even one of the others in your family in the background. But there was no one in any of the pictures.

You read the article twice, including the quotes from a number of unnamed people, annoyed and disappointed that members of the Flock would reveal so much about themselves to outsiders, including intimate details of religious practices, like the use of the sacred ashes from cremated remains of elders to make the sign of the Shepherd.

You shook your head several times with disbelief, lost in thought until the bus stopped for a meal break.

Later, back on the bus, you dropped off into an exhausted sleep, awakening only after finally arriving in Chicago. You thanked the woman next to you for letting you keep the paper and got off the bus.

It would be only an hour or so before you stumbled accidentally into your new job, becoming almost immediately involved again in the Lord's work with a seemingly inexhaustible supply of lost souls to save. An ideal situation.

4

Later, back at your apartment in the Tenderloin, you are restless, unable to go right to sleep, tossing and turning for what seems like hours.

At 3:30 a.m. you awaken suddenly and sit up in bed, your chest tight, your mouth bone-dry, hearing again the earlier sound accompanying the disappearing shadow at the mouth of the alleyway. You hear it very clearly now, and, of course, you recognize the sound. Roller skate wheels *scrunching* away on the concrete sidewalk.

It's the sound of a scooter-board skating off into the night.

You gasp, for in your heart, you are certain that you have been observed in the Lord's work tonight. After all the care and planning executing the dispatches, markings, and prayers of the last eight months since coming to the city, you have again been seen by someone as you performed your duty.

You get up, go to the sink in the kitchen, and drink a glass of water, trying to ease the painful dryness of your throat, relieve the tension in your stomach.

No question in your mind, you have been spotted.

After another minute of stomach-knotting anxiety, you finally smile wryly and begin to relax, because you realize that you know the identity of the skateboarder.

The smile turns to a wide grin.

It could be only one person that time of night. Oh, yes, you have seen him a number of times in the Tenderloin collecting aluminum cans and bottles. Or just hanging out with street people. Come to think about it, you have seen him during the day, too, over at the Greyhound Bus Depot. Tomorrow, you will try to find out his name, maybe where he lives, follow him, and detail his habits.

Maybe he hasn't told others what he saw. Not yet. But he will sooner or later. Of that you are sure. And by doing that he will be directly interfering with the Lord's work. Of course that cannot happen. No.

A surge of anger overwhelms you.

Calming down after a moment, you vow that you will not let a cripple, a small-time black hustler, stop your work, your duty. It is too important. No, if he did see you, he must be shut up somehow before he talks to anyone about it.

You suddenly feel very calm, now that the necessary course of action has been clearly defined in your mind.

SCORIN'

Smart junkie always has a good inside connection.

—Beechnut

After the meeting at the P.I. office, Richie takes Katy out for the second installment on their agreement.

He drives over to Mission Street just as it begins to get dark, explaining that tonight they will focus on scorin', how a junkie gets his dope. He parks his Volvo, then they get out, and Richie walks Katy half a block to the corner, telling her, "Along here is one of the easiest but most dangerous places to score in the city, 16th between Mission and Valencia... Yeah, here, and over at Eddy and Jones in the Tenderloin."

The detached, cynical, hard edge is back in his tone, his game face on.

Katy notices it's actually quite pleasant out, an unusually warm night for the city, many people still comfortable in T-shirts, tank tops, and shorts. But as she turns the corner and sees the mob of people, she senses a sudden temperature shift. Almost like the chilling effect of going into an unfamiliar place in Sacramento after a murder suspect, with her gun drawn, her pulse racing, every muscle tense. The electrical tension in the air on 16th is palpable, making the short hair on the back of her neck stand up.

Katy knows that what she senses is *evil*.

She stops to take a deep breath, control her apprehension.

"You okay?" Richie asks, touching her arm.

"Yeah, just a passing strange feeling, you know like pre-game jitters," Katy says dismissively, smiling at him. "How are we going to know who's a dealer in this big crowd?"

Dropping his hand, Richie snaps sarcastically, "That's easy, they're the ones with tombstones in their eyes."

He smiles at her before they begin to move along again, obviously trying to soften his expression, but his forehead remains deeply creased, his eyes cold and sad. He adds in a slightly gentler tone, "Don't worry, they'll find us, Katy."

She nods back and shifts her gaze.

They begin to walk along 16th.

"Ya lookin', Mama?" a black man hanging onto a nearby parking meter says to Katy in a sinister whisper from the corner of his mouth. "Ya lookin'?" He's old, unkempt, his clothes smelly, tattered, and filthy, and his dark eyes are indeed dead.

She clears her throat but does not respond.

Richie whispers in her ear, "He ain't a dealer, just a derelict hoping to get a finder's fee," and clutches her arm tightly, guiding her away from the shabby old man a few paces along 16th into the people flow.

Actually, Katy notices that the people divide into two distinct groups. Those bustling along quickly, dressed casually for the weather, but obviously in a hurry to be somewhere else: *The Citizens*. And then loitering on the fringe are the others, mostly dressed in pants and long-sleeved shirts, some actually wearing coats or windbreakers, their clothes wrinkled, dirty, and not fitting well, their expressions wary, alert, predatory: *The Hustlers*.

A young Mexican guy steps out from the shadowed fringe and says in heavily accented English to Richie, "Hey, mon, *coca, tar, outfit?*"

They keep walking, Richie explaining to Katy, "Coca is cocaine as you probably know, tar is heroin, and an outfit or rig is a complete kit for fixing, including cotton balls, a syringe, and cooker made from the concave bottom of an aluminum soda can."

Walking the remaining short distance to the corner of Valencia they're solicited twice more, once by a scroungy bearded, white hippie, and again by a skinny, young Mexican kid, not even old enough to go into a bar.

At the intersection they stop, turn around, and pause.

"This is the absolute tail end of hard times, here," Richie says to her. "Most of these dudes are junkies doing a *four-for-one*. That means they sell four balloons and their dealer gives them a free one. It's a risky place to score. You can get completely ripped off, buying a balloon with no dope, or even arrested after the deal by lurking undercover narcotic agents. At best you're going to buy a balloon that's probably been stepped on by the junkie dealer—"

"Stepped on?"

"*Cut*. Normal balloon is a quarter gram. Junkie can't help but take a little taste from each customer's balloon."

"What's a balloon worth here in the city?"

"Quarter gram normally is twenty bucks, but the word right now on the street is that dope is cheaper—maybe half the regular price. The big sale intended to increase the customer base, make up for the declining market for cocaine. Sometime soon though, after the new customer base is established, the price jumps back up. You understand the supply and demand economics here? Dope is a completely controlled market."

Katy nods, looking back along 16th, watching a transaction right out in the open, a blue balloon exchanged for green dollars. "Why the balloon as a container?" she asks, watching to see if the buyer and seller get away clean. They both turn and quickly walk away in opposite directions, no one apparently paying any attention to what went down.

"Oh, the dealer or junkie can easily hide it in his mouth, and if he has to, he can swallow the balloon, then pass it later. The dope protected, still good."

"Yuk."

"I know," Richie agrees, his face even harder in the fading light. "That's nothing though. Strung-out junkie will go to any lengths to scrounge up a fix—wringing out used cotton balls and cigarette filter tips used to fix from the littered, filthy floor in a shooting gallery, whatever."

"Yeah, I know what you mean, I saw the movie, *Trainspotting*," Katy says, remembering the disgusting scene when the junkie dives in the toilet bowl after his dope.

Richie begins to lead her back toward Mission and the mustard-colored station wagon, saying, "A good rule here on the street is to only buy from Mexicans."

"Why is that?"

"Your chances of getting ripped off are probably higher with whites and blacks," Richie explains. "Almost all heroin in the city is Mexican tar, the low level dealers and distributors all Mexicans. Oh, there may be some China White somewhere over in Chinatown, but you need to be Asian to deal or buy there. So the legit dealers in the Mission, Haight, and 'loin are normally Mexicans."

"I see," Katy says as they reach the car.

"We need a phone, now," Richie says, sliding behind the wheel.

"Right back there on the corner," Katy says, pointing at a beat-up phone kiosk covered with graffiti.

"No, we need one we can get a call-back on," he says, starting the Volvo. "Most street pay phones here, in the 'loin, and in the Haight you can't get a ring back. There's a test number you can call on a phone to see if it will ring back, but I don't have it anymore. There's a cafe ahead I know that has an inside pay phone that's probably good."

2

A few minutes later, Richie is slipping coins into the phone at the back of *The OK Corral*, a narrow little diner with no tables, only a long counter and stools. "I'm calling a beeper number," he explains, after flipping through his notebook. "This number is new and worth money on the street—used to be ten, even twenty bucks to buy one, probably more now. Listen when he rings me back…"

After waiting a few minutes, the phone rings back, and Richie picks it up, holds the receiver tilted away from his ear so Katy can hear too.

"Yes," a voice snaps.

"I need a quarter," Richie whispers back into the phone.

"Ol' Mint, fifteen minutes," the heavily accented voice orders, then hangs up abruptly.

"Come on," Richie says, hurrying back to the street. "We've got to be there waiting."

They head back downtown to the old U.S. Mint Building on 5th Street, luckily finding a nearby parking spot; then they get out and wait in front of the dark and dilapidated government building. Twenty minutes pass, nothing happening. "They're always late," Richie explains. "So, you, needing your fix *now*, wait here getting really twisted, your paranoid thoughts jumping all over the place: Did I get the right address? The right time? Did he forget me? Is he lost? Where is he? Maybe he is out of dope? You watch the street both ways, more bent out of shape than a little kid with a dollar, waiting for an ice cream truck that is really late."

Fifteen minutes later a beat-up '69 Toyota brakes to a squealing halt on the street near them. The driver, a young Mexican with a bandito mustache and badly broken nose stares suspiciously out the open window at them for just about five seconds, then roars off without saying one word.

"Guess you don't look quite right, because the dude made us," Richie says with a thin-lipped smile and a shrug. "Anyhow, this calling a dealer is a little safer than scorin' on 16th Street. We might still get ripped off or busted, but the percentage drops a little. After the driver grabs our money and tosses us a balloon, he still peels out just as fast as that guy. They don't wait around to give receipts. And that's how *they* get hustled. You know, they get shortchanged. Maybe the junkie has cut the corners off a twenty, glued them on a one, or some other goofy scam. Rip-pin' 'n' runnin' all the time. Rule two on the street: You can *never* trust a junkie."

They head back to the station wagon.

3

"I want to take you to this vacant lot because it actually will play in the next installment, too," Richie explains as they head south on 4th Street, slowing when they reach China Basin and the recently completed Pac Bell Park, the new home of the Giants.

They park near the darkened stadium. Then Richie leads Katy in a swing back up 4th and around the block almost to Townsend. "China Basin used to be an office, warehouse, industrial area up until recently. But, since the selection of the baseball park site, it's being gentrified with upscale restaurants, bars, condos, townhouses, as you can see."

Katy glances around. The area is indeed well lit, lots of people still coming and going into the restaurants and clubs, new construction going on in a number of places.

"But ten years ago it was quiet here at night, and I used to come over to this old warehouse back in there." He points across a vacant lot at a two-story building, a red brick wall showing through patches of white stucco siding, the front of the building partially demolished, a nearby lot full of heavy equipment. "Used to be a chain link fence with a gate right about... here, I think, secure-looking with a big lock on a heavy chain, but always left unlocked."

He leads Katy around a KEEP OUT sign and temporary fence, back over the rubble, past the cranes, dozers, and backhoes, and along a remaining sidewall of the building, a rough, reddish background for fresh tagger cartoons and four-letter words, some of the older, fading graffiti on the wall appearing dated but still easily readable:

Tricky Dick a social disease.

Edgar mama stoop for the group.

Make love not war.

Emma Mae do the nasty with Little Anthony—and an obvious later addition—*and Big Henry and JoJo and Baby Junior and...*

Acid is a trip!

Jose sucks the big Juan

"You'd walk along the front warehouse, then here to the rear into the dark, and back to these shaky stairs, only *after* you'd phoned first from the street." They pause, looking at a lopsided, crumbling wooden stairwell at the rear of the brick building leading up to a door in the second story. "Chained under those steps to a pole in the ground was the biggest, baddest pit bull I'd ever seen—Homeboy. If you didn't call, Homeboy was out on a twenty-five-foot chain, and he'd tear an unannounced intruder's leg off if he came anywhere close to that staircase." Richie nods to himself, his gaze distant, lost in thought for a few moments.

"But if you called first?" Katy prods.

He glances back at the stairs.

"Well, Sweet Jane would yell down, 'Friends, Homeboy, friends,' or something like that to the dog from that door up there—a kinda code. Then that gray and white, bigheaded devil would lie down by the pole as you entered the premises. You still had to brave the stairs, with Homeboy watching you intently with his black eyes. He never barked or growled, just glared, as if thinking, *I'd love to tear your balls off, sucker, but you got one free pass.* Didn't take you long to scoot up to the door to the loft with the huge number 8 spray painted in black on it. I think a numeric symbol for the letter H. It was one of my long-time inside contacts and a shooting gallery, but we'll talk about that part next time."

They stand there for a few minutes in silence, then Richie glances about, adding, "Actually there used to be quite a few old vacant lots and empty buildings here South of Market, where people squatted, sold drugs, drank beer, smoked, and shot up. Not anymore, though. Undeveloped real estate anywhere in San Francisco is getting really scarce now with all the dot com stuff going on and stimulating new building."

4

Back at the car, they just sit for a while and Richie explains a little more about scorin'.

"An apartment location in the city for a connection eventually draws too much attention, with all the traffic going in and out. It soon gets busted or robbed. I was in a place back in '88 or '87 over on Grove, just off Divisidero by *Brother-in-laws BBQ #2*, when two dudes in ski masks with AK-47s busted in the door, scared the shit out of everyone, and made us lie face down on the floor. Then they stole all the drugs and cash in the place. That's why a savvy dealer keeps no cash and only limited supplies of dope on hand where he hangs out."

"But an inside connection is best, specifically because... ?" Katy asks.

"Well, it's still safer, you're not so vulnerable as on the street in the open. And an inside dealer is supported by repeat business, he knows his customers personally, so you normally get a fairer measure for what you pay for. Sometimes you can actually fix there, too, like I used to at Sweet Jane's in China Basin."

"What happens when the dealer gets busted, goes out of business?"

Richie shrugs. "You try and find a new inside dealer. Usually introduced by another hooked-up junkie. Word gets around pretty fast when you're living on the street."

Starting up the Volvo, Richie forces a thin smile and adds, "Of course, if you're using it's best to be the bagman your own self. That's probably every junkie's dream."

"Bagman? To deal?"

Nodding, Richie turns out into the fairly heavy, nighttime traffic.

Swinging back uptown, he says, "That's right, and it isn't really hard to do, at least small-time. You can buy in quantity and get a discount from most any beeper dealer. Then go into business. It takes some heavy discipline though to get established; you buy, say, two grams, and you're tempted to use it all yourself. Most junkies can't resist. No good, because you're soon out of business with no hustle... And larger amounts, big-time dealing, including most inside dealers, takes a really good connection up the line. Maybe someone you met in the joint or like that. Someone who trusts you not to give them up in a bust."

He stops and glances over at Katy, still wearing his serious game face. "Of course every junkie who gets his hands on more drugs, uses more, discipline or not, steadily increasing his habit. So inside dealers who are using, and most are, always pack a heavy jones, some as much as $500 retail a day. They don't go on vacations or take off holidays or go to the doctor or anywhere else. So they're there when you need them, you know what I mean?"

Katy nods. "You were never a bagman, were you, Richie?" she whispers in an almost accusatory tone.

He glances her way and smiles wryly. "Actually, I worked legit for most of those years while using. Blue collar. Held a carpentry union card for about ten years, but couldn't hold a job the last year or so of heavy using. No, I never sold dope. Instead, I ran a couple of pretty chicken shit hustles, including selling fast passes in the projects, and burglarizing some little old ladies in my apartment building, but I can say I was never the bagman..."

For some reason, Katy feels better when she hears that Richie was never a junkie dealer. Still, at the same time, she feels sheepish about the judgmental nature of the question and apologizes, "Sorry, I probably had no right to ask something like that."

"Nah, it's okay," Richie says, his tone softening.

J

Early Wednesday morning, the phone ringing awakens Katy.

She glances at the bedside clock and groans: 6:55 a.m.

"Hello," she mumbles, rubbing her eyes.

"Hello, Katy, sorry to call so early…"

It's Hap, she mouths to Johnny, who is awake and looking at her questioningly from his side of the bed.

"Just got a cell phone call from the uniformed officer who wrote up Jaime's IDS," he explains, a hint of excitement obvious in his tone. "He's got a dead body of an old wino in an alley over in the Tenderloin, and he thinks there are some *definite* similarities with Jaime's corpse. So, maybe our boy was out doing his thing again last night."

"Wow, that's a break, the blue taking the trouble to call you, especially at this time of the morning," Katy says, fully awake now. "Where exactly is the body?"

Hap gives Katy the address in the Tenderloin.

"Okay, we'll meet you there in ten, fifteen minutes," she says, already pulling on her jeans with her free hand, signaling for Johnny to get dressed.

"We'll try and keep the Coroner's boys at bay until you get here," Hap replies. "See ya soon."

A wino? she thinks, remembering Richie's idea that the perp may've been hitting others in the underclass. Then she has a brilliant flash. I wonder if this old guy was turned away from Brother Timothy's last night like the three boys? She asks herself. *Good question, girl—file it!*

Alert and dressed, Katy and Johnny get in the car to drive downtown through the thick early-morning fog, the clock on the dash of the Mustang reading 7:01.

2

Hap, the cop, and the Coroner's men are at the end of the alley, standing idly in front of a large, blue dumpster, blowing on their hands and hugging themselves, when Katy and Johnny arrive. The big guy introduces everyone, the two white-clad orderlies looking bored, impatient to bag the body, and get inside out of the cold, wet air.

Katy stares down at an old man wearing a greasy, threadbare, navy-blue overcoat, lying on his back on a sheet of cardboard. He appears to be sleeping peacefully, she thinks, but knowing better and moving closer.

"I didn't disturb nothing after I spotted the *J* on his forehead," the policeman explains with a frown on his face. "But before that I had pulled the cardboard away from the dumpster maybe three feet, so I could more easily check around him without getting too close and having to smell the old geezer. Didn't think it was a big deal at that moment. Sorry."

"It's okay," Katy says absently, pulling on a pair of latex gloves.

"Yeah, we appreciate the call," Johnny says, patting the cop's back.

"Hey!" he says to Katy, a surprised expression on his face, as he takes his first close look down at the victim's features. "I think I've seen this guy before... somewhere."

"You have?" she says, watching Johnny tug roughly at his broken nose.

He stares for a few moments thoughtfully, and then he snaps his fingers and nods, still looking down intently at the dead man's face. "Yeah, I've got it. But it was some time ago... Six months or even more. I saw him at my Thursday night AA meeting."

"You knew him, then?" Katy asks.

"Nah, not really," Johnny answers, pulling on his latex gloves. "Just a nameless old guy among the fifty or so others meeting there each week. Don't think I ever spoke to him or heard him speak at the meeting. He only stood out because, unlike many of the others at meetings, he *looked* like the stereotypical wino. You know—a bulbous red nose, seedy, disheveled appearance. And I remember seeing him two... maybe three more times at those meetings. After that not seeing him again until now."

Hap steps forward and says, "Well, I'm going to get a couple of Polaroid shots of your friend, Johnny, then I'll get out of your way." He straddles the dead man's head, points the camera straight down and takes a close-up shot of the face and the smudged *J*. He waits for the shot to develop. Then, canting a little to his left, Hap snaps a second picture of the deep scratch on the victim's neck. While the photo develops, he sidesteps around the body and cardboard to the old guy's feet. From there he takes a shot of the entire corpse. Moving back another ten feet, he finishes with a fourth picture that includes the body and immediate surrounding area.

After Hap is finished, Katy edges in closer, and carefully kneels down.

She adopts a kind of wide-angle camera-view herself that includes the entire scene: The body resting on the piece of cardboard, the empty wine bottle a few feet to the left, the blue dumpster at the heavily littered end of the alley. She maintains her viewpoint there for a moment, trying to project herself back a few hours to when the old guy was still alive, trying to get *his* feel for it all: The darkness, the night sounds, the cold fog slipping into the alley, the faint but ever present smell of urine, the filthy litter, being all alone except for the bottle of wine, then... *nothingness.*

Katy blinks.

Jesus, she swears to herself, a sour taste in her mouth, feeling almost overwhelmed by the sudden onset of sadness. What a helluva depressing way for someone to end up in this beautiful city: a corpse in a filthy alley in the Tenderloin. She shakes her head. How could someone steal what little time this old guy had left? And Why? For what possible gain?

Then, with a mental effort, Katy gets down to business; she centers, shifts aside her depressing thoughts, and concentrates on the task at hand, focusing in on the details of the murder. Okay, creepo, let's see what *you* left behind in addition to a dead old man.

"Check out the fresh scratch, kiddo," Johnny says, pointing at the approximately seven-inch-long, deep scrape from just below the left ear down the side of the old guy's scrawny neck.

"Looks similar to Richie's description of Jaime's scratch, only in a different location and deeper, you know."

"Yeah, you're right," Katy says, wondering what the perp is using to make the scratches. And how does he introduce the poison? Certainly not a knife dipped in a substance. The wound is too shallow, not really a cut, puncture, or even a slice. No, not a knife or anything else razor sharp. Just a deep scrape, like from one of those old beer can openers—what were they called? Don't remember... Or maybe just a very sharp, tough fingernail like Richie suggested about Jaime's scratch.

Johnny opens the scuffed-up black briefcase he's carrying and takes out a Q-tip and a clean plastic sandwich bag. "Let me get a swab of the wound, maybe we'll get lucky and find some residue left of the substance that killed him." Gently he rolls the Q-tip over the entire scratch, then carefully puts it in the sandwich bag. "Okay, Katy, got it." He stores the potential evidence back in his briefcase.

Trying to check for some kind of distinctive smell, Katy leans close over the victim's neck, just above the scratch and takes a whiff. Instantly she twists her head to the side and pinches her nostrils, the scent of stale, sour body odor too strong and overpowering, almost sharper and more biting than a broken ammonia capsule held under her nose.

"Jesus," she gasps aloud, her eyes watering up.

"Yeah, old dude's pretty stinky like I said, could've used a bath or shower in the last month or so," the uniformed policeman says sympathetically, handing Katy a clean handkerchief.

She wipes her eyes, takes a breath of fresh air, centers herself again and focuses her attention. "Thanks," she says to the Blue. She glances back down at the old man, staring at the smudged forehead.

Okay, Katy decides tentatively, I agree with Richie: it does indeed look like the letter *J*—although uncrossed which is strange. Maybe drawn with an artist's stick of charcoal or perhaps a piece of chalk. But as she begins to mentally file her observation, she feels the familiar unsettling sensation grabbing in the pit of her stomach—her crap detector waking up.

Uh-oh.

What?

What's wrong? she asks herself self-consciously, mentally backing up and taking another, closer look at the dirty, blurred smudge on the victim's forehead.

Not charcoal or chalk or any kind of stick marking, Katy decides, after making the closer examination. No, the shape is not sharp or uniform enough to be made with a drawing instrument of any kind. And not really the right color for charcoal, or right texture for chalk either. The material and writing method here is much cruder, almost like a kid's finger-painting. Not any kind of paint though... But, yeah, that's it, she finally decides, after touching her gloved forefinger to the marking and staring at the tiny flakes of dark gray residue on her fingertip. The perp probably dipped or rubbed his finger into some substance, than scrawled the mark with that finger.

What substance?

Gray ashes of some kind, she guesses, after rubbing her thumb back and forth over the residue.

From where?

She glances around the immediate area quickly, spotting nothing appropriate, then shakes her head sheepishly, chastising herself. Of course not from here, you friggin' nitwit, she says to herself. He's marked each of the previous bodies too, so he has to be carrying the gray ashes with him. Carrying them in some kind of container.

Why?

Obviously because they have some significance to him.

Where do gray ashes come from?

Cigarettes?

Fireplaces?

Barbeques—?

There are just too damned many possible common sources, she thinks, shifting attention away from the ashes.

Okay. What about the uncrossed *J*?

What could it mean?

Ockham's Razor.

Her favorite professor in Police Science at Sac State, Dr. Siobhan Keene, often wrote that on the blackboard, reminding the class: *"The simplest explanation is often the best explanation."*

Could it possibly be the first letter of the perp's name? she asks herself, remembering that Jeremy did indeed begin with a capital *J*.

Nah, that's too simple, too damned revealing, she thinks, her crap detector stirring in the pit of her stomach again. Better put Ockham's Razor on hold for now.

But an uncrossed *J*, what could it mean?

A lot of things.

Frustrated, Katy sighs and shrugs her puzzlement.

Man, it would definitely be a lot easier if we had the benefit of some of SFPD's forensic people, she complains to herself silently.

No such luck. At least for now, anyhow. Guess we were really spoiled up in Sacramento where we had immediate access to forensic techs, medical examiners, everything in the department. That's the problem with being unofficial civilian investigators. You have few technical resources.

She again sighs deeply, relaxing concentration, glancing away from the body for a moment. "Johnny, we need a sample of the stuff he uses to make the *J*," she says, gesturing back toward the victim's forehead.

"Right."

He takes a fresh Q-tip and sandwich bag from his briefcase and carefully picks up a tiny sample of the gray ash from the old man's forehead.

Katy stands up and stretches, letting her gaze travel slowly down the body, noting the rumpled, ill-fitting clothes under the dirty overcoat, before directing a question at the uniformed officer. "Any identification on him? Or did you have a chance to look?"

The policeman replies, "Yeah, I did, right before I noticed the *J*. Surprisingly, he had a wallet in his outside coat pocket, empty of everything of course, *except* for his Social Security card. The name on it is Peter Miller."

"Well, that's a good break," Katy says, breathing through her mouth as she kneels down again and continues to closely check over the victim, pulling up the sleeves of his overcoat and faded Pendleton shirt. She carefully inspects his skinny, pale arms and both of his hands, turning them over. No defensive scratches, so he probably didn't have the opportunity to struggle. She places the old man's hands back on his chest, deciding that it's impossible to tell much about anything picked up under the fingernails. They look like animal claws that have never been cleaned.

"Hey, come look at this, Katy," Johnny says from behind the dumpster, where he's wandered away to.

She steps around the large container, pinching her nostrils again, realizing the smell of urine reeks even stronger behind the dumpster. Tough to take so early in the morning on an empty stomach.

Johnny points at the ground, a fresh pair of knee indentions into a thick piece of cardboard, probably taken off the stack in the dumpster to shield the kneeler from broken glass and other litter on the ground in back of the container. "Bet this was the perp who kneeled here, hiding. Must've been waiting to ambush the old guy, you know. And if that's right, then he would've stalked him previously, known the old fella's habits. Like where he came to crap-out for the night, maybe even where he usually bought his nightly medicine."

"Yeah, that makes sense," Katy agrees. "Must've remained kneeling, waiting for the old man to drink his nightcap and go to sleep, before he attacked him. No fuss, no muss. That would explain the complete lack of defensive scratches on the victim's hands and arms."

They both carefully check around the area, Johnny eventually poking through the dumpster contents and stack of cardboard, Katy checking through the litter around the body.

Hap asks, "You two seen enough of the victim for now?"

Katy answers, "I have," examining several shards of glass, before shaking her head and moving on to sift through a little stack of sandwich paper wrappings.

From the dumpster, Johnny replies, "Yeah, we're through with him, Hap."

The big guy signals the waiting Coroner's men.

While the two orderlies bag the body, Hap thanks the uniformed police officer, asking to be advised of whatever information becomes available on the name check. Then he lights up his first cigar of the day, the strong, rich tobacco smell quickly reaching Katy's nostrils, thankfully masking the latrine odor loitering in the fog at this end of the alley.

"Okay, Katy, you've been awful quiet for the last few minutes," Johnny says, after pulling off his latex gloves. "What are you thinking about?"

"Well, obviously the smudged *J* is a critical piece of information," she replies, staring absently at the now bare piece of cardboard lying in front of the dumpster. "I think he's finger painting them with some kind of dark gray ash he carries with him. But from where, I don't know. And exactly what does the marking mean? It has to be significant to the perp. And the gray ash, too."

"Yeah," Johnny says, "maybe Richie is right about the religious connotation. *J* for Jesus or something like that, you know."

Katy nods half-heartedly, considering the idea.

A *J* for Jesus or Jehovah?

Didn't seem to ring right with her, the *J* being uncrossed.

Katy turns to Hap. "Can I look at your pictures?"

The big guy hands her the four Polaroids.

Sometimes a photograph from the scene cuts off your other senses, making you focus visually, something popping out in the picture that may've not been obvious in real life. She thumbs quickly through the first three, staring for a long moment at the fourth, the one of the old guy's forehead with the marking.

Something about the placement of that *J* on the victim's forehead strikes her as odd—not quite setting off a tingling in her gut, but damn close.

Katy hands the Polaroids back to the big guy.

Johnny takes out the pair of evidence bags from his briefcase and offers them to Hap. "Think you can talk someone in the crime lab into doing an analysis on these two swabs for us? Save us paying a bundle for a private lab workup."

"Maybe," Hap says, puffing on his stogie. "Yeah, I can probably con someone into a favor." He flashes his jovial, used-car-salesman, I-will-sure-try smile—another visit to the sales manager.

"Okay, you see what you can do on that and follow up on whatever the blue turns up on background on the old guy. And maybe the latest IDS and copies of your photos will pique Homicide's interest. We'll check the liquor stores right around here, see what the clerks remember. I'll call Richie and tell him about the latest hit and the similarities. I'm going to a noon Capp Street meeting and see what people remember about the three boys. Then, Katy and I are going to kick some stuff around, and we'll see you at the 7:00 meeting at the office tonight."

Hap salutes and takes off.

Katy and Johnny pause at the alley mouth to the street and discuss strategy for a few minutes.

"Yeah, I think we definitely need to see what background we can dig up on Jeremy Featherstone," Katy says. "Maybe we can go over to Brother Timothy's this afternoon or when we have time and interview him again. We also need to remember to check if Peter Miller was turned away from that shelter last night, and if so what anyone there remembers about him."

"Okay, and I need to ask about Peter Miller at the AA meeting tomorrow night, see what people there remember," Johnny replies, jotting stuff down in the notebook he carries. Suddenly he frowns, rubbing his nose. "Maybe checking out Walden House yesterday and the Capp Street NA meeting this afternoon are a big waste of time. This old dude was an alkie, probably never went near either place. No one will even know him there."

"Maybe, but we know for sure that all three boys were at *both* those places," Katy says absently, something still sticking in her mind about the forehead placement of the uncrossed letter *J*.

They discuss Katy's preliminary conclusions about the scratches and *J* markings, Johnny not adding much, except he doesn't think the scratch is made with a church key or that the gray ash comes from cigarettes.

"... Uh-uh, seems to be darker and kinda oily in texture, you know," he says, referring to the ashes as he leads her up the street to the nearest liquor store, *Ray's*.

Katy smiles thinly, following along, "Well, if nothing else, we've got a lot of good questions for your Progress Board tonight, pal."

"How 'bout Spaghetti Western for breakfast after we check in up here?" Johnny asks, referring to the popular breakfast spot in the Haight.

"Sounds good."

TLACHTLI

Katy gets in a good basketball practice with the other two members of Little Women at 5:00 on the empty court in Pacific Heights. They work a lot on *blocking out*—turning and screening their opponents away from the basket after each opposition shot—knowing it will be critical on Saturday to give the team from Silicon Valley only one shot and no offensive rebounds on each possession. Sidney goes over the tendencies of the ex-star from Arizona, suggesting that she get some backside help whenever Jamie Worley is inside and rolls quickly toward the bucket. Both Katy and CeCe acknowledge their understanding, agreeing to help, as the practice and discussion winds down an hour later.

CeCe takes right off from the court to get ready for a hot date, someone she met at work—she's an ESL teacher at the adult school in the Mission. "Dude is a gorgeous PR," she says over her shoulder, faking a swoon. "A real Ricky Martin look-alike, you know what I'm saying." She slips into her blue Ford Escort, grins lecherously, makes an obscene *Yes* gesture by pulling a doubled fist to her chest, then waves goodbye.

But Katy hangs out a little while longer with Sidney, accepting an invitation for a cold drink at her friend's apartment across the street from the park's basketball court. She considers bouncing some of the questions in the murder case off of Sid, who has been really helpful with creative suggestions in the past, whenever Katy has discussed ideas and rough drafts of some of her articles for the *San Francisco Bay Guardian.* But she decides against even mentioning the case, both of them too relaxed after the workout to address the puzzling questions.

"You know basketball really does relieve stress," Katy says, walking up the apartment building's front steps. "At the very least it makes you divert your attention from your worries. Even short practices like this one are so involved, you forget all about your problems. It's like time-out from the real world. Do you know what I mean?"

Sid laughs, leading Katy into her place. "Yeah I do. And you got that right."

In the hallway, Katy glances at the African mask collection on the wall on either side of a striking painting depicting Swahili women at an outdoor market in Lamu, Kenya, their traditional black *bui-buis* contrasting sharply with the colorful fruit and vegetable displays. She has seen the painting several times before, but always enjoys checking it out. Sidney can afford African paintings and artifacts decorating her expensive apartment and even driving a silver BMW convertible, because she's a top graphic designer with one of the big advertising firms down on Montgomery Street.

"Yeah, I'm sure glad James Naismith put up those peach baskets at the YMCA in Springfield, Mass back in the 1890s," Katy says, following Sidney into the kitchen. "The game has come a long way since then and really means a lot to me. I love it. Hope I can play forever."

"Basketball has been good to me, too," Sid agrees, "giving me the opportunity to go to a top university."

Katy knows that Sidney grew up in Houston and though heavily recruited by a dozen schools including the University of Texas at Austin, she decided on a full ride at UCLA to play four years of basketball for the Lady Bruins because of the school's renowned graphic arts and design program. And even though Sid was somewhat disappointed at never playing for the Monarchs in the WNBA after college because of her lingering Achilles tendon injury, there was never any question about the quality of her education at UCLA.

"But you know, a form of basketball was actually played long before that peach basket went up in New England, maybe as early as six hundred years ago, in Meso-American culture," Sidney says, pouring Katy a big glass of home-made lemonade. "I incidentally ran across some interesting background on the game researching Central American hieroglyphic designs on ancient steles." She smiles half-apologetically, raising her eyebrows questioningly, and asks, "You got time for a quick basketball history lesson?"

"Sure," Katy says, taking a sip of the cold drink. "I'd love to hear it."

"Well, this one form of basketball was called *Tlachtli* by the Aztecs. And there are several ruins indicating the Mayans also built long *Tlachtli* courts sunk down below spectator seats with raised vertical stone rings at each end, in present-day Honduras and Guatemala. They used a small rubber ball that registered a score when thrown through the center of a vertical ring. But this was a much rougher game back then than we have now.

Players wore protective gear, gloves, padding, helmets, so it must've been a full contact sport."

Katy laughs, then jokes, "Sounds like a Dennis Rodman kind of game."

"Yeah, really," Sid agrees, grinning and taking a drink. "But I guess it was even more violent than even his wildest NBA escapades. Supposedly, the early Meso-American priests actually sacrificed members of the losing teams…" She pauses, then adds, "How about that for playing in a meaningful game. In *Tlachtli* you lose, you permanently snooze."

Katy grimaces. "Wow, I guess that's what you call really serious team motivation," she says. Her grim expression changes to a sly grin. "Now days we've really evolved, we just sacrifice the losing coaches." She drains her glass before setting the empty on the counter. "Good lemonade."

Sidney follows Katy to the door.

Katy pauses for a moment at the door, then says, "I promised

myself I wouldn't even think about an investigation Johnny and I are
working on, and I haven't. But you know…" She shrugs, throwing her
hands up: what-are-you-going-to-do.

Sid smiles and nods. "How can I help?"

"Have you ever heard of anyone drawing with some kind of gray
ash, like a substitute for charcoal, doing body painting or marking faces
with it… something like that?"

"Gray ash, burned from what?" Sidney asks.

"Don't know."

"Hmm… No, I don't think so," Sidney says, shaking her head
slowly. "It would have to be from something with an oil base, to make
it stick to human skin." She shrugs. "Don't think I've heard of any art
form using any kind of oily gray ash as the base for body painting. But
almost anything is possible, you know, especially if you take into
consideration other cultures." She shrugs a kind of apology to Katy.

"Hey, that tells me the medium isn't common, anyhow," Katy says,
grateful for Sid's expertise. "And thanks for the drink and setting me
straight about *Tlachtli*," she adds, before giving her friend a hug, and
heading for the Mustang parked across the street. She files the odd
name for Meso-American basketball away in her store of mental trivia.

She has to hurry now to get home, shower, and make the 7:00
meeting at the Geary office on time. But the practice and visit with Sid
were just what she needed to keep her mind away from obsessing on
the investigation questions, she thinks, starting up the car and heading
for the Marina. Even if she did slip up for a few minutes at the end.
Actually, she hasn't really obsessed about the murders for over an
hour. Good going, girl.

Double S

Katy and Johnny arrive a few minutes late for the 7:00 p.m. meeting at the office near Japantown. Hap is already there waiting patiently, feet up on his desk, puffing on a cigar stub, a layer of blue, rich-smelling smoke hovering in the air. But Richie isn't there yet.

"He called about five minutes ago," Hap explains, after noticing Katy's quick scan of the office. "He'll be a little delayed. Said he was hoping to bring along a nice surprise for us. Maybe donuts, huh?"

Katy laughs, realizing Hap definitely has a good sense of self-deprecating humor.

After waiting a few more minutes, Johnny decides to begin the meeting, asking Hap to bring them up to date from his end.

The big guy takes the stogie from his mouth, a serious expression on his face. "We finally found the missing IDS," he says, sliding the sheet of paper across the desk to Johnny. "Unfortunately no scratches or forehead smudge marks mentioned. Haven't been able to run the blue down yet, so I don't know if he noticed anything not reported. And my best connection in Homicide agrees that the other IDS's and especially the copies of my Polaroids of the old wino are *sorta* interesting. After he gets a hold of the most recent IDS of the old man, he'll bring it up with his boss. But he isn't too optimistic about them opening up a new case, says they're really logjammed at the moment. You know typical old bureaucratic downfield juking." Hap makes a dismissive face and shrugs. "Not anything about this on the street, at least from my C.I.s. Oh, and it'll take at least another day or so to get anything back from the crime lab on your two Q-tips, Johnny—they're working in your analysis between official jobs. They're pretty busy, too. Probably be another day before I hear anything on Peter Miller's background check." He roughly stubs out the cigar butt in his ashtray, then says, "You guys making any better progress on anything?"

Johnny shakes his head and glumly admits, "We got nothing checking the nearby liquor store where the old fella was killed. Owner said he'll check with the night clerk, but he didn't sound too reliable or really interested in recontacting us. And nothing much from my Capp Street NA meeting this afternoon either. Only two people even remember the three boys. But I put the word out to a couple of close friends to keep their ears open."

Then he pulls out a folder from his briefcase, and with a bit more enthusiasm he continues, "Our friend, Jeremy Featherstone, has a kinda unusual background for a hippie. He was arrested for assault on a male roommate two years ago. The DA didn't prosecute after a preliminary investigation so nothing much came of it. The roommate, a young guy named Steven Boyer, only nineteen then, didn't want to press charges. It was all written off as a lover's quarrel. So I checked with the landlord mentioned in the report, and learned our boy has quite a temper. Because that incident wasn't the only time there had been a hubbub at the apartment. There'd been a number of complaints, including a month or two before the assault, a neighboring tenant complained to the landlord of a late night loud fight between Jeremy and his roommate that went on for over an hour. The landlord said that, when he checked personally the next day, the roommate apologized for the noise, but didn't want to get into details, and seemed to be absolutely terrified of Jeremy. Then a month later, after the cops investigated the assault, the two moved out and the landlord thinks they went their separate ways. Katy and I will be seeing Jeremy Featherstone again tomorrow morning at Brother Timothy's for a follow-up talk. We'll also check to see if Peter Miller ever stayed there and was turned away the last night before his death, like the three boys. And tomorrow night I'll see what people remember about Peter Miller at my AA meeting. Can we borrow that Polaroid shot of his face?"

Johnny pauses, while Hap digs out an envelope from his sport coat inside pocket and tosses it over. Then Johnny slips out one photo, making sure it's Peter Miller's face. "Okay, good. Thanks, Hap."

Both men shift attention to Katy.

"Well, I've been thinking a little more about pitching the article to the *Guardian*, suggesting that SFPD is dragging their feet on these murders because they only involve members of the underclass. The *Guardian* loves that type of antiestablishment stuff, so I think I can make it fly. But maybe we can do more with it, poke the perp in the butt. Suggest his motive here is maybe homosexual in nature or something like that. Stimulate a response from him or someone who knows him. We did that a couple of times in Sacramento, Hap, where we had the cooperation of the media. It worked fine in at least one case. Perp's mother contacted us after she read an article in the *Sacramento Bee*, which eventually led to an arrest and conviction. In the Red Chief case, he saw us on a TV show, realized he knew me personally from long ago in San Diego, and contacted us by phone. Things moved fast after that, and he eventually busted into my apartment, where Johnny got him. So, sometimes media communication flushes something out…"

Katy pauses and raises her eyebrows slightly.

"But it can be kinda dangerous and scary," she adds, remembering struggling for several *long* minutes in her apartment with Red Chief, who was armed with a straight razor he'd used on his three victims. Only her athletic skills initially preventing her being cut and then Johnny still had to come to her rescue. "Gotta be handled carefully, I know. What do you guys think?"

Johnny says, "I don't know, Katy, about jabbing this perp in the ass. What do you think, Hap?"

The big guy shrugs, then makes a frown and says, "I'd like at least one more day before you pitch an article, Katy. Maybe Homicide will be on board by then. Then the piece just has to focus on the perp, you know, without pointing fingers at the cops. Sure will make my life easier in the future."

Katy understands and agrees. "Okay, but I *am* going over tomorrow morning to see my editor at the *Guardian*. Maybe do some background work on the number of non-homicide underclass deaths in the last year, including ODs, homeless people, and winos. That type of potential victim stuff. See if my editor remembers anyone else with a *J* smudge. Then I'll start the rough tomorrow afternoon for pitching on Friday. And even if homicide is on the bus, I still plan on focusing the article on the society-doesn't-care-about-these-people angle. I'll think some more about directing something at the perp then, Johnny."

Hap says, "Fine, I appreciate that, Katy."

Johnny nods, then shifts the discussion. "Katy also has a number of questions she wants to write in on the progress board, revising a couple of earlier ones."

She gets up and explains to Hap as she chalks in her items under the *Questions* column:

How is the poison delivered?
What is the poison?
What are the gray ashes?
What is the significance of the ashes?
What is the significance of the J?

As Katy is finishing her last question, the door opens and Richie comes in, followed by a surprising sight—a very short man, his legless trunk resting on a kind of wide skateboard.

2

"Hello," Richie says, out of breath. "Sorry I'm late, but I've been talking my friend here into coming over tonight, maybe becoming part of the team." He introduces each of them to Damon Dupree.

The black man, in his mid 30s, is wearing short dreadlocks and a 49ers red, white, and gold sweatshirt—Jerry Rice's number 80—with the arms cut off at the shoulders. He has the upper body of a football player—a massive chest and muscular arms. But no legs, which makes his huge arms appear too long for his body. He's wearing a set of dark gloves just like a wide receiver, and holding a pair of wooden blocks, obviously used for propelling himself. He rests easily on the skateboard that actually resembles a padded version of the scooter-board used by mechanics for getting around under cars.

After pulling off his gloves, he shakes hands with everyone, Katy noticing his grip is firm, dry, but not overpowering like so many weightlifter types.

In a deep confident tone, he says, "It's a pleasure to meet you all. But only really old friends like Richie still call me Damon; most folks on the street know me as Double S, a nickname. It stands for Short Stuff. And I'm down with that." His smile is authentic and engaging, his dark eyes bright, sincere, and very intelligent.

"Damon and I go back almost twenty years to Mission High football," Richie explains, ignoring use of the nickname. "He was an all-city tight end on our championship team when we were seniors—"

"And Richie was one damn fine quarterback, and shoulda played with me the next year for the Rams at City College," the black man says, reaching out and lightly tugging Richie's trouser leg. "Man could throw and run like a right-handed Steve Young."

"Yeah, well a lot of things went wrong for both of us after high school, which seems like the distant past now anyhow," Richie says, the smile thinning on his face. "Damon *did* play two games in his freshman year at City College, but lost most of his legs the night before his third game when a drunk ran a stop sign in a heavy fog over on 11th Street, South of Market."

"Yeah, I guess you're right, those football days were a long time ago," Double S admits, still smiling, but his tone not quite so bright and cheerful. "A different world."

For a moment there is a strained silence.

Then, after unfolding a chair for himself, Richie goes on, "Anyhow, that isn't why I talked Damon into coming over here with me tonight, to talk over football or old times. He gets around now, knows what's happening in the Mission and the 'loin. And last night he just may have seen our killer."

"You did?" Katy asks, her short question slicing through the hanging cigar haze.

"Yeah… well, I think so," Double S answers, nodding at Katy.

"You *think* so?" Hap says loudly, dropping both legs to the floor with a thud, leaning forward on his desk, a questioning look on his face.

"Okay, okay," Johnny says, putting both hands up, as if slowing traffic. "Let's start at the beginning. You were obviously in the Tenderloin last night?" he asks, pointing a finger at Richie's friend.

"Right," Double S replies, pushing his hands flat against the floor, flexing his heavily muscled arms, and lifting himself up off his scooter-board, then easing back down onto the platform, an apparent stretching or relaxing maneuver for his knee-length stumps. "I live over in the Mission on Shotwell in a basement apartment with my brother and his son. But every Tuesday I make my aluminum can and bottle run through the 'loin—coupla bars and restaurants save me stuff special, and I check a few other spots, sometimes able to beat out the other dumpster divers. Except last night I was late and it was way after dark before I even got started—"

"Why Tuesday nights?" Katy interrupts.

Double S glances at her, smiles, and patiently explains, "Garbage trucks pick up next day in the area, you understand, nothing left to raid after they sweep through on Wednesday morning."

Katy nods, shrugging, making her *sorry-dumb-me* face.

"So about what time did you finally make your run through the Tenderloin?" Johnny asks.

"Oh, it musta been a little after 8:00 at night, I guess, so that by a quarter after, I was at the mouth of this alley on Leavenworth, just off Eddy. Big dumpster back in there, usually full of cardboard, but sometimes I dig out a few cans or bottles."

"What did you see?" asks Johnny.

"Well, at first I didn't know. They were at the end of the alley near the dumpster in the dark. I thought it was a sex thing, a couple of guys, you know. This one dude was lying down, and this other guy was bending over him. So I just sat there on my board, not wanting to go back to the dumpster just then. But he froze kinda funny, the guy standing, and I could just make out this strange expression on his face… looked like a dude getting his rocks off, if you'll excuse the language?" He pauses and glances over at Katy who is staring back at him.

She makes a dismissive gesture, encouraging Double S to continue.

"But then I ain't so sure it's a sex thing, 'cause the dude on the ground ain't moving, and the other guy just stands there frozen, staring into space, kinda goofy-like—"

"Into space, where into space?" Katy interrupts again.

"Well, I was still at the mouth of the alley, quite a ways away from the two, but I think he was gazing at a spot just above the guy's chest laying on the ground. Looking at... nothing, really."

"Did the guy standing have a weapon in his hand?" Johnny asks. "Church key maybe or something sharp like that?"

Double S slowly shakes his head. "I didn't see no weapon. Dude was just froze in place there for two maybe three minutes. Then he seemed to suddenly wake up. He kneels and pulls something from his pocket, a little round container, like a snuff can. And he dips his finger into that can and reaches down with that same finger and touches the other guy's forehead. Yeah, just touches it... Oh, now, thinking back on it, seeing it all again, I think the dude's other hand was gloved."

"He's wearing only one glove?" Katy asks. "You sure?"

After a moment's thought, Double S says, "Yeah... a white glove on his right hand, bare left hand. I kinda notice gloves, you know. Anyhow, *before* taking out the can and touching the other guy's forehead, he strips off the one glove and slips it in his pocket, but being real careful pushing it in, like he's afraid of... I don't know, breaking it or something. Then he does the thing with the can. After that, even though I can't hear nothing, I'm pretty sure he was saying a prayer over the guy stretched out on cardboard. Had that kinda posture, anyhow. The whole scene is really weird, you know what I'm saying."

Double S pauses for a few moments, looking down at the floor thoughtfully before continuing. "I guess that's about when I figured this definitely wasn't no sex thing. The guy laying on the cardboard still ain't moved. The other dude finally stands, turns my way, and stiffens up like before, but his face looked real pained now, like a tooth ache or something hurtful hitting him sudden-like. He just freezes, his eyes closed. For a full minute or maybe more, then he blinks and looks at his watch. Dude laying on the cardboard still ain't moving. By now I *know* something bad has gone down, something that ain't none of my business. So I do my imitation of one of them X Games skateboard racers down on the Wharf this summer, and get out of there real quick, you understand what I'm saying."

"Did he ever see you?" Johnny asks.

"I don't know," Double S replies. "All I cared about was getting my raggedy ass outta there fast. Went right home, forgot about the end of my can run."

"Tell me," Katy says, getting Double S's attention again, "do you think you can describe him?"

Double S says, "Yeah, I think so. Let's see… A tall, white dude, young, in his twenties, maybe twenty-five or twenty-six. Kinda handsome, but not pretty, you understand. He was wearing a black windbreaker—no team emblem or nothing on it, just plain—Levis… and, yeah I'm absolutely positive, only *one* glove, on his right hand, like Michael Jackson. But he took it off before touching the other dude's forehead, like I said. And that's about it, I guess." He pauses, then there's a twinkle in his bright, dark eyes. "Not the greatest description, I know. But you gotta understand that all you white people look alike to us black folks."

"Hey, that's pretty funny, man," Johnny says, grinning for a moment. "But it looks like you remember enough for a police artist to get something down." He turns to Hap. "Can you talk someone into seeing Double S tomorrow, get us a likeness drawn and some copies made up?"

"I'm not sure, but I'll try and arrange something," Hap replies to Johnny. Then to Double S he adds, "I'll call you in the morning if I can set it up, okay?"

Double S nods his head. He writes a number on a piece of paper and hands it to Hap. "That's the Greyhound Bus Station over on Tenth. They'll page me. I work the shoeshine stand there from 7:00 a.m. until 1:00 p.m. on Wednesdays, Thursdays, Fridays, and Saturdays, Sundays from 9:00 until 6:00—part of the city's Opportunities For The Disabled Program."

Katy has remained quiet during all the description part, waiting to ask Double S her last question. "And the guy didn't have a beard?"

He thinks for a minute, pulling on his own gloves. "No beard, no mustache, dude was clean shaven."

A few minutes later as the meeting is breaking up, Johnny asks

Double S to keep his ears and eyes open in his travels around the Tenderloin and Mission, and he invites the legless black man to the next meeting.

"… Back here tomorrow night at 8:00, okay?" Johnny says to the group, adding, "that'll give me time to check out my AA meeting at 7:00."

GREEN HORNET
DOES A 180

Often during the early part of an investigation, Katy finds her libido stimulated, sex one of the few intense-enough distractions to take her attention away from the obsessive and puzzling questions that plague her thoughts. That night she ambushes Johnny in the shower, after flipping off the bathroom light. Even after being together four years, she's still self-conscious about being naked in light.

"Hey, pal, need your back scrubbed?" she asks, pressing in tightly against his naked, wet body.

"You bet," he answers, making more space for her in the cramped stall. "But you should have left the lights on in order to see your work." He laughs. "I think you have a terrific shape, you know." He leans over and gives her a peck on the nipple of her left breast.

Katy responds by kissing him roughly, her tongue exploring his lips, then his opened mouth, their bodies fused together, now. She soon feels Johnny's aroused state pressing above her upper thigh.

In a husky voice, she jokes, "Doesn't feel like you're really into a back scrub right now, pal?"

Johnny doesn't answer immediately, just kisses her back enthusiastically, clutching both of her buns tightly, as if appreciating their size, and mumbling, "Uh-huh, uh-*huh*," before he nuzzles her breasts.

Then he leans back and, with a grin in his voice, replies hoarsely, "Too late for that now, kiddo. I need some therapy, but it ain't gonna be on my back."

A few moments later in the bedroom, only partially dried off, they both tumble onto the bedspread, giggling, kissing, touching, licking, fondling, and gasping for breath. Usually when they make love, they are slow and considerate, like two professional ballroom dancers, familiar with and anticipating the other's physical moves. Johnny usually puts on some of his music—often the Eagles—and they make love slow and tender to something like the mournful "Desperado" or hauntingly mysterious "Hotel California."

But not tonight, no time for music—slap, slap, wet, frantic, and tense, until finally both burst out an explosive groaning surrender into the pressing quiet of the bedroom.

Therapy, down and dirty.

They lie together quietly in postcoital bliss for several minutes, as their breathing gradually returns to normal.

Johnny finally breaks the silence and confesses, "Much more relaxing than an old back scrub," before his breathing begins to thicken.

He soon dozes off, still holding Katy in his arms.

I should be completely relaxed myself, doing my snoring duet with him, she thinks. But Katy doesn't feel the least tired. Just the opposite in fact. She recognizes the problem, slides out of Johnny's unconscious grasp, and rolls over onto her back on her side of the bed.

The minutes tick by.

Her mind remains alert, churning over the investigation questions about the delivery instrument, the poison, the gray ashes, and the letter, *J.*

Again and again her attention comes back to the letter, *J*, especially its positioning on the old guy's forehead. For some reason that intrigues her, she feels intuitively that the *position* of the mark may be the key.

She tosses and turns.

Finally, in the wee hours of the morning, exhausted by it all, Katy manages to slip into that twilight zone just before dropping off to sleep...

Suddenly, with her eyes closed, she clearly sees herself again in the alley in the Tenderloin. She's staring at Hap's photo of the victim's upside-down head and the uncrossed *J*. In her mind she slowly rotates the Polaroid photograph 180 degrees. Now she is looking directly at the old guy's face, forehead, and upper chest, just like the perp must've done after he administered the fatal scratch. Then, she imagines the perp taking out the snuff tin, dipping his finger, and marking his victim's forehead...

But now it's not an upside-down, uncrossed *J*.

Uh-uh. Not at all.

It's a, a... ?

She blinks, staring now for the answer into her darkened bedroom.

What's it called?

A staff.

Or sometimes, a... crook?

A crook.

Yeah, that's it.

A *shepherd's crook*.

She roughly shakes Johnny awake.

"What is it, what's wrong?" he mumbles, struggling into consciousness, and sitting upright in bed, rubbing his eyes.

"I've got it, pal," she says, smiling. "Oh, yeah, I've finally got it. The old light bulb just blinked on over my cartoon head."

"What do you mean?" Johnny asks, leaning across her and glancing at the bed stand clock on her side of the bed: 2:25 a.m. He makes an annoyed face. But he looks alert now, waiting for her to answer.

"He's not marking his victims with a capital *J*," she replies, unable to stifle a smug grin. "No, sir. It only looks like an uncrossed *J*, if you always see it *upside down*. But that's the wrong way to look at it. He wouldn't've marked his victims that way."

"Well, what is the right way then?" Johnny asks impatiently, pausing to rub his broken nose.

"Turn Hap's Polaroid shot 180 degrees in your mind," Katy explains. "What do you see, now?"

After a moment, he says tentatively, "A, a... stick with a hook on the end?"

"Right, except I think it's usually called a shepherd's crook."

Johnny squints his eyes, pulling at his nose again. Then he nods slowly.

"Yeah, I think you've got something about the placement anyhow, kiddo," he says, appearing thoroughly engaged now. "If I were going to mark someone's forehead right after I killed them, I'd do it looking at them square in the face—"

"Especially if you'd just bent over and scratched them on the arm or neck with a lethal substance, right?"

"Right, but what do you think it means, this shepherd's crook marking?"

"Well, I think Richie may have got it partly right," Katy says, slipping out of bed and pulling on her blue kimono with the silver dragon on the back. "A shepherd's crook is a religious symbol. You see them in a number of places, like in those Christmas manger scenes, you know."

Johnny looks puzzled for a moment, rubs the brow of his broken nose again, then finally grins. "Yeah, okay. I think I see it now, what you're driving at. Like those kids plays at Christmas time, everyone in costume, the nativity scene with the wise men, and the shepherds are always holding those crooks in hand, right?"

Katy replies, "You got it." She stops at the doorway of the bedroom and asks, "How about a drink? This kind of analytical detective work always makes me thirsty."

Johnny slides out of bed and follows Katy into the kitchen, after pulling on his dark blue terry cloth bathrobe and slippers. "So, we got ourselves a religious nut running loose, a serial murderer marking his underclass victims' foreheads with a shepherd's crook," he says, a studious expression on his ruggedly handsome face. "Okay, I can go along with all that; but, now, tell me, what's the significance of the gray ashes? What do they have to do with a shepherd's crook?"

She frowns, reaching into the fridge for some mango-orange juice. "I've thought of that, but I don't really know the answer…"

She mentions asking her artist friend Sid about the origin of the ashy substance at basketball practice earlier in the evening, and drawing a blank, except that Sid thought the ashes probably come from an oily source. "But I bet we'll know more about their significance after we figure out exactly where the ashes do come from. Maybe Hap's lab analysis will help us do just that."

Johnny smiles thinly, glancing at the clock near the stove. "Katy, here it is the middle of the night and your mind is still going 100 miles per hour. You never fail to amaze me when we're on a case, you know."

She grins broadly back at him. "Hey, pal, we're actually not too bad a team at this detective stuff. That's why *we* both got those super hero nicknames from the *Bee* and the TV up in Sacramento, right, Cato?"

"Yeah, but I gotta admit that I'm not always at the top of my game at 3:00 in the morning, for crissake," he says, reaching up and getting two glasses down from the cupboard.

They sit down at the kitchen counter and drink a glass of juice together, neither saying much more. Both just relaxing and enjoying the moment, Johnny punching in a tape on the player—the Eagles are rocking and singing, "Get Over It."

Katy smiles to herself at the irony of the words.

A little later, they go back to bed, and not surprisingly, she easily falls into a deep sleep.

JEREMY
FEATHERSTONE

Katy raps on the entry door to Brother Timothy's at around 10:00 on Thursday morning. Both her and Johnny wait for a couple of minutes before Jeremy Featherstone finally peeks out through the yellowed Venetian blinds, then unlocks the door.

Katy immediately notices that the young man is now freshly shaved.

"Hello, Jeremy," Johnny says in a neutral tone.

"Hello. Ah, Brother Timothy won't be in for another hour or two," Jeremy answers back in his soft-spoken voice. "Maybe 1:00 or so would be a better time to catch him."

"Actually we wanted to talk with you," Johnny says, smiling. "If you don't mind? Take just maybe five minutes."

Jeremy Featherstone, looking slightly concerned, says, "Okay. C'mon in. We can sit right here at the screening desk." He pulls two of the folding chairs in front, and takes a seat in back of the table. The homeless shelter is quiet, apparently no volunteers about as yet.

Katy and Johnny sit down across from the tall, young man dressed again in sandals, faded jeans, and an old green USF sweatshirt with DONS spelled out on his chest in white, block letters. He is really a good-looking guy, Katy decides, if you ignore his kind of generally scruffy appearance and nervous mannerisms.

"What's this about?" Jeremy asks, his tone a little higher pitched.

Johnny doesn't answer right away.

Instead he takes out Hap's Polaroid of the prone Peter Miller from a file folder he's carrying. He sets it down on the table and stares at it a moment, before he explains. "There's been another murder not far from here on Tuesday night," Johnny says, pushing the photo across the table. "We were hoping you could tell us something about the victim."

Jeremy glances at the photo and shakes his head. "No, I don't know him."

"Never saw him, here at the shelter?"

"Don't think so," he replies, taking a more careful second look at the photo.

"So you don't think he ever stayed here?" Johnny asks, his voice growing a little impatient.

"I'm not sure about that, we get so many just like him," Jeremy says. He raises his right forefinger as something occurs to him. "What's his name? I'll check back through our recent nightly logs, if you want me to? Everyone is required to sign in, you know."

"Peter Miller," Johnny replies. "And we would like to know if he did stay here recently, and especially if he was turned away from here on Tuesday night."

"I can check back for his name if he stayed, but we don't keep a record when someone is turned away. I suppose we could ask the counselors that were on duty Tuesday night if they remember him. I think that was Felix and—"

"When did you shave off your beard?" Katy interrupts, her tone challenging, confrontational.

Jeremy is taken aback by the accusatory nature of her voice and stammers, "Ah, I-I-I… actually just last night."

"Why?" she snaps back.

He shrugs, reflects for a moment, frowning, then replies, "No reason really, just got tired of it, I guess. Been wearing one for a long time now. Too long."

Katy nods very slowly, as if it takes her a moment to comprehend the answer. Then she abruptly says, "Okay, let's talk about Jaime O'Brien, D.L. Mathews, and Joey Bartkowski."

For a moment Jeremy just stares back at her, a blank expression on his face. Then, he finally says, "Oh, you mean those younger guys that were at the shelter a couple of weeks ago. The ones that left here and then OD'd?"

"We don't think they OD'd, Jeremy," Johnny says, his tone becoming edgy and sharp, matching Katy's.

The young man frowns again, looking a little confused, more nervous. He just stares back at Johnny in silence for a moment, and then abruptly shifts his gaze and position on his chair, looking over at Katy, as if she might be more understanding of his situation.

She just peers back coldly.

Eventually, Jeremy clears his throat, and then volunteers in a barely audible tone, "I don't know nothing about those three guys, if they OD'd or were really murdered or what…" His voice trails off completely.

"Okay, maybe we should talk about another of your old friends, Steven Boyer?" Johnny says, taking out the folder from his briefcase and glancing down at it. "The one you assaulted two years ago. By the way, what happened to him? He still around here, living in the city?"

"Now, wait a minute," Jeremy says defensively, his confused, anxious features darkening, slowly reddening with anger. "I wasn't convicted of anything. You two have no right to snoop around into my private life. Brother Timothy told me you're not with the police department or really have any official capacity. You're just private citizens. So, I think I would prefer—"

"We *have* an eye witness from Tuesday night," Katy says, interrupting Jeremy's mildly indignant rant, pointing at the photo sitting on the table between them. "Where were you at 8:15 that night?"

"8:15, Tuesday night?" Jeremy sags limply, the question suddenly deflating his puffed-up, angry state, like a pinprick letting the air from a balloon. Then, partially recovering his poise, he replies in his almost normal, soft-spoken tone again, "I was at The Cedars in the Western Addition, the facility for old people with Alzheimer's disease, visiting my father around that time... At least from around 8:30 to 9:00. I usually go over every Tuesday night about that same time."

"Anyone see you there?" Johnny asks, moving his chair closer to the table, his rugged face looking confrontational now.

"Ah... yeah, sure, my father, of course." Jeremy thinks a moment and adds, "And I spoke to two of the orderlies."

"Their names?" Johnny demands, taking out his notebook.

Jeremy looks stricken. "I don't really know their names. Just two of the guys, whoever was on duty that night. You can check that, right?"

"Does your father have a roommate?" Katy asks.

Jeremy shakes his head, looking really concerned now.

"And your father," Johnny says, pressing even closer. "How serious is his disorder? Does he always remember your visits?"

"No, I guess he normally doesn't remember any of them," Jeremy confesses, his voice almost a defeated whisper.

A moment's awkward silence.

Then, the tall, young man suddenly grins broadly at Johnny and Katy, after he recalls something. "Oh, hey, you have to sign in with the time of visit at the front desk," he says, his guilty, strained expression almost gone. "*That* will verify my visit, right?"

Johnny nods and says, "Okay, we'll check that out, Jeremy. But it will really help if one of those orderlies remembers seeing you Tuesday night around 8:30 or so. Is that your log, there?" He gestures at the three-ring binder Jeremy has absently taken out of a drawer under the table.

"Yes, it is," Jeremy answers, opening the binder and pushing it across the table for Johnny to look at. "Residents for the last week, back to last Saturday night, the pages for each night separated by a colored tab."

It's quiet as Johnny traces his finger down the three pages of signed entries for Tuesday night. "Nope, no Peter Miller signed in here," he says, glancing up at Katy.

"You never answered about whatever happened to your old

roommate," she says to Jeremy, as Johnny continues checking back through the other colored tabs in the log.

"I haven't seen him for almost a year," Jeremy answers, frowning. "I think he moved out of town. Vallejo, someplace like that in the North Bay. Yeah, he's going to Solano Community College up there near Fairfield."

Johnny finishes checking the week's entries for Peter Miller's name. He shakes his head. "He hasn't been here, at least in the last week."

"And you don't ever remember seeing him?" Katy asks Jeremy.

The young man glances again at the photo and shakes his head. "I don't. Do you want me to check back in the past logs for his name?"

Standing up from the table, Katy answers, "I don't think so, right now, maybe later sometime."

"We'll be seeing you, Jeremy," Johnny says, his tone neutral again, as he rises slowly to his feet. He picks up the Polaroid from the table and slips it back into the file folder. He doesn't offer to shake hands with Jeremy, but says almost sarcastically, "Nice talking to you."

Johnny and Katy leave Jeremy Featherstone sitting by himself at the table, looking more than a little worried by their visit and interrogation.

2

Outside, Johnny says, "What do you think, kiddo?"

Katy answers, "I'm not sure. He seemed exceptionally nervous. But so do a lot of people when we question them. Especially digging hard like we did."

"I agree."

They walk around the corner to where they parked the Mustang.

"We need to follow up though, check out his story carefully," Johnny says, as they stand in front of the car. He jots down a note in his notebook. "Actually go over to The Cedars."

Katy nods and adds, "And maybe it would be a good idea to talk personally with Steven Boyer. See what he can add to our profile on Mr. Featherstone."

"Yeah, good idea," Johnny says, rubbing his crooked nose. "Maybe we should split up this afternoon. I have to make that AA meeting early this evening, but before then I can check out the sign-in sheet for Tuesday night and the orderlies at that rest home in the Western Addition. Think you can make it up to Fairfield okay by yourself and talk to Steven?"

Katy makes a face. About an hour and a half each way, she thinks. Then tracking him down through Solano Community College records. Probably take me all the rest of the afternoon. No research for me over at the *Guardian* today. She sighs inwardly. "Sure, I'll do that, but I'll need the car," she says, holding out her hand for the Mustang keys.

"Okay, you can drop me off at The Cedars in the Western Addition before you take off."

3

After leaving Johnny at the nursing home, Katy drives east across the Bay Bridge. She plans on taking Interstate 80 all the way up to Fairfield, remembering that the community college is located off the highway just past the community of Cordelia.

SEVENTEEN

But the souls of the righteous are in the hand of God.

—Ecclesiastes 3:1

The old Greyhound Bus Station in the middle of 10th Street just south of Market is huge inside, and even though it is still early—a little after noon—it's crammed with people, some just wandering about aimlessly. Crowded and noisy. You're wearing sunglasses, a Giants black and orange ball cap, and an old gray sweatshirt, hoping the black half-man won't recognize you in different garb. You search around for fifteen minutes, without spotting him on his scooter-board. About ready to give up, you idly watch a man hoist a huge traveling bag up and squeeze it into one of the hundreds of lockers in the gray bank that extends back along a corridor toward the restrooms.

That's when you spot him.

He's working at the shoeshine stand near the men's room, which surprises you. You didn't expect him to be working here at the station at a straight job, but rather to be involved in some kind of crowd hustle or scam.

You move a little closer, watching for an opportunity to use the tiny Minolta in your coat pocket.

He's working next to an old-fashioned two-seat stand, but he's sitting on his scooter-board, his customer sitting on a folding chair resting one foot off the floor on a kind of kid's shoe-shine box.

An old, white-headed, black man is working next to the cripple at the conventional stand, his customer sitting up high, feet resting on a pair of metallic gray foot supports extended to about chest level of the standing shoe-shiner.

The half-man is talking, joking, and laughing with his fellow worker, over the sound of his shine rag popping above a cordovan dress shoe, while his customer studies the green sports pages from the *Chronicle*. You are not near enough to hear the conversation, so you ease closer and lean against the corner of the last row of the 50-cent lockers, pretending to watch the steady flow of mostly men in and out of the nearby restrooms, but too exposed to use the camera. You hope you appear to be just another idle hustler, blending into the background.

"Yeah, y'all right on that, son," the old guy says in a kind of southern drawl, bending down to get a can of *Kiwi* black shoe polish and brush applicator from a tray of supplies under the base of the stand's foot extenders.

"I know, Big Gramps, *no* politician in this town gonna touch that man. No, sir, Willie Brown gonna slip through that next election without being touched, just like my man, Jerry Rice, running a quick slant and slipping untouched through the secondary against them Atlanta Falcons."

You remain in the spot for a while longer, learning little of significance, except for the cripple's apparent nickname, Double S. You do not get a good opportunity to use the Minolta, not even taking it out of your pocket.

2

At about 1:00 p.m., Double S is relieved by a young Latino who takes his place next to the white-headed old man. The new guy has a kind of permanent empty grin frozen on his face, his speech noticeably hesitant and slightly slurred.

Double S neatly stores away his little box and shining supplies into the tray under the stand's foot extenders. He folds up the chair and slides it behind the shine stand. Then he scoots around and pauses for a moment in front of the stand.

"Big Gramps, Octavio, my man, catch ya later."

"See ya, son," the old man responds, smiling and nodding.

"S'long, Double S," Octavio says, saluting at the cripple with his shoeshine brush.

On the way out of the station, Double S suddenly stops and parks in the aisle at the corner of the lunch counter to bug one of the waitresses, who is leaning over getting salads from a stainless steel refrigerator, her white uniform dress pulled tight against her shapely buttocks.

"Yo, Sadie, you looking *good*, girl."

"You never mind about that, *boy*," the young black woman responds with mock anger, looking back over her shoulder at the man on the scooter-board leaning in and leering at her from the aisle. "I'm too busy to be messing with y'all right now, ya unnerstand."

"I hear ya, you sweet thing," Double S says, then laughs loudly and takes off out of the Greyhound Station.

3

You follow him, which requires you to jog to keep up as he speeds south on 10th toward the Mission, the cripple on his scooter-board moving almost as fast as a kid on a bicycle.

He finally slows after reaching tree-lined Shotwell Street, cruising past the colorfully painted Victorians, all divided now into apartments and mostly occupied by Latino families.

In the center of the second block, Double S turns in, coasting to a stop before an entryway along the side of a three story, well-maintained building. He maneuvers himself down a short stairwell to a basement apartment, pausing at the bottom of the stairs to reach up and unlock the apartment door. You snap off a shot from the Minolta and wait patiently across the street in the shade of a large elm tree...

4

About an hour later Double S emerges from his apartment and you follow him out of the Mission, uptown to a diner on Bryant in the 800-block near the courthouse. He meets a big, unkempt man with a cigar and a young, well-dressed lady carrying a briefcase and a black folder under her arm—one like an architect or perhaps an artist might carry. Feeling confident that you haven't been noticed by the trio, you snap off a pair of shots with the camera. They go into the diner, which is not crowded at this hour, and sit at a big table near the front window.

You wait outside, leery about going into the almost empty place and exposing yourself. As you watch them talk, the woman is drawing something in her opened black folder. She glances up often and appears to be listening intently to Double S, who is sitting next to her. Then, after a moment or so of sketching, she points at the work with her pen. Double S nods or shakes his head, sometimes pointing down at the drawing himself.

Obviously the woman is an artist of some kind... maybe a police artist?

Yeah, she reminds you of one you saw on TV, drawing a face while listening to a verbal description by a witness. That's what she is doing.

The thought chills you, reinforces your lingering concern that the black cripple did indeed spot you in the alley last Tuesday night. They may be making a sketch of *you* in there at this very moment, or at least what Double S remembers about your appearance. It was dark and he was twenty or thirty yards away. Maybe he didn't see enough to accurately describe you. But maybe he did.

You shift your attention to the third person in the booth. The big guy looks like a cop—

But, if he's a detective and she's a police artist, why are they meeting Double S out here in a cafe instead of headquarters, where they would have better sketching conditions, equipment, and lighting?

Maybe they aren't cops?

Then, who are they?

You rub your face, puzzled.

You resist an almost overwhelming impulse to rush into the diner, lean across their table, and grab a quick peek at the artist's sketch.

Instead you wait nervously in place, a hand clutching the Minolta in your pocket, the minutes ticking by so slowly, your stomach muscles in a tight, painful knot. You close your eyes for a moment and suck in a number of deep breaths, relaxing, easing the cramp, but unable to speed up the movement of time…

Finally, at 3:30 or so, the three come out of the diner and immediately split up.

Double S scoots away southeasterly, back toward the Mission, with you trying to keep up behind him.

Fifteen minutes later, he disappears into the basement apartment on the side of the beautiful Victorian on Shotwell.

By now you're out of breath, but have fully regained your composure. You are resigned to the fact that this black man has definitely witnessed you performing the Lord's work. After catching your breath, you decide the important question is—*What should you do about it, if anything?*

Of course you need to protect yourself, but how?

As you wait at his place pondering the problem, you decide to check the names on the mailboxes at the top of the front steps of the elegant building. You climb the stairs, listening carefully for the door opening at the side of the Victorian.

The box for the downstairs flat, 745 D, is neatly labeled in black paint: *Dupree*, David and Damon. The name Damon is fresher paint, obviously added at a later date. You have his last name now, probable first, and his photo.

You can think of nothing else to do at the moment but wait, so you return to the shade and cover of the elm tree across the street. The day is warm and bright, birds singing and flitting about, children home from school now and riding their scooters and bikes up and down Shotwell on the sidewalks, chattering noisily in Spanish as they dart past you. Occasionally one of the youngsters playing catch in a front yard nearby runs out into the street to retrieve the ball. The cheerful nature of the neighborhood lifts your spirits.

5

Early that evening Double S leads you northwesterly out of the Mission, across Market Street, then up Geary Street to a small, private investigator office near Japantown. He moves at a more leisurely pace than this afternoon, and you keep up easily. You stop and watch as he disappears into the office, asking several questions.

Why would Double S need private investigators, if he saw you in the alley?

Why not just go to the cops?

Even more puzzled now than earlier, you wait outside *Sullivan, Cato, & Associates*, snapping pictures of everyone who enters the office after Double S.

Then you wait.

After fifteen minutes or so, you consciously shift your thoughts, recalling the other occasion when you *may* have been spotted doing the Lord's work. The incident that forced you to abandon an almost ideal situation in Chicago before heading west, two years ago...

6

Six years ago you had arrived in Chicago from St. Louis in the afternoon.

After leaving the Greyhound Bus Depot on Harrison Street just west of the downtown area, you paused to gain your bearings. Then, you wandered around for a while, just getting the feel of the heart of the city. After a half an hour, you found yourself on Division Street, looking at two clasped hands painted in white on a storefront window. Over the hands, an arc of capital letters read—WE CARE SHELTER: RESPITE FROM THE STREET. But it was a hand-lettered sign in the corner of the big window that really captured your attention: *Custodial help wanted.*

You entered the shelter and were hired on the spot as the nightshift custodian/handyman for the facility.

You soon learned that WE CARE was a nonprofit corporation that owned and ran four social service facilities at different locations in Chicago, with an annual budget of over ten million dollars.

During the next two years you were promoted twice, first to a working custodial supervisor at the WE CARE shelter for abused women on the Southside, and then to working custodial/maintenance supervisor for the two drug rehab residential facilities, one downtown and the other in Inglewood. Eventually you became the number one man in custodial/maintenance supervision for WE CARE, Inc., responsible for on-site management of all four facilities, including supervision of sixteen custodians and two maintenance men. Occasionally you filled in when one of your men was sick or needed time off, especially at night when it was difficult to hire subs. This was when you found the best opportunities to continue your practice of the Lord's work, experiencing the Deathflash and guiding souls to the Hereafter.

But two years ago, you were filling in at the downtown men's shelter when you were probably spotted by a fellow worker as you used the Hand of God.

It was just after 8:00 p.m., a line of clients still coming in the door at the WE CARE shelter. You were getting ready to leave, after filling in for four hours for the evening custodian, who had attended a wake for a relative, but would return by 8:30 to finish his normal 4:00 to 12:00 shift.

"No, no, Murray," the intake counselor was saying to a client, an exasperated expression on his face as he shook his head. An old man, obviously drunk, was at the registration desk near the outside door, trying to sign into the shelter. Behind him he held a line of string, stretched out ten feet or so, the end tied to a resting skate. On the skate was an item wrapped tightly in a brown paper bag—obviously a bottle he was trying to nonchalantly smuggle in behind him.

"Take your skate and bottle outside," the unamused counselor impatiently ordered Murray. "Come back tomorrow, *if* you are sobered up by then."

The old man, despair permanently carved into his lined face, just nodded sadly and turned away from the desk; then, with slumped shoulders, he shuffled back outside, dragging his skate behind him.

You followed.

The old drunk turned eastward back toward downtown, eventually ducking into an alley near the city bus stop three blocks from WE CARE.

You watched from the mouth of the alley.

The old derelict already had a cardboard box set up among the debris along the far wall of dirty bricks. At the end of the alley was a cluster of three more cardboard *tents.* You hoped they were unoccupied this early in the evening.

You waited and watched... for at least ten minutes.

No one else came or left the alley.

Nothing moved in the cluster of cardboard shelters.

It was very quiet and dark now—about 8:20.

You crept along the brick wall, stopping at the old man's shelter and listening.

Snoring.

You took the Hand of God from a plastic sandwich bag in your pocket and carefully slipped it on, extending your forefinger snugly against the bulb in the glove finger, glancing down at the lethal drop of moisture that appeared on the tip of the metallic talon. Satisfied with your quick preparation, you kneeled and crawled into the cardboard opening. Stopping at his side, you remained on your knees, watching the old man's face for a moment. He continued snoring, unaware of your presence. You leaned forward and scratched the sleeping man's exposed lower arm.

In his sleep, he groaned, made a slight face, and rolled away from the talon on the Hand of God.

After another minute or so, the Deathflash exploded from his chest, basking the inside of the cardboard tent and you in its wonderful brilliance!

Minutes ticked by as you remained on your knees, all your senses keenly stimulated by the magnificent hovering dots... Eventually, you roused yourself from the almost trancelike state, sucked in a deep breath, and attended to your Shepherd duties. You withdrew the tin from your jacket pocket, made the Shepherd's mark with the sacred ashes, and then prayed the old sinner's soul on to its maker.

Backing out from the opened tent and exposed shell of the old man, you hesitated, the onset of the now all-too familiar spell suddenly overwhelming you, including the excruciating pain when the sliver of steel stabbed above your left eyebrow into your sinus cavity.

Momentarily paralyzed but hanging onto consciousness... Then, at the edge of your perceptual field a distinct sound separated from the evening noise: a vehicle noisily taking off just behind you out on the street.

With an effort you twisted around and stared dumbly.

Coming completely to your senses, you realized that a city bus had just pulled away from the stop. And anyone who had got off a few minutes earlier and glanced down the alley into the open cardboard tent could have spotted you engaged in the Lord's work. Of course they would've misinterpreted what they saw as a plain homicide; they wouldn't have understood the nature of your task. No, indeed not.

So, pulse racing with nervous anticipation, you shuffled clumsily the few yards to the street and glanced in the direction of the departing bus.

No one on the sidewalk for several blocks.

Thank God! Your rubbery legs almost gave way with relief.

Then, you looked back up toward WE CARE and gasped with shock, as you saw the familiar back and gait of Danny O'Connor, your swing shift custodian. He was hurrying back toward work after obviously arriving on that very bus.

Oh, my God!

Had he looked down that alley getting off the bus?

Into the tent?

Had he seen you doing your duty?

As you finished the last silent question, Danny stopped three blocks away at the shelter door and glanced back in your direction, probably not actually seeing you in the shadows.

But, even at that distance, you recognized an uncharacteristic look on his normally cheerful features: puzzlement, concern, perhaps even fear.

Then he disappeared into the building.

He'd seen something unsettling.

Seen you dispatch the old sinner and all the rest of it?

And did he recognize you?

Possibly not at that distance in the dark.

But you weren't sure. You couldn't convince yourself that Danny O'Connor had *not* seen you at the Lord's work.

Making a decision, you hurried home and packed quickly.

Then, you left Chicago that very night, fortunately catching a ride out of town… And eventually hitchhiking your way across the country to San Francisco, leaving a twisted trail of false names at a half dozen brief stops along the way. Unlike St. Louis, this time you insured that tracking you would be extremely difficult.

That time two years ago is so similar to what happened last Tuesday night.

The office door opens at 8:30 p.m. and five people leave the P.I. agency, including Damon Dupree on the scooter-board. Hoping there is still enough light, you snap off a group photograph. You recognize Richie O'Brien, who is followed by the guy with the fighter's face, John Cato, the tall Katy Green, and finally the big guy with the cigar you'd seen earlier down on Bryant Street… probably the Sullivan of the agency's name.

O'Brien, Cato, Green, Sullivan, and Dupree. You snap off individual photos of the first four, just before the group breaks up—

Katy Green and Richie O'Brien hurry off for an old mustard-colored Volvo station wagon parked nearby. From the Volvo, they wave to the three others remaining on Geary Street, as the two of them head off in the direction of downtown.

As you continue to spy on them, Cato, Dupree, and Sullivan casually head up the street a block and a half to a parked Mustang. They store the scooter-board in the trunk before the three of them climb in and take off in the same direction as the others.

You are left in the shadows, the early fog thickening around you as you weigh the situation.

Obviously Dupree hadn't gone to the police with what he saw in the alley Tuesday night. For whatever reason, he has come to these three private investigators… who must now be working with Richie O'Brien, investigating the loss of his brother and two friends. They were obviously putting everything together tonight, maybe even aware now of the others. And sooner or later they would have to share this information with the authorities, bringing your work to public attention and scrutiny.

You shiver in the cold.

Then sigh.

So, pretty soon it may be too late to maintain anonymity, you think, nodding as if agreeing with someone else's conclusion.

Now, either you must run again… or if you stay you will be compelled to protect yourself, in order to continue the Lord's work?

To run?

Now?

God knows there is *so* much work remaining to be done in this city. You really are needed here. San Francisco is awash with a multitude of sinners past the point of salvation, many backsliders, their souls requiring guidance. And with the headache spells so devastating now, you're just too tired, perhaps incapable of running and starting over again.

No question, you have to stay.

So, you conclude that it is really out of your hands; the fate of *all* five meddlers now must rest in the Hand of the Lord.

All five.

Of course you realize that you must help, and the situation dictates that you work quickly before the problem grows even worse, including the authorities and the public spotlight.

Quickly, *but* very carefully.

A FEW ANSWERS

Thursday night everyone is assembled in the cramped office off Geary Street near Japantown when Johnny arrives from his AA meeting at about 8:05.

"Well, let's get right to your reports," he announces, moving to the Progress Board. "I know it's late, and Katy and Richie have another research date tonight." He picks up a stick of chalk. "I'll save time, making a few additions, deletions, corrections, whatever as we move along. Okay?"

Everyone nods.

"Okay, Hap, what do you have?"

The big guy places an unlit cigar in an ashtray on his desk and opens a manila folder. "Got a note back on Peter Miller from the officer who discovered his body, with a resident hotel address in the 'loin. I backtracked from there. Petey, as he was known, lived on Social Security here in the city for the last five years, maybe some situational panhandling at the end of each month when his money ran out. No family. No friends to speak of. And no enemies I could determine. Used to be a cab driver, but struggled even back then with the sauce. Apparently, he fought it though, going to lots of meetings until a few months ago. Finally gave up, began really hitting the juice. Just another member of the city's underclass like the three boys." He looks up from his folder. "Speaking of the boys, talked on the phone to the blue who wrote up the IDS on Bartkowski. Nothing unusual *except* he found no drugs or drug paraphernalia at the death scene—"

"How'd he figure an OD then?" Katy asks.

"Blue assumed it after noting fresh tracks on the kid's arm. Said he thought maybe the kid fixed in a shooting gallery nearby, then wandered into the alley and died… I dunno about that though." He looked skeptical, glancing over at Richie.

Richie shakes his head. "No way, man. If you OD on heroin, it happens immediately after using, right on the spot. Your lungs, heart, everything begins shutting down. You have time to make a funny grunt, period."

Johnny agrees, "You guys are right, Bartkowski did not OD in that alley three weeks ago." He makes a quick notation on the board, turns back and gestures for Hap to continue.

"Nothing back yet on your Q-tips from the Miller hit. I'll prod the lab tomorrow morning, see if I can get some quicker action. Don't have quite as much pull as when I was packing a shield, you know." He glances back again at his manila folder, shuffles the papers.

"Ah, let's see, still nothing important from my C.I.s on the street, but I'll keep checking… That's about all I've got," Hap concludes, closing his folder.

"Richie?" Johnny says, after making a couple of additional notes on the Progress Board.

"Nothing unusual noticed by my people at 815 when Jaime and the other two boys split from the program. No one paid particular attention or concern. Except maybe their orientation counselor—the new guy that you…" he paused, pointing at both Katy and Johnny before continuing "… met the other day. Seemed pretty shaken for a day or so when they went out. But he's new and that reaction is normal; he'll toughen up soon. People relapse. It happens all the time, you know." Richie's angular features remain deadpan, as he shifts direction. "There is *something* going on out on the street though. Nothing really said by anyone, nothing you can put your finger on, but I'm picking up a level of tension, a paranoia, kinda like when there's bad dope circulating out there or a dope shortage for some reason. Major negative vibes, you know what I mean?" He glances at his friend on the scooter-board. "Damon, you sensing any of this?"

"Yeah, I think you're right, man," Double S agrees, nodding. "I been picking up a similar feeling when I was scooting around the 'loin last night, up in the Mission, too. I'll check out the Haight, see if it's the same there. And there has been some dude checking around, asking questions, kinda same as ours, like he's looking for someone, you know what I'm saying. White guy, tall, maybe thirty or so. Dude might be our hitter."

"Why would he be asking questions about himself?" Katy said aloud. "That doesn't make sense."

Double S shrugged and shook his head.

Johnny stopped writing on the board, taking time to pull at his nose. "See if you can get some more info, maybe a better description of the guy, Double S. Exactly what is he asking? Maybe he's hunting for potential victims."

The black man nods. "Gotcha."

Johnny gestures to Richie, who continues, "Okay, so, maybe there is an awareness of something wrong coming down out there... a kind of unspoken heads up. If that's true, someone else out there has to know something." After a moment or two of silence, he turns up his empty palms. "And of course this strange guy Damon heard about, checking around—who is he, anyway?"

"Yeah, that is odd, don't sound like it's a cop, even undercover," Hap adds, setting his cigar in the ashtray. "People on the street would make him quickly. Maybe it's not the killer, either. But even if he ain't a cop, he could be someone *else* looking for our guy?"

"Yes, but who exactly?" Katy says, frowning. "Why would anyone else be looking for him? Someone like Richie maybe, a relative or friend of one of the victims? Someone out of prison, looking for an old cellmate, maybe recognizing an M.O.? "

Hap frowns uncharacteristically. "I dunno. I guess it could be any of those?"

"You got anything else, Double S?" Johnny asks, glancing down at the man resting on his scooter-board.

Double S says, "Yeah, a hooker on Capp Street says she's missing two friends, disappeared separately during the last two or three weeks. I checked around a little on that... But aside from the vague sense of increased street tension like Richie said, I get nothing definite on either missing hooker. They just seem to be gone—"

Then he snaps his fingers and pulls some papers from a brown paper bag. "Almost forgot. These reproduced sketches by Hap's lady friend look pretty good to me of the guy I saw Tuesday night in that alley over in the 'loin." He scoots around the room, handing out four copies of the police artist's sketch of the perp Double S saw wasting Petey Miller.

The room is quiet, as everyone checks over their copy of the drawing.

Katy's first impression is a vague sense of familiarity. Maybe I *have* seen this guy, she tells herself.

But where?

When?

Who is he?

She finally shakes her head, nothing solid surfacing, and looks up.

"Well Katy has something important," Johnny announces, dropping his sketch copy down on the desk, standing and picking up the piece of chalk at the board.

Katy thumbs through a couple of pages in her Spiral notebook then looks back up. "I ran down Jeremy Featherstone's ex-roommate, Steven Boyer, up near Fairfield today. He's going to Solano Community College there. Didn't get much from him, except that he believes Featherstone is capable of a degree of violence, maybe even murder. But sudden, impulsive stuff, nothing like using poison, that kind of thing... And my basketball teammate, Sidney, a graphic artist, thinks the gray ash the perp is using to mark his victims is not any kind of common artist material. Might be something the perp is mixing up special." She closes her notebook, unable to stifle a little smirk of satisfaction. "Here's the topper though, what Johnny means. Last night Johnny and I figured out the mark is not really a *J* like we thought. We think it's probably a shepherd's crook."

Katy explains about the most logical positioning of the mark by the perp, demonstrating to each of them with Hap's Polaroid, positioning it correctly.

"Yeah, I think you're right," Richie says, handing Katy back the photo of Peter Miller's marked forehead.

"Yep." Hap agrees that the shepherd's crook mistakenly looks like an uncrossed *J* only when viewed upside down. "Be unnatural for the perp to move around to mark his victim, after scratching him."

Everyone studies the progress board for a few moments, looking over Johnny's growing list of questions with a few more answers now, including the proper interpretation of the mark—a shepherd's crook.

"Well, I didn't make much progress today," Johnny admits, rubbing his broken nose. "I did confirm that Jeremy Featherstone was signed in for a visit between 8:00 and 9:00 Tuesday night at his father's rest home, like he explained to Katy and I yesterday. But one of the orderlies on duty Tuesday evening did not remember seeing Jeremy anytime that night, and the other thinks that *maybe* he saw him early in the evening, just after dinner. Of course the old man remembers nothing. So, Jeremy could have signed in anytime really. We need to sweat him again, maybe tomorrow morning."

Johnny again tugs thoughtfully at his broken nose before continuing. "And the AA meeting I just came from was a bust. Most of the people I talked to didn't even remember Peter Miller, even after I showed Hap's Polaroid photo around. And those who did remember did not have much to add in the way of information. I'm not really sure when he last attended a meeting. That's about it." Then, as an afterthought, he turns toward Richie and says, "Oh, I saw Jackson Williams at the meeting. You know, our new coffee guy from Capp Street. He just stuck his head in, looked around, saw me, and quickly left without speaking. Funny, huh?"

Richie agreed, explaining to the group, "Yeah, young guys usually don't go to both kinds of meetings, NA and AA—"

"Unless they're looking for someone," Katy interrupts, glancing up with a thoughtful crease between her eyes. "He *is* white, tall, and in his late twenties, right? Maybe he's the guy Double S is hearing about on the street. Looking for the killer, too? Wonder if anyone named Williams has been a victim?" She reopens her notebook and scratches a reminder to herself: *Jackson Williams, related to a past victim?*

No one says anything more, but Double S smiles at Katy and nods his head—*You may have something, girl.*

Johnny nods, too, turns, makes a note on his board adding the name Jackson Williams under MISC. followed by a question mark, mumbling, "Could be something here, I guess... Could be?" Then, after turning back to the group, he asks, "Anybody got anything else important to add up here?"

No one volunteers anything.

They discuss strategy and assignments for a few minutes, agree on assembling again tomorrow at 7:00 p.m., before the meeting finally breaks up.

On the street, Richie and Katy head off in one direction to do more research on Katy's writing project and the other three climb into Johnny's Mustang for a ride home.

USIN'

Junkie gotta be the loneliest man alive, cuz he flat-ass wears out all his friends.

—Beechnut

After the meeting on Geary, Richie drives Katy back to the little diner in the Mission, *The OK Corral,* where they'd called the dealer's pager number a couple of nights ago. The counter and stools are full when they walk in, people mostly drinking coffee and talking. After waiting a few minutes for a couple to leave, Richie and Katy squeeze onto the vacant pair of adjoining stools.

Richie orders two coffees, his face taking on its grim, hard-edged cast again—his imitation of a scuffed-up Clint Eastwood after getting his ass kicked, and looking for revenge. He adds cream and sugar to his coffee, before explaining why they came to this cafe tonight in his detached, sharp tone, "Old Beechnut used to say, 'A strung-out junky ain't trying to get high, he's trying to get well'." He nods, smiling thinly. "And that's about right. When you're hurting, you will *try* to fix just about anywhere, anytime, even a busy diner, like this one right here."

Katy quickly glances around, not knowing what to expect. She sees nothing unusual—at least no one fixing—and looks back at Richie with her eyebrows arched.

He notices the look, but first tastes his coffee; then he suggests to Katy, "Go on, check out the head."

"The bathroom... ?" she says in a reluctant voice, not feeling especially enthusiastic about going into the restroom here in this crowded place filled with rough-looking street people. But she gets up, before even touching her coffee, and makes her way, careful not to bump anyone on a stool, to the one door labeled WC, back near the payphone.

Inside, Katy squints to see and glances about the darkened, cramped cubicle, expecting to be confronted with bloody used needles on the floor, cotton balls in the sink, discarded cookers, or whatever; but she is surprised, not really finding anything unusual except for a trash can overflowing with dirty, wet paper towels. So she flips on the light switch and blinks because everything is instantly bathed in blood, the dark room now illuminated by an unshaded high wattage *red* bulb extending out of the wall just over the commode. *Wow, that sucker is bright,* she thinks.

But, except for the colored light, there's really nothing else to see in the tiny restroom. Not a frigging thing. *What's up with that?* she asks herself, making her way back to their place at the counter, a little peeved.

Back on her stool next to Richie, Katy asks, in a slightly annoyed tone, "What was I supposed to find in there? That bright red light bulb?"

He nods, his expression still grim. "That's right."

"Why?"

"Junkie tries to use in there, he can't see a *register* in his needle. You know the stringy backflow of blood into his dope, indicating he's hit a vein. He needs to find a register."

"Yeah, okay, I understand now..." Katy says, leaning out and glancing down the long row of peoples' backs to the WC door. She smiles kind of sheepishly at her slowness to catch on, thinking, *Pretty clever of the cafe owner.*

When Katy tucks back into the counter, Richie is holding up his spoon for her to take a closer look. There are maybe half a dozen tiny holes in the bowl of the utensil. She frowns.

"Can't cook dope with this spoon, girl," he explains, "but you can still eat pie or stir your coffee with it. You see, in this area, cafes like the Corral do whatever they can to discourage junkies in a hurry to fix. Most won't even give a free glass of water to anyone off the street, because they know addicts ain't gonna drink it, they're gonna mix it with tar." He shakes his head. "Dope fiend is pretty lonely even here in the Mission, shunned by everyone. His own fault, because he's just a royal pain in the ass. And that's a fact."

She nods, feeling a momentary twinge of sympathy for the hapless plight of the addict, absently taking a drink of her black coffee, the sip of hot liquid almost scalding her tongue. Katy carefully blows on the cup of steaming liquid before tentatively sipping it again.

"Actually we're getting a little ahead of ourselves, here," Richie says. "Some stats about usin' may be in order before we go too much further."

He pauses, sipping his coffee and gathering his thoughts. "There are probably 13,000 heroin addicts here in San Francisco alone, out of a nationwide population of as many as 750,000 to 1,000,000. The scary thing is in recent years the average age of an addict has dropped ten years from an average around 30 to about 19, as of this last year. And we ain't just talking black dudes or hookers or kids from the projects either. We're talking both white boys and girls, from all over, the problem spreading into even little towns in the Midwest. This increase in use by kids has been accompanied by an alarming increase in heroin overdoses. For example, on any given weekend, SF General alone might deal with two, three fatal ODs, seeing over 150 a year." He finishes the last drink of his coffee before adding, "We're talking about an epidemic here. Something not recognized by the general public, yet."

Richie pulls out a dollar and some change and drops it on the counter for the coffees. "Okay. Ready to go?"

Katy nods, stands, and follows Richie out to the mustard station wagon.

2

"Of course kids don't begin shooting up, hooked from day one," Richie continues, sliding into the Volvo. "They usually start out experimenting, you know like snorting or smoking the stuff at parties with friends." The starter grinds a moment before finally catching. "Some quickly graduate to *chasing-the-dragon*. You do that by holding a flame under aluminum foil, and breathing the evaporating dope fumes with a cut-off straw—"

"I saw Harvey Keitel doing that in a movie once," Katy interrupts, as Richie goes around the block, then back uptown on 16th for a couple of blocks, slowing down and searching for a parking space as they near Mission.

"Yeah, *The Bad Lieutenant*, something like that... pretty good flick, realistic," Richie replies, after finding a parking spot.

He sets the brake, remaining seated, the crease between his eyes deepening. "Anyhow, pretty soon, kid is shooting dope, and he ain't just usin' on weekends at parties. Two, three, four times a week now. Everyday. But he thinks *he's* different, you know, he ain't getting hooked and strung out. No way, man, he can handle it, quit anytime he wants. Yeah, sure, fool—"

Richie snorts derisively, making a kind of sour, disgusted face, like he'd bitten into something rotten. "Yeah, we were all really the same, you know, but thinking we were special, *different*. The rules just did not apply to us."

He slides out of the Volvo and leads Katy around the corner on Mission and 16th. "No one is different at all. It's the same path once on the point... sooner or later you're hooked big time, strung out, and then dope-sick more often than not. It ain't recreational anymore. Soon, it's like ol' Beechnut said about just trying to get well. When I see a hamster running on one of them caged wheels in a pet store or on TV, it always makes me think of a dope fiend... except the hamster can stop anytime and get off. An addict keeps on running."

They stop and Richie points at the dark green kiosk with gold trim on this side of the BART square near the curb. "Ever been in one of these?"

Katy shakes her head. She's never used one of the newly erected

French toilets, but she has read a lot about them in the *Chronicle*. And, of course, the criticism of Mayor Willie Brown for buying them. Kind of an expensive political hot potato. She walks around the toilet. The attractive, oval-shaped stall is about nine or so feet high, looks more like a well-kept newspaper or classy flower kiosk than a public restroom.

Katy gets in line with Richie, waiting for the stall to become vacant.

"These were much needed, especially for the tourists in the downtown area, but they're also a haven for junkies," Richie explains, dropping a quarter into the slot, after the previous customer steps out.

The green, metallic oval door slides around exposing the freshly washed-down interior.

They step inside and close the door, Katy noticing water still draining through the slatted floors, but the toilet, the sink, and all the stainless steel appearing clean and sanitary.

"You can stay in here up to twenty minutes, which is plenty long enough to fix and nod out for a few minutes," Richie says, opening the sliding door. "Time to get well."

As they step out, the next customer, a young bag woman, steps up, a quarter in one hand, the concave end of a soda can gripped revealingly in her other hand. Richie glances over at Katy with raised eyebrows, making sure she has spotted the cooker—a *see-what-I-mean-look* on his hard face.

Katy nods back.

They walk in the direction of the parked Volvo.

"She'll be in there the full twenty minutes," Richie says. "That particular location isn't a good one, if you need to go to the toilet real bad. I've seen as many as six junkies lined up there in broad daylight, all with their cookers in hand, and anxious to fix."

After they reach the station wagon, they sit a minute, Richie kind of summarizing, "So, an addict needs a place off the street to fix. Alley ain't safe, cops or someone ripping you off either before or after you begin nodding out. Public restrooms are the usually preferred spot, but the owners of cafes—once the most common locations—are getting smart, taking measures to discourage use of their facilities. And now Willie Brown rides to the rescue, erecting French toilets all over the city at high traffic locations. His political foes may be whining about the money. But the junkies say, Man, you can't beat a French toilet with a belt—need even more of them all over the city. You get the picture?"

"I got it," Katy says, looking out the window across 16th Street, watching a gaunt, filthy 4-for-1 dealer slipping a small green balloon to a well-dressed, college-aged guy, the customer quickly hiding the balloon from sight in the pocket of his blue herringbone sport jacket. *Yeah, you're slick, dude,* Katy thinks. Probably only fifty or so people could've spotted the transaction, if anyone here in the Mission really gave a shit.

3

Richie eases the Volvo out into traffic, turning downtown on Mission. At Fourth, he turns south toward China Basin, slowing and eventually finding a parking spot just off Townsend.

"C'mon," he says leading Katy toward a familiar area—the location of the demolition site and old brick building. Most of the front and sides of the structure have been knocked down in the last day or so, reduced to a great pile of brick and mortar. A back loader with its large scoop grounded, rests next to the pile, like a metallic animal with its mouth open, ready to begin eating bricks.

"Ah, good," Richie says, pointing to the wooden stairwell still standing against the remaining back brick wall. Nothing else is left of the old location, including the long sidewall with all the colorful graffiti.

They make their way around the pile of rubble, the lights from surrounding buildings providing ample illumination of the hazardous footing.

At the bottom of the stairwell Richie stops.

"Wonder how many times I actually climbed these stairs?" he says, staring up the rickety stairwell, scratching his chin thoughtfully. After a moment he shakes his head and answers his own rhetorical question, "Too many, I guess."

Then he glances at Katy, his angular face deeply creased in the dim light. "Like I mentioned the other day, this was a shooting gallery in the old days. Bought my dope here from Sweet Jane, then often used the facilities to fix right here. She was a long-time user-dealer and had once been quite pretty, I think…"

Richie pauses a moment, looking up the stairs as if he can actually see the woman standing there in the darkness at the top of the stairwell, shouting down to the pit bull, Homeboy. He smiles thinly to himself. "Sweet Jane always gave fair measure, and she had a kind heart for a dealer… Yeah, this was a good setup off the street. And the place wasn't like what you might have seen in movies. No, actually it was half-ass clean—Sweet Jane and her daughter lived up here, and she tried—"

"A daughter?"

"Yeah, Twinkle…"

He paused again and laughed, remembering something, his features softening noticeably. "Twinkle, like the song. You know, twinkle, twinkle, little star. A cute kid. She must have been five or six when I started coming to see her mom—"

Abruptly, the hard-guy frown is back on his face.

"I remember this one time in '88 or maybe it was '89… Sweet Jane was about thirty or so by then, been usin' since she was a teenager, been dealing for two or three years by then. Skinny as a rail, her arms and legs all tracked with scar tissue, most spots too ropey for a fix. Anyhow, around that time I used to help fix her pretty regular. She'd stick her thumb in her mouth, blow hard, until the veins popped out in her neck… But this time in her room, I'm just ready to hit her in the neck and in walks little Twinkle, hugging her beat-up Raggedy Ann doll. I freeze, as if waiting for a photo to be snapped, thinking, Holy shit! What do I do, now? But Sweet Jane just spits her thumb out and says in an everyday mom voice, 'Sweety, you go on and play in the kitchen, Momma is taking her medicine.' And there I *am*, the doctor, right? Well, after a moment, Twinkle just smiles sweetly and says, 'Okay, Momma,' and trots out of the room, like it was a routine everyday mother-daughter exchange at the doctor's office. Man…"

Katy watches, as Richie pauses again and stares up at the door ajar at the top of the stairs, the spot apparently bringing back so many memories. She doesn't say anything, the lingering image of the little girl and the bizarre shooting-up scene so vivid in her mind's eye. *Jesus*, she swears silently to herself. What a fucked-up kind of life for both that poor kid and her mother.

Finally, Richie sighs loudly, as if agreeing with Katy's silent judgment.

"Yep, that was just another day in the life of a junkie. But I remember telling myself, a little later that night, when I was fixing by myself—Man, that's it, I'm quitting for sure... first thing tomorrow morning."

"And did you?"

Richie glances at Katy with a smile dripping cynicism, as he leads her back away from the rubble. "Oh, yeah, sure I did... a year or so later in the slammer, after I got my ass busted for holding."

"What happened to Jane and Twinkle?" Katy asks, following him around the rubble.

"I don't know," Richie replies, shaking his head. "Like so many people in the life, they just suddenly disappeared one day. And I haven't heard anything about either one for years. That's why this shepherd guy could of whacked out a lot of people, nobody really knowing how many, if all his victims are in the underclass. Dope fiends, alkies, hookers, homeless, they just naturally come and go, no one caring enough to check on them. So the cops, their relatives, no one knows."

"You could be right about more hits," Katy says, as they leave the demolition site. "I'm going to check out recent deaths at the *Guardian* tomorrow morning. See if by chance the shepherd's mark has been noted on other ODs or supposedly routine deaths—see how many are suspicious."

4

Back in the station wagon, heading for Katy's townhouse in the Marina, Richie describes the kind of obsessive-compulsive ritual-like behavior involved during usin'—like following a recipe step-by-step. Then, he adds, "Hell, after a while, if I followed my routine, I could start getting off soon as I scored, or just seeing the dope and needle, or for sure watching another dope fiend tying off. A junkie goes through his ritual, everything determined, even the number of times he thumps a vein to raise it. The routine becomes part of what Beechnut called, 'getting well.' Sounds crazy, but I know the ritual really has a physical effect on you. Even now, thinking about going over to Sweet Jane's place, the old days, I get a familiar twinge deep in my gut."

As Katy watches him, Richie sucks in a deep breath.

After a moment, he continues. "There's some legitimate research indicating that addicts may have actually changed their brain chemistry through drug use. Maybe junkie ritual behavior triggers something up there neurologically. Who knows? There is still a lot of scientific work to do. In fact, considering the epidemic nature of the heroin problem, we're not getting enough money for research. But I guess that is another topic for another day."

They ride along quietly, until they reach the Marina.

"Yes, research is definitely something else we need to talk about another time," Katy finally says. "And thanks, Richie, got some good stuff to think about here," she adds, sliding out of the old beat-up mustard Volvo in front of her place on Chestnut Street.

She waves to ol' Clint as he drives off, chuckling to herself, thinking, *A guy that famous ought to be able to afford a better car.*

REVELATIONS AT
THE GUARDIAN

L ate Friday morning Katy meets with Jessie Warner, her editor and primary contact, at the *San Francisco Bay Guardian* offices.

Jessie Warner is almost as tall as Katy, a middle-aged, attractive black woman, very fit and lean, looking like a gym rat or a distance runner of some kind. And she had indeed once been a world class track and field athlete, a member of the Olympic sprint team in Montreal—placing fourth in the 200 meters and taking a gold medal with the other members of the championship 4x100 meter relay team. After a messy divorce, she came to San Francisco from St. Louis a year and a half ago, about the same time Katy moved from Sacramento.

Katy has done several feature articles and an interview of a best-selling science fiction writer friend for Jessie, working closely and developing a high degree of respect for the editor, the two eventually becoming good friends during the process. Jessie has been over to their apartment in the Marina a number of times for lunch, once for dinner. She reminds Katy a little of her old friend and mentor in San Diego, Gerri Robinson—both women all business on the outside, but with hearts of gold.

Katy takes a seat beside Jessie's desk and glances around the familiar office, her gaze resting for a moment on the three photos on the desk. Her friend's grown daughter, Angie, a screenwriter in Hollywood; son, Desmond, a dot com executive here in San Francisco; and the third picture of a much younger Jessie in her red, white, and blue USA track uniform, smiling proudly and wearing her gold medal around her neck.

"*Oh-oh*, you've got that I-have-a-major-story gleam in your eye, girl," Jessie says half-jokingly, grinning and handing Katy a hot mug of raspberry herbal tea before taking her own seat at the desk.

Katy laughs. "You're pretty sharp, Jess, this visit is only partly social. Actually I did want to talk some business."

"What's up?"

"Well, I've been conned into a little investigative work again with Johnny and his partner, Hap Sullivan, for their agency," Katy explains, after taking the first sip of her tea and nodding her approval. "We think a serial murderer may be operating in the city with impunity, hitting junkies and winos, maybe other members of the underclass, too. We really don't yet know how many or how long he's been killing people."

"Uh-huh," Jessie says, nodding. "You're thinking about a Guardian feature on this killer? What kind of human-interest slant? Him preying on the forgotten members of society—something like that?"

"Well, partially, yes, but maybe initially also the piece designed to get a response from him, something like hinting the hits may be pathological, partly homosexual in nature, and at the same time we want to put some pressure on the SFPD," Katy replies, then places her steaming tea mug on the edge of the desk. "Homicide absolutely refuses to get involved, not too interested in junkies getting whacked. Explaining the deaths as overdoses. So far anyhow. So we want to stir them up, too, in the article. You know, kind of like you mentioned, but taking it even a step further: Why is the SFPD Homicide Division dragging their collective feet when members of the underclass are being stalked and murdered? An exposé, I guess."

"Well, that all sounds real promising," Jessie says, a thoughtful expression on her face. "How do you want to structure it? One big feature or are you thinking about a series? Several articles."

"I think one article will do it for now," Katy says. She explains about the timing of the article's release, and holding off a day or two on criticizing SFPD until Hap okays it. Then she says, "Perhaps most importantly for now, I'd like you to help me do some research, dig back in your files, see if we can spot any other potential victims. You know, hookers, bums, homeless, any member of the underclass that died from undetermined or suspicious causes with no police follow-up. Maybe we can get a handle on how long the perp has been operating here in the city, how many people he may have hit? Statistics we can also use in applying public pressure on the SFPD. What do you think?"

"That may be a lot of careful digging, because we will have to include *Chronicle* and *Examiner* articles in the search, probably scanning for one paragraph or even one line obits for potential leads," Jessie says slowly, a slight crease separating her eyebrows, marring her attractive features. "Exactly how far back do you intend on searching?"

"Well, I guess it depends on what we dig up at first? Probably not more than eighteen months initially, though, would be my guess. Maybe not that long."

Jessie nods, the frown easing a little. "Still might be a pretty good number of different leads to check out. You got anything yet that will narrow the search. Maybe gender? Race? Age? You mentioned a homosexual angle? Are all the current victims males of a certain age and race? Or maybe something more about the killer's M.O.? Anything like that may help us focus the search, save a little time?"

"The victims may not all be male. The homosexual bit at this point is just a ruse to try and raise a response from him, you know the drill. And, yes, I do think we have a defining M.O. Perhaps a religious angle. He leaves a kind of signature mark behind, finger-painted with dark, greasy ashes on his victim's foreheads—"

"What kind of a finger-painted mark?" Jessie asks sharply, her usually slow, thoughtful tone abandoned.

Katy picks up a pen from the black and orange SF Giants cup-holder on the desk and draws the inverted, uncrossed *J* on a piece of scratch paper. "It looks something like this, the line of course a little thicker and more uneven. Placed on the victim's forehead. We think it may be a shepherd's crook, like something you see at kids' Christmas plays—"

"You're kidding?" Jessie interrupts again, a look of shocked disbelief on her face.

Surprised by her friend's uncharacteristically emotional reaction to the mark, Katy shakes her head. "No, I'm not joking, Jess. We think that's what the mark is anyhow, probably a shepherd's crook, representing a religious symbol, you know. We could be wrong. At first we thought that it was the letter *J*, uncrossed at the top but—"

"No, it's a crook alright," Jessie states, her voice dropping in pitch, her tone confident, "definitely a religious symbol and the young man drawing it is actually a religious figure, known as The Shepherd."

"What do you mean?" Katy asks, setting down her tea mug again on the desk, confused now. "You've heard something about the perp and these murders already here at the Guardian?"

"No, not really anything about these murders locally…" Jessie pauses, takes a deep breath, and sighs.

"When I was back home, I saw this exact symbol used before. And no question it's meant to be a shepherd's crook. I came across it when I was doing a series of investigative articles for the *St. Louis Post-Dispatch* on a bizarre religious cult and its leader, a person called The Shepherd."

"Just like this, you mean?" Katy asks, pointing down at her sketch on the scratch pad, unable to contain her own sense of confusion and disbelief. "Drawn on who… murder victims in St. Louis? And what's the connection to our killer here in San Francisco?"

Jessie laughs humorlessly. "I can hardly believe this myself. It's crazy. The guy finally surfaces after all these years, right here in the city." She shakes her head in amazement.

"Come on, come on, tell me about it," Katy snaps impatiently, gesturing for her friend to continue her explanation of her odd remarks.

"Okay," Jessie says, closing her eyes, taking another breath and collecting her thoughts. She blinks, absently gazing out her draped office window at the cloudy sky, before slowly beginning her explanation in her characteristically measured tone.

"Let's see, six... almost seven, years ago, I was doing Sunday Features for the *St. Louis Post-Dispatch*. At the same time I was also teaching a graduate Journalism course at Washington University. A student had a proposal for an assignment, an article on something unusual in her home life..." Jessie pauses for a moment to take another sip of tea, then shakes her head again, obviously still finding this connection of events distant in time and place almost too much to believe.

Katy squirms restlessly in her seat, waiting, frowning impatiently.

After a moment, Jessie looks directly at Katy, and then continues, "That student assignment proposal was so intriguing that it would develop into a feature series for the paper. You see, this student, a young woman, was raised in an isolated part of the Ouachita Mountains in Arkansas, near a strange religious cult that was named simply, The Flock. This cult's leader was called, The Shepherd, and back at that time, about seven years ago, the reins had recently been turned over to a new Shepherd, a young man picked from the small congregation. My journalism student, whose family at this time still lived nearby the cult, had heard that the new Shepherd had suddenly disappeared, abandoned his Flock after being in charge only part of a year, leaving them leaderless. The more I listened to my student, the more fascinating I found all this material—the cult itself, their rituals and beliefs, and the cult's plight without a leader. After setting it up through my student, we visited her family whose residence was less than half a mile from the holler where the cult headquarters was located. Soon after the visit, we did actually write three feature articles, all of them appearing in consecutive Sunday editions of the *Post-Dispatch*." She pauses and chuckles. "The student and I were even interviewed on a local TV channel, a controversial talk show, something like Sally Raphael but small-time, about religious cults like The Flock and its weird beliefs—"

"But exactly how could this wayward Shepherd match up with our serial murders of the underclass here in the city, and more importantly, why?" Katy interrupts, expressing her puzzled thoughts. "A man of God from the backwoods of the South turns up here in San Francisco, murdering people?"

Jessie holds up her hands, palms out, in the traffic cop slow-down gesture.

"Just chill out a minute, girl, let me develop this possible connection my own way, okay? You're worse than Arnie Lieberman, my old city editor at my first journalism job out of college on a weekly in Alton, Illinois. He wanted every story condensed, 'Get to the point, get to the point,' he always blurted out too loudly at potential article meetings. Drove me absolutely nuts."

Katy chuckles, gets up, and adds a little sugar to her tea. "Hey, Jess, you know me by now. Sorry. Do it your way."

"Yeah, I do know you pretty well by now," Jessie agrees, nodding and smiling kindly.

"Okay, back to the Ouachita Mountains. This cult evolved slowly after the Civil War, really beginning to practice its beliefs only about eighty or ninety years ago, involving never more than a couple of hundred isolated settlers, mostly subsistence farmers, hunters and gatherers. A Fundamentalist Christian offshoot with some unique beliefs and practices. For example, they believed their leader, The Shepherd, possessed the Gift of Sight, able to actually see the soul leave the body at the exact moment of death. They called this the *Deathflash*. The cult believed that only specific timely prayer at this special moment could guarantee the soul would be guided to its maker. And like a lot of peoples barely scratching out a living in a hostile, isolated environment—the Eskimos come to mind—this cult dispatched its enfeebled elderly, chronically ill, severely disabled, and a few—"

"Dispatched?"

"Yes," Jessie replies, frowning again. She took a long sip of tea.

"They *killed* them in a special sanctioned ceremony, The Shepherd marking the victim's forehead with his special sign, a shepherd's crook, after using The Hand of God—a sacred white glove with a metal talon that dispensed a quick acting poison into a scratch. Immediately after the victim died and the Deathflash left the body, the Shepherd, with the help of the congregation, prayed the soul to Heaven..."

Jessie pauses to pour herself and Katy a little more of the raspberry tea.

"Poison?" Katy says, noting that the description of the Hand of God matched the glove description Double S saw on the perp's hand in the old man's killing in the Tenderloin. "Ah, Jess, exactly what kind of poison was this?"

"Not sure specifically," Jessie answers after searching her memory a moment. "I *think* it was from the Nightshade class, a local plant anyhow, growing exclusively in that region of the Ouachita Mountains, a root the Indians there had used for hundreds of years to poison fish. In a highly concentrated form it's apparently quite lethal to humans, effectively shutting down the heart, lungs, and respiration in a few minutes—"

"Sounds like a heroin overdose," Katy interjects. "Oops, sorry, Jess," she apologizes again, making an overly contrite face. "Continue, please. This background is all very fascinating, and I think it is going to be extremely helpful to our investigation."

"Well, there isn't too much more to tell," Jessie says thoughtfully. "Except for the first few formative years, the Flock had one leader for most of their existence; then after he grew old and feeble, he used the Hand of God on himself, passing the Gift of Sight on by holding the hand of the new Shepherd as he died, the young man selected by the Council of Bishops from the congregation. This new Shepherd is the one that disappeared six or so years ago, taking along the Hand of God, a supply of poison, sacred ash from cremated ancestors, and of course the Gift of Sight, if that part is even remotely believable. He has to be your guy, operating now, here in the city, dispatching sinners for whatever reasons, probably religious in his mind."

Katy sits quietly for a few moments, and then she nods and says, "No question you're right, this has to be the same guy. What you say fits everything we know to date. For instance, we have an eyewitness, who describes him as a tall, young, white man. Says he wore a white glove on one hand, dipped his finger into a can of ash and drew the crook on the victim's forehead, then appeared to pray for his victim after gazing spellbound at something unseen just over the victim's chest. Must've been looking at the Deathflash, or what he *thought* he saw at that moment. Kind of a self-induced trance state."

"Yes, that sounds like The Flock's Shepherd alright," Jessie says, agreeing with Katy's description.

"You have his name?"

"No names allowed in the articles, as you might have guessed, and I don't really remember specifically, if I ever really knew… Yes, I did know it. And I think I might have the family name somewhere in my notes for the three *St. Louis Post-Dispatch* articles."

"Where are those notes, now?" Katy asks anxiously, then snaps off another pair of related quick questions. "And how about photos of our guy? Did you take any of him?"

Jessie's expression breaks into a wide smile, displaying her beautifully even, white teeth. "Oh, you are living right, girl. I still have the notes saved in a filing cabinet at home, got rough and printed copies of those three *Post-Dispatch* articles, too, I think. We didn't publish any photos of cult members in any of those articles, only the Big House, the official cult headquarters and home of the Shepherd, and the family tar paper shack of the new Shepherd… couple of other holler views, too, as I recall, all pretty bleak shots—these are really poor country folk just scraping by. Anyhow, the Council of Bishops insisted we not take any specific pictures of anyone in The Flock. But I think I had an old photo given me by someone there, a photograph of the new Shepherd and his entire family long before his appointment, standing in front of their little shack. Yes, I remember now, it was a picture of a mother and four kids—two girls and two boys—but the photo had aged poorly, turning brown, not real clear as I recall."

"But this is all terrific news!" Katy says, really excited now, not even trying to contain her growing enthusiasm. For the first time in the investigation, she has that special tingling sense in the pit of her stomach; a familiar feeling that she recognizes from past investigations in Sacramento, signaling they were getting close to the perp. Real close. "Just what we need to help break this case wide open, Jess," she adds, hugging her friend. "Let's go over and take a look at your material. Then, I'm springing for lunch at *Greens*, if you want." She knew her friend was a vegetarian, and the famed restaurant out at Fort Mason in the Marina her favorite place to eat in the city.

"You got yourself a date, girl!"

Katy tries to call Johnny on his cell phone with the good news before heading out to Jessie's apartment on Noe Street, with no luck. She isn't able to even leave a message. Must not have it on, she decides. He'd planned on going over to Brother Timothy's to talk to Jeremy Featherstone again. Not like you, pal, to forget your cell phone or not have it on, she thinks, frowning to herself. What's up?

2

Jessie's stuff is well organized in a filing cabinet at her apartment. She doesn't find the family name of The Shepherd, but she easily finds the three articles, her notes, and the old photo.

Katy is disappointed at first by the quality of the photograph, obviously taken by an amateur with a cheap camera. Brown, brittle, and cracked. The family is standing too close to the ramshackle cabin, their faces heavily shadowed by the tin roof overhang... except for the youngest girl, maybe two or three, and the boy on the far right, who is standing in direct sunlight, staring back at the photographer with a serious expression on his teenage face. She examines his features carefully, his intelligent gaze, something stirring at the back of her mind. At first, she tries to imagine a beard, seeing a younger Jeremy Featherstone. But that doesn't work. Then for a moment she visualizes one of the young counselors she met at Brother Timothy's. No, way too short.

"Jesus, Jess!" Katy finally blurts out after studying the photo for almost a full minute. She points at the boy on the far right of the family group. "I know him! I've seen him right here in the city."

Jessie glances over her shoulder at the old photo. "You sure this is the same person? This was taken some time ago. He was just a kid then."

"Yeah, you bet, he's our boy!" Katy says, the tingling sensation almost electric now in the pit of her stomach.

"You positive, girl?"

"I'm sure," Katy answers confidently. "He's much older of course, actually a young man now in his mid- maybe late-twenties, and I've even talked to him very recently—"

She breaks off, staring at the photo again, and making a decision.

"I need to get this to Johnny, right away," Katy says, indicating the photo and Jessie's whole file on The Flock and The Shepherd.

"No problem," Jessie says, "take all the stuff with you, and make copies of anything you want to keep."

"Rain check on Greens," Katy says over her shoulder apologetically on the way out of the apartment. "I won't forget. We'll do it real soon."

Jessie smiles, shouting out at the closing door. "Get him, girl."

3

Katy repeatedly tries to get Johnny on his cell phone with no luck. She even rings their apartment phone twice with no answer. And the office on Geary. Nothing there either.

Where in the hell could he be? she asks herself, remembering he only planned on visiting Brother Timothy's this morning to sweat Featherstone again. He'd even mentioned meeting her for lunch. But they hadn't really set a time or place.

Katy is worried.

TWENTY-ONE

Fear not them which kill the body, but are not able to kill the soul.
Matthew 10:28

Early Friday afternoon, you are at your place in the Tenderloin.

You should feel great fear now that the hunters are closing in, because you know they will not understand. And the authorities will probably be getting involved soon, too. They will try to put you away, perhaps send you where they will execute you for what you have done. But a strange calm has come over you, now that you have decided what must be attempted to protect the Lord's work as long as possible. In any event, your mind is at rest, able to study scripture, and you take great delight and solace in what you have just been reading in Matthew in the Good Book about the soul, even your own soul.

Glancing up from the Bible still open in your lap, you smile wryly. They may be close, but they haven't caught you yet. No, indeed.

Setting your reading aside, you move into the kitchen, where the printed black and white copies of the digital photographs are stuck with magnets on the fridge door. Under control, you stare thoughtfully for a moment at each face, and then glance over the notes under each photo, what you have learned about them, the hunters:

Hap Sullivan: Retired SFPD Detective, mostly in Burglary, 28-year career, several commendations from the department. Divorced, no children. Private investigator now. Lives at 1632 B Fulton (not far from Richie O'Brien).

Katy Green & John Cato: The Green Hornet and Cato of Sacramento fame, once homicide detectives par excellence, favorites of the media as their super-hero nicknames imply. Credited with catching a number of high profile murderers. Her a writer now, and he a private investigator in business with Hap Sullivan. Live together in Marina at 1124 Chestnut St.

Richard O'Brien: A recovering addict himself. And brother of one of your recently dispatched Flock, the boy Jaime. Well respected in the rehabilitation community, especially at Walden House, Inc. Unmarried. Living on Divisidero in an upstairs apartment at 2131 C.

Damon Dupree: Legless man, black, well-known on the street in the Tenderloin and Haight. Works part time at Greyhound Bus Depot on 10th and collects aluminum cans in the Tenderloin. Living with his brother and nephew in the Mission at 745 D Shotwell.

All five of the hunters are a very clear danger to you now.

Of course your duty is clear.

But which one first, who is the most dangerous hunter at this point—who will be the most helpful to the San Francisco Police Department when they get involved...?

You pause for only a few moments, finally leaning forward slightly, and placing your finger firmly on one of the photos, as if squashing a bug.

"Yes, you will be first, of course," you say aloud solemnly, as if a judge pronouncing final judgment.

Then, you smile, feeling an inward peace. The die has been cast.

Turning, you leave the kitchen, stop momentarily in the bedroom to pick up a pair of needed items from their hiding place in the shoebox hidden at the back of the closet. You carefully place the can of ashes and Hand of God, both protected by heavy-duty sandwich bags, in your jacket pocket.

Ready now to perform your duty, you nod to yourself, and leave the apartment.

Your next stop is within walking distance of the Tenderloin.

SURPRISES

Anxious because she still hasn't heard a word from Johnny, Katy goes over to the office off Geary Street early, around 6:45 p.m. Richie is already waiting outside for the meeting to begin at 7:00. He hasn't heard from Johnny either.

Katy unlocks the door and lets them into the little office.

Before they get the lights on, the front door bangs opens.

It's Johnny.

Thank God!

Katy hugs him, and then pushes him away from her. "Where the devil have you been all day, pal?" she asks, not even trying to contain the concerned anger in her voice.

Johnny, looking slightly sheepish, pulls at his broken nose and then explains. "It's been one of those days, you know what I mean. I went over to Brother Timothy's in the Tenderloin this morning to shake down Jeremy Featherstone again. I waited and waited, but he never came to work. Finally, early in the afternoon, Brother Timothy showed up and opened the shelter. I talked him out of an address and phone number for Featherstone, after a big argument—Brother Timothy just being obstinate. Of course, I could never rouse an answer to my calls, so I went over to 18th and checked out the apartment. It was empty, the closets obviously cleaned out in a hurry. I spent the rest of the afternoon tracking down the landlord, a Mr. Lee. Featherstone had given Lee no notice or forwarding address. He'd just split, not collecting his security deposit or anything. I took a chance and swung by the Greyhound Bus Station on my way here, with no luck. None of the ticket clerks recall seeing anyone looking like Jeremy Featherstone today. So, a big nothing, kiddo." He makes a hapless shrugging gesture, holding up his empty hands.

"What about your cell phone?" Katy asks in an accusatory tone. "You haven't been answering it all day."

Johnny pulls out his cell phone. "Battery went dead, so I clicked it off." He shows it to Katy. "I planned on stopping and getting batteries, but you know how that goes when everything seems out of whack—"

At that moment the office phone rings.

Johnny answers it.

"Hello, Sullivan, Cato, and Associates."

He covers the mouthpiece and silently mouths to Katy and Richie, *It's Hap.*

"No shit?" Johnny says too loudly, a frown creasing his rugged features. After listening a moment and looking badly stricken by what he hears, Johnny writes something on a scratch pad. He adds in a shaken voice, "Okay, Hap, I got the address. We'll be right over after I break the news."

He hangs up the phone, a mixed expression of sadness, regret, and anger on his face. He sighs, then explains, "Hap is over on Shotwell. The perp has hit again, and it isn't good." He stops, leans over, and clasps Richie's shoulder. "I'm sorry, man, I'm afraid our perp has murdered your friend, Damon."

Richie looks shocked. He shakes his head and stares down at the floor. "Man, oh, man," he murmurs, still shaking his head in disbelief. "Not Damon, too."

After an awkward moment, Katy points at the scratch pad and asks Johnny, "Hap is there now with the body?"

Johnny nods.

"Okay, Richie," she says softly, "why don't you wait here. Take it easy, get your bearings, you know. Johnny and I will be back shortly, bring you up to speed after we find out what happened to your friend." Then she adds in a respectful whisper, "I'm really sorry. He seemed like a great guy."

Richie looks up, Katy realizing he is pulling on his street-game face. "No," he says hoarsely but emphatically, after clearing his throat. "Let's all go see Damon."

2

Hap is waiting for them in the Mission on Shotwell, in front of a colorfully painted Victorian. The ever present cigar unlit, but in hand.

He leads them around the corner of the building to a basement flat side entrance, where a pair of uniformed cops are waiting, talking quietly with a black man. "He's down here," Haps says, pointing out the short stairwell leading down to the basement apartment. "This is Damon's older brother, David. They lived together in the flat with David's son, Leon. It was David that discovered Damon's body." Hap turns and points back to his three colleagues. "This is Johnny Cato, Katy Green, and Richie O'Brien."

David Dupree shakes hands politely, nodding slightly at Richie in recognition.

Hap explains, "David says that Damon left the apartment about 6:15 or so, right after dinner, apparently heading out for our meeting at the office. Then David took the garbage out about fifteen minutes later and found his brother just like you see him. He immediately called 911. Ed here—" Hap indicates one of the blues "—responded and called me when he spotted the marking on the forehead. He's the same patrolman called before, when he found the old guy, Petey, in the alley over in the 'loin."

"Still can't believe it," David murmurs, the sadness weighing heavy in his tone. "My brother…"

"We are truly sorry, Mr. Dupree," Katy says kindly to the grieving brother, scratching out their Marina phone number on one of Johnny's business cards and giving it to David. "Your brother was a good man. If there is anything we can do to help you, please call us. Our home phone is on the back. Anything, okay?"

No one says anything for a moment or two.

Hap takes a puff on his unlit cigar. Then he clears his voice. "Ed says someone from Homicide is on their way out now," he announces to the group. "Be here real soon."

They would have to be quick, before the detectives take over the crime scene.

Johnny and Hap talk to the blues, as Katy slips down the stairwell and kneels beside Double S. He's crumpled over backward, his special scooter-board along his left side, staring sightless up into the descending fog.

What happened here, friend? she asks silently.

Did you see him coming?

Hear him?

Recognize him?

Was it the same guy from the Tenderloin alley?

Did you have time to put up a fight?

Double S has a long bleeding scratch on his left cheek and the now familiar shepherd's crook drawn with ashes on his forehead. In addition, he has a large lump just above and back of his right ear.

"Looks like he struck you with something as you came out the door," Katy murmurs to herself, continuing to check around the foot of the stairwell... noticing only the abandoned bag of garbage that Hap mentioned. Probably didn't know what hit you. No defensive scratches on those arms. And I know you would've put up a good fight, too, if you had seen him.

After another moment or two checking around the stairwell where the perp probably stood, without finding anything, the ground too hard for even a partial shoe print, she turns back to the group hovering a few steps away.

"Hap, maybe you can stay here, be some help with Homicide," Katy suggests. "You know, they'll probably want to canvass the neighborhood for potential witnesses? Or whatever? I bet your Polaroid photos may be of more interest to them now. Share them, bring the detectives up to speed. See what you can get back from their folks in forensics. They will probably process our swabs from Petey faster now, too, right?"

Hap nods, chewing on his unlit cigar as a siren approaches.

"Okay, I'll stick around," he agrees. "See what I can do to help."

Katy gestures toward Richie and Johnny, who have finished talking to the blues. "C'mon," she beckons them to follow her. In a confidential tone, she explains, "Let's head back to the office. I have some startling new stuff to show you both about our boy. We're much closer to him than you think. And his name isn't Jeremy Featherstone, despite Jeremy's apparent abrupt departure from his job at Brother Timothy's and his apartment."

"Okay, give me a minute," Johnny says, excusing himself to go back to the stairwell. He bends down near his dead friend. Remains there a moment with his eyes closed. Then, he stands up, and after a sigh of resignation, he joins the other two.

Katy explains to Hap where they are headed. Then the three of them take off in Johnny's Mustang.

3

Back at the office near Japantown, Katy begins to run through what she's learned about The Shepherd and The Flock from her friend Jessie Warner at the *Guardian*. She hands both Richie and Johnny a copy of each of the three articles on the cult from the *St. Louis Post-Dispatch*. Then she pauses for a few minutes, letting them both peruse the articles.

Johnny finally looks up from his reading, points at the article, and asks, "You think this is our boy, this new Shepherd guy here?"

"Yes, I do," she replies.

"But why would he come all the way here from Arkansas?" Richie asks.

"I don't think he came here directly," Katy answers. "Jessie's articles don't say anything about subsequent events after he left the cult, but she heard from her student that he may have actually gone to live in St. Louis after leaving his family. But he left there abruptly, realizing he was being tracked by a pair of Bishops from the Flock. That was maybe six years ago, and she's heard nothing more about him since that time."

"But here in the city—?" Johnny says skeptically.

"I know he's *here*, pal," Katy interrupts, smiling confidently. "This is an old photo of him." She puts the picture down on Johnny's desk, both men leaning over for a closer look. "Of course that photo must be at least ten or twelve years old."

After a moment, Richie glances up at Johnny with an amazed look, like a student finally figuring out an elusive answer and checking his teacher's face, as he pronounces loudly, "Man, I think it's our new coffee guy from the NA meetings over on Capp Street. You know the guy?"

Johnny leans closer and carefully studies the old photo. "Yeah, you're right, Richie," he agrees, the excitement cranked up in his voice also. He looks over at Katy "Our boy has got to be Jackson Williams!"

She just grins, feeling the tingling in the pit of her stomach.

"You saw him at your AA meeting the other night, too, remember?" Richie adds, picking up the brown photo again.

"Yeah, that's right," Katy says, unable to restrain her excitement now. "And I just bet he's the same guy Double S saw in the alley. Probably the same guy he heard about on the street. You know, the one asking questions and nosing around like some kind of odd detective?"

"Maybe scouting out more potential victims," Johnny says, playing with his crooked nose.

"Oh, man, I got that special feeling, you know," Katy says, rubbing her stomach and grinning broadly.

Johnny laughs. "Me, too, kiddo." He explains about the feeling to Richie—a kind of tingling premonition they both seem to get in the pit of their stomachs when they are closing in on a perp. Something they first noticed as Homicide detectives in their days on the Sacramento Police force.

Katy steps up to the blackboard and makes some additions, including adding Jackson William's name in capital letters as their number one suspect, drawing a line through the name of Jeremy Featherstone.

"I'm guessing you may have access to a phone number, maybe an address, right?" Johnny asks Richie.

He thinks a moment. "Yeah, I'm sure I do, but it's over with all my N.A. meeting stuff stored at the office on Capp Street. But we can—"

He glances down at his watch. "Shit," he says, frowning, "the center is probably closed for the night. No one around until 7:30 or so in the morning. We might be able to get a hold of someone in charge of maintenance…"

"Maybe Jackson has a phone listed," Johnny suggests, indicating the bank of Bay Area phone books, reaching for San Francisco.

"Call Information," Katy and Richie say almost simultaneously.

Katy picks up the phone, punches in the number. "San Francisco, please… Jackson Williams… Okay, thank you." She makes a face. "Maybe we should call other informations around the Bay Area? We don't know that he's staying in San Francisco proper."

"Nah, I'm pretty sure he lives here in the city," Richie says thoughtfully. "I wrote down the address when he volunteered to do coffee a couple of weeks ago. I think it was a residential hotel in the 'loin. And I don't think he had a private phone, either." He shakes his head. "Damn. Can't remember the hotel name, though." He shakes his head, looking disgusted with himself. "We might just have to wait until early tomorrow. May have better luck catching him at the hotel early in the morning anyhow. Those places are pretty depressing. Bet he doesn't hang around much there in the evening."

"Okay," Katy says, shifting thoughts and mood. "You guys can run him down early tomorrow. But I have to get ready for a ball game tomorrow morning. Little Women in the semifinals of the big basketball tournament."

"Hey, that's right," Johnny says, making the double thumbs up sign. "Good luck, kiddo."

He gestures toward the phone. "I better bring Hap up to speed about tomorrow morning." He calls his partner and talks for a minute or so. Then he turns back to Richie and Katy. "Okay, Richie, he's meeting us at the Capp Street Center at 7:15 in the morning."

Before they split to go home, Richie asks, "Katy, you want to do your next research installment Sunday morning, got some places I can show you then, if you want?"

She thinks a minute. "Yeah, sure, but we need to do it real early," she says, before catching herself, then continuing with a slightly sheepish grin. "You know, just in case the team does win tomorrow, and we make the finals, which will be Sunday afternoon over at the Marina courts."

The two men chuckle at Katy's understated confidence.

"What time's the game Sunday?" Johnny asks.

Katy replies, "1:00 p.m."

"We won't take long," Richie says. "Pick you up at 8:30 early. Then I'll drive you over to the Marina courts after we finish. I'd like to see you play, anyhow. A writer and a basketball player—seems like a pretty unusual combination, isn't it?"

"Oh, I don't know."

Katy shrugs, thinking, *Not really*. Probably just a common stereotype—the nonintellectual jock. There have been a number of good writer/athletes, she thinks, although they usually write nonfiction about sports. Jim Bouton comes immediately to mind, and his great book about the Yankees. *What was the title…?*

Oh yeah, *Ball Four*.

But there has also been some good fiction done by jocks, too, she thinks, like Pete Gent, the colorful Cowboys tight end who wrote *North Dallas Forty*, which they made into a movie. Just a matter of interests, she decides. Basketball and writing are two of the three loves of her life. She glances up at Johnny.

They leave the office, all headed for home.

LITTLE WOMEN
VS. CERTEK

Again Katy is surprised by the large turnout for a game early on a Saturday morning at the Panhandle courts. Stands packed, standing room only—maybe three hundred or more people. Joking and boisterous, apparently quite a few coming up from San Jose to root for the team from CerTek. Katy searches the stands because she does not hear or see Sidney's number one fan, the black dude with the falsetto voice. No, he's not here yet. And of course Johnny, Richie, and Hap are absent, chasing down their prime suspect, Jackson Williams. Early this morning Richie called, after looking through his NA stuff and finding a residential hotel address for Williams in the Tenderloin—a Hotel Reo on Jones Street.

But all the investigation stuff clears from her thoughts as she begins to warm up, doing some stretching first, then concentrating on short jump shots, working her way around the key to the foul line and back down close to the bucket.

"Hey, you bring your Eddie Fuller game?" CeCe asks smirking, from under the basket, catching and flipping the basketball back to Katy.

Smiling at her, Katy nods, not responding aloud, knowing damn well that CeCe knows Eddie Felson is the name of the pool shooter in the movie, *The Hustler*, played by Paul Newman—she's corrected her a number of times. Her husky teammate is just trying to loosen Katy up. Earlier CeCe had introduced her new PR boyfriend to them with a straight face. "Don't he look just like Ricky Martin?" Everyone laughed, because the guy had glistening black hair and a dark goatee, looking more like a younger version of the Ricky on the *Lucille Ball Show* reruns.

But CeCe's scam works, Katy finds she is actually relaxed and loose.

Swish… swish… swish.

Three straight from the top of the key. She has the touch in practice—that feeling in her fingertips that flows back along her arm and up to her brain as she releases each shot, absolutely confident the ball will drop through the rim and net. Now if it just carries over into the game, she hopes. Because the touch can mysteriously disappear when the real game starts. It's happened like that before. Katy warming up well, then throwing up bricks when the game starts. You never know. She goes under the basket, throwing balls back out to CeCe.

What she calls being in the zone, having her Eddie Felson touch, has recently been studied and written about formally. Katy has just read a book called, *Flow: The Psychology of Optimal Experience*, by a Professor at Claremont, who thinks it is the result of a state of focused and heightened attention—associated not only with sports performance, but relevant in sex, the creation of art, problem solving, even serious reading. Katy has often wondered if *flow* is related to what John Gardner, the famous writing teacher, calls the fictive dream. Gardner thinks good writers project themselves into a special state, which he calls the fictive dream. Readers can easily reach that state, too. And clunky writing can jar them out of the fictive dream.

Anyhow, she hopes she's in the flow when the game starts.

Swish. CeCe is looking good.

Sidney gathers the three together just before the start of the game, and reminds them to remember their Wednesday night practice. "Box out. Move your feet on defense. And give me offside help away from the pass, each time Jamie Worley drops down into the low post position. Okay?"

CeCe and Katy both nod their understanding, everyone dead serious now. Game faces on. Everyone working themselves into a state of focused and heightened concentration.

The game starts with CerTek in possession.

One of the smaller players, a star guard last year with San Jose State's championship team, makes a nifty entry pass to Jamie Worley. She's flashed in down low, catching the bounce pass, then stopping suddenly and spinning back to her right, away from Sid, making an easy left-handed lay-in. CeCe did not drop back fast enough to help. And the ex-Arizona star is really quick and always moving without the ball. Just like the desert bird, *The Roadrunner*, which had been Jamie Worley's media nickname at Tucson. CeCe pats her chest, indicating—*My bad; I'm on it now.*

0-2.

Winner's out.

The third CerTek player, a 5'-10" small forward on that same San Jose State team, fakes a set shot, then attempts another entry to Worley who is moving back into the low post. But Katy has dropped back from her opponent with offside help, and bats the ball away. It rolls back toward the free-throw line, where CeCe scoops it up.

A turnover.

Little Women pass the ball back out to the top of the key, as is customary, then begin play on the offense. They try to pass it around and make sure everyone has the feel of the basketball.

But CerTek has scouted them well, and the ex-San Jose State forward follows Katy like a shadow, making it tough for her to even touch the ball. Eventually though, CeCe gets Katy the ball outside, when Sid picks off the shadow. After setting the screen, Sid quickly rotates toward the basket, catching CerTek in a switch, Worley now blocking Katy's drive, but Sid loose behind the other CerTek player for an easy uncontested layup after Katy drops her a lob pass—the classic pick-n-roll.

2-2.

Ball back out to the top of the key to start play again.

Katy begins with the ball by faking a jump shot from the top of the key, drawing her CerTek player even closer, over-guarding; then Katy jukes left and drives right around the player who's been caught crossing her feet to compensate. The shorter CerTek player slides over to block the drive, and CeCe goes back door for another easy lay-in.

Take what they give you, Katy hears her old PAL coach, Gerri Robinson, shouting at her from long ago in San Diego. *If they take away your outside shot, drive on them. If they double you, hit your teammate. If they drop back, then shoot outside. Every time they take away something by overcompensating, they are exposed somewhere...* Find *that somewhere. Take what they give you.*

Katy smiles, the old advice ringing in her ears as she bounces the ball out to CeCe to start play again.

4-2.

Top of the key, CeCe makes a short bounce pass to Katy, then sets a rugged pick, springing her teammate free for an uncontested fifteen-footer. Ball hits the rim, rattles around and out, but Sid leaps and tips it in, out-rebounding the shorter Worley.

6-2.

At that point, CeCe misses a jumper near the foul line and Worley, who has boxed-out Sid nicely this time, easily snags the rebound.

Out to the ex-San Jose State guard at the top of the key...

The teams exchange baskets and then both go through a dry spell, missing a pair of shots, turning the ball over to the other team after each miss. Back and forth, the crowd jumping up and down, yelling loudly whether the basket is made or not. The partisan rooting about evenly split in the three hundred people.

CeCe recovers a loose ball.

"Hey, way to go, Little Women, sick 'em!" a high-pitched voice shouts over the other crowd noise. Their number one fan has arrived, the black dude and his sidekick taking a place up front with the fans milling around, both standing between the nearest two sets of stands and shouting loudly through cupped hands. Sidney has heard him, and grins her recognition at Katy.

Moments later as if on cue, Katy breaks loose from the defender mirroring her movements and shoots another long jumper, the ball leaving her fingertips in a high arc with beautiful rotation, coming down dead center and swishing. A thing of beauty, a thing of touch. Oh, yeah, she feels it coming now: the *flow*. ol' Eddie Felson.

Katy grins at CeCe, as they take the ball to the top of the key. Catching her breath, she whispers, "Knock, knock."

CeCe, holding the ball, frowns but cooperates, asking, "Who's there?"

"The Fuller Brush dude!"

"All right, girl!" CeCe says, passing again to Katy and almost knocking over the CerTek player with a middle-linebacker quality screen this time. *Thud.*

Loose with the ball, Katy shoots another long-arcing jumper.

Swish.

12-4.

But an entry pass down low to Sid goes astray, CerTek claiming the turnover.

And Little Women soon find out why Sidney was so overly concerned about Jamie Worley.

The ex-Arizona star makes four straight short jumpers, capitalizing on her explosive quickness and grittiness in traffic near the basket. Tough, smart, slick, and unstoppable. Her crowd contingent thunders after each basket, roaring as she finally ties the game on her fourth bucket.

12-12.

But Sid is no slouch either, as far as quickness and smarts. She deftly fronts Worley on a sideline pass, intercepting the ball. Firing it back out to CeCe at the top of the key, who quickly bounces a pass back into Sid.

Who *stuffs* it.

The Little Women rooters go wild.

"Oh, yeah, Homes, my big-ass, super-bird!" The black dude shouts shrilly over the crowd, giving his pal a high five.

14-12.

From that point the game begins to turn, Little Women working the ball around smoothly and confidently until Katy works herself loose—just a half step from her shadow at the top of the key, where she elevates... and shoots up a rainbow.

Swish.

16-12.

CeCe picks Katy's guard again, a slight brush this time, but enough for Katy to get off another beauty. The crowd goes nuts, the arcing shot coming from NBA three-point distance and touching nothing but net.

18-12.

A chant for Little Women from the stands, led by the black dude, the crowd drowning out the CerTek supporters.

The game remains hard fought, still contested by CerTek, despite the chanting fans, Jamie Worley slipping out and actually partially blocking a third straight long bomb by Katy. But Sid grabs the errant shot, works around down low, and goes up and over her smaller opponent for an easy three-footer off the board.

20-12.

Game time!

Bedlam in the stands, people cheering, high-fiving, chanting, *Little Women, Little Women* and holding up one finger. The court is mobbed with well-wishers, slapping the winners' backs, some consoling CerTek. It's several minutes before Katy manages to catch her breath. It hits her then: Little Women will be in the finals tomorrow at 1:00 over in the Marina. She's stoked, big time, her pulse racing wildly.

Still, Katy manages to search out and find Jamie Worley in the mob of well-wishers. "Great game," Katy says, shaking the woman's hand. "You're a player for sure."

"Good luck, tomorrow," the CerTek star, a good sport, shouts over the crowd noise.

"Thanks."

Then Katy turns and works her way back to CeCe and Sid, who are surrounded by admirers, including Sid's number one fan. "Hey, no pressure tomorrow, girl," he says to Sidney in a serious tone of voice, "but ya'll better bring it, 'cuz I'm bettin' my purple Cad-mobile convertible on Lil Women, ya unnerstan' what I'm sayin' here, Swoop?"

Everyone laughs.

As the well-wishers eventually thin out, disappearing in all directions, the three winners towel off and ease down from their high, able now to hear each other speak without shouting.

"Sweet game, Katy," CeCe says, proudly patting her friend's shoulder. "You had your ol' ya-ya going, girl."

"Yeah, but you were setting some great picks… And Sid, your boxing out Jamie Worley was really outstanding. A great team win. We can all be proud of ourselves."

Sid's smile suddenly dissolves, replaced by a frown. She slumps down on the side court bench by her gym bag, and pulls off her right Converse sneaker. Obviously in some kind of pain, she massages her upper heel, carefully inspecting her ankle.

"Twist something?" Katy asks guardedly, keeping the concern from her tone, sounding almost nonchalant.

Sid nods.

"Not the same old, nagging Ach—?" CeCe asks, cutting herself short without completing the question.

Sid looks up. "Yeah, it's a little tweak in my Achilles tendon alright. That's the bad news—" She interrupts herself with an encouraging wide grin, the frown fading away. "The good news is I don't think it's serious. No swelling, no redness, no real pain, just a momentary tweak, I guess. Maybe I just overreact now to even the slightest grabbing sensation, you know."

"Well, that's good you don't feel it's serious," Katy says, breathing a sigh of relief, knowing the tendon has been an ongoing problem for Sid, ever since her senior year in college. In fact tendon problems delayed and finally caused Sid to abandon her plans for a promising WNBA career—she'd been a high draft by the Sacramento Monarchs after graduating from UCLA.

"Yeah, I got this prescription stuff in my bag I'll rub on for now, maybe ice it down as soon as I get home. You know, just as a preventative measure."

She takes a tube of stuff out of her bag and gently rubs some onto her ankle.

"Well, glad you're okay, girl, but I gotta go, now," CeCe says, giving Sid a hug. "Ricky Martin is waiting to take me to lunch. See ya'll tomorrow over on the Marina courts. Lil Women rule!"

They wave goodbye to CeCe and the boyfriend.

Sid slips her shoe back on. Tests the ankle, smiles, and makes a thumbs-up to Katy.

She gives her friend a hug, before Sid takes off.

That's when Katy spots Johnny coming from the direction of the intersection of Haight and Stanyon.

2

"Hey, kiddo," he says giving her a peck on the cheek. "Heard all the commotion even way over where I parked. You guys must've won?"

"Yep, we play tomorrow for the championship over in the Marina."

"Great!" Johnny says, waving at the departing Sidney. He picks up Katy's green and gold Sac State gym bag, leading her back along the path to Stanyon. "Sorry I missed the whole game."

"Where's Hap and Richie," she asks, then adds before he replies, "and what happened? You get Jackson Williams or what?"

Johnny shakes his head, pulling at his broken nose. "No, we didn't, kiddo. He wasn't at Hotel Reo. But we checked around and another resident thought he'd moved over to the Hotel Majestic last Thursday. So, we beat it over there. He's currently checked in at the Majestic, but wasn't in his room. Desk clerk said Williams doesn't spend much time at the hotel. I left Richie and Hap, staking out the place. If they catch up with him, they're going to call us, and Homicide, too. I hurried back here, hoping to see at least the last part of the game. Dammit, too frigging late though."

"Well, pal, you missed a good one," Katy says. "C'mon, I'll fill you in on the whole deal. Then I need a shower before we go down to the Majestic, see what's happening there."

"Sounds good, kiddo."

3

Just as they enter their apartment on Chestnut Street, the phone rings.

Katy rushes to the kitchen and picks it up. It's Hap.

"Bad news, Katy," Hap says, disappointment heavy in his tone. "Jackson Williams came back to the Majestic, just about half an hour ago. But he spotted Richie and me through the front window, and apparently quickly put it all together and took off, hauling ass toward Union square. Guy is some kind of fast, too. Bottom line is he got away in the crowd. But all his stuff is here at the Majestic. He isn't going far."

"Oh, I bet he won't come back there," Katy says, disappointed herself. "He knows either us or the cops will be watching for him."

"Yeah, but he left an envelope in the hotel safe," Hap explains. "Clerk thought it was money. So, like I said, he isn't going far. No bread, no place to stay. If it's money, he's got to try for it."

"What now?"

"Well, we think he'll probably stick around figuring how to get to his envelope. Probably send someone for it, something like that. In the meantime, maybe show up at St. Anthony's to eat, hit one of the shelters for a bed to sleep, even your boy's place, Brother Timothy's. We're going to share this with Homicide, get some help staking all the places out. Meet you and Johnny tonight at the office, 7:00?"

"Sounds good," Katy replies, then hangs up. She shares the immediate bad news with Johnny.

4

Johnny, Katy, Hap, and Richie meet that night at the office on Geary at 7:00. Nothing yet on Jackson Williams who hasn't been sighted at any of the stakeouts—no one coming in for his envelope either. They do little more than touch base and mourn the loss of Richie's friend, Damon Dupree. Then they break up.

KICKIN'

Every junkie plans on kickin'... first thing tomorrow. Oh, yeah, count on it.

—Beechnut

The fog is thick the next morning when Richie picks up Katy in the Marina, the day matching his grim expression, his game face already tugged on—the scuffed-up, Rowdy Yates look. They drive a block over to Lombard Street, then turn south on Divisidero Street, before he says much of anything.

Katy remains quiet, enjoying the ride.

Richie finally nods to himself. "Okay, we're talking about kickin'..." he says absently, as if reminding himself of the morning's tour topic. With a kind of half-apologetic look, he glances over at Katy and smiles thinly. He looks back out the windshield and whispers in a resigned tone under his breath, "Okay."

The street is almost empty of anything except parked vehicles.

"Every junkie starts kickin' a number of times, most often not by design, instead forced by his inability to score," Richie begins, his voice as hard-edged now as his angular, lined face. "Usually, even if it is by design, withdrawal sickness forces them to use again after they begin kicking. Being dope-sick ain't any fun. It's like having a serious case of the flu. In fact the aching joints, muscular cramps, are what you're trying to get rid of. Stretching and *kicking* out the cramps like a runner—that's where the expression comes from. In addition, your nose runs, eyes itch, and you are twitchy all over. Can't sleep, staying up for at least three nights, sometimes four when really kicking. Can't eat, except some people can keep down milkshakes, ice cream, and cold sweet stuff like that. But mostly you're too nauseous the whole time, no appetite. Nope, a kicking junkie ain't a pretty sight."

He glances over to see if Katy is with him.

She nods.

As the Volvo climbs up and over the crest of Divisidero Street in Pacific Heights, the mist is thinning, and by the time they reach the flat, lowest point of Divisidero where McAlister crosses, the sun is already breaking through the fog. A beautiful morning, boding well for Katy's basketball game later on. She's relaxed, feeling very upbeat despite Richie's grim description of kicking.

He doesn't appear to notice the improving weather, still focused on his thoughts, wearing his dead-ass, hard-guy game face, and continuing to speak in a sharp-edged monotone. "Tough part about kicking is there is *no* relief. You don't quit hurting for those three or four sleepless nights, absolutely no respite. You pace, swear, sweat, shiver, and at some time beg those around to help you score. You're strung out, big time, really miserable. So, kicking cold is a tough row to hoe—harder than a pimp's heart. But a situation every junkie is forced by circumstances to face sooner or later during his addiction."

He breaks off, slowing the station wagon as they pass Fulton Street and creep by Grove Street, finally finding a parking spot just before reaching Hayes Street. Like Market, which cuts mostly east and west, Divisidero divides San Francisco in half, running north and south. He maneuvers the old beat-up mustard Volvo into a spot almost at the exact center of the city.

"That's why very few can completely make it through those first four days without some kind of help," Richie says, setting the parking brake. "Unless they're forced to by a situation, you know, like being arrested, locked in the slammer, and having no choice." He snorts humorlessly. "Right now down at 850 Bryant, I bet there are several junkies in the drunk tank, kicking, getting real sick, ralphing up their guts, sweating, ranting and raving like lunatics. The cops hate the sight of a kicking junkie and are not likely to be much help. Usually just looking the other way. So, by choice, few people elect to kick cold like that, fewer successful… Except for a guy commemorated by this place right here."

Richie points at a storefront in the middle of the block. Apparently some kind of church that sits next to a colorful-looking African restaurant, the rest of the block normal storefront businesses.

They get out, walk the half block.

"Beechnut brought me here to the Church of St. John just before he checked out, a few years ago," Richie explains, as they stand on the sidewalk outside the place. "Named after John Coltrane. You know his music?"

"Yeah, sure, a great jazz saxophone player," Katy replies, watching a steady stream of dressed-up folks, a mixed racial group of mostly black and white, enter the oddly-located and nondescript church front.

"Coltrane had been a heroin addict years ago, long before rehabilitation programs or NA or anything like that," Richie says, lowering his voice, not wishing to attract attention from anyone on the street. "And he kicked by himself, no help from anyone or any program, drawing on a strong, inner, spiritual strength. So, he became kind of a legendary figure back then to a small group of musician heroin addicts—like Beechnut who knew him—then later to a slightly greater population struggling with dope. And eventually a few people here in the city started this church in his memory. It's become kind of a half-assed tourist Mecca, you know, a little like Grace Cathedral but on a much smaller scale. C'mon, let's go in."

Richie takes Katy's arm and guides her through the open door to the church, stopping just inside in the small foyer, temporary partitions screening off the greater church proper—

Tap, tap, tap, tap.

Katy's attention is drawn to the far right—the sound of a drummer setting a beat—to an alcove near the big front window. A bandbox with seven musicians squeezed tightly together with their instruments, just striking up the song, "When the Saints Go Marching In." Katy smiles, one of her favorites. Various instruments, but a clarinet, trumpet, and a sax featured up front, all the musicians dressed casual, rocking and rolling, sweating, bright-eyed, and obviously enjoying themselves.

Listening to the music, Katy shifts her gaze beyond the foyer past the partitions to the inside of the church proper. It's a long, narrow room filled with folding chairs, the packed congregation on its feet, in front of their seats, but turned away from a small stage and lectern up front, back to face the music blasting away from the rear of the church—everyone clapping, keeping time, and smiling.

Richie and Katy remain standing in the foyer, listening to the energetic band ripping through a quick medley of stuff.

The music is mostly jazzy renditions of gospel favorites or some straight Dixieland Jazz, including Katy's favorite.

She finds the Church of St. John to be an unusual place, not anything like any church service she's ever visited in the past. More like a celebratory revival, a raucous, joyous excitement hanging in the air, buoyed by the uplifting sounds of the instrumental chorus…

Eventually, during the first break in the music, a woman holding a bible to her chest approaches Katy, Richie, and several other recent arrivals clustered together, inviting them to move on into the church proper, pointing to some standing room available along the far left wall.

Richie smiles, shakes his head, and drops a bill into a collection basket sitting on a stand in the foyer near the center aisle into the church. "Thank you kindly, but we aren't going to be able to stay very long."

They listen to the beginning of another medley for a few more minutes, and then Richie leads them back outside the church. "Preaching, talking, and some singing will begin soon," he explains, "more normal church stuff, like you've seen often before."

Grinning, Katy says, "Wow, that's some inspirational church music!"

Richie nods. "The congregation is its own choir, but the singing is usually overwhelmed by the band. Sometimes they have some pretty good guest speakers, too, their minister acting like a master of ceremonies. The upbeat spirit of the place reminds me a little of the feel of a good NA meeting, but without being quite so serious in tone. Beechnut spoke here in the old days, even played in the band a couple of times."

He glances at his watch, then back to Katy who is watching people still stream into the church, the music blasting out of the door louder than any Mission bell tolling in the flock. "We need to get going," Richie says. "Over to a clinic, a small program in the Haight, not far from 815. Got to be there before 9:00 when they open though. It'll get pretty damn crowded after that."

They head for the parked Volvo station wagon.

The weather is indeed sunny and glorious.

2

"We're going to visit a methadone clinic now," Richie explains as they drive south on Divisidero. "Methadone, as you probably know, is a government controlled substance. Clinics and a few private doctors are licensed to dispense it by the State. I think there are currently eight clinics operating here in San Francisco—that's a lot for a city this size…"

He pauses, waiting to get around a double-parked van, the driver unloading produce boxes destined for a nearby organic grocery store.

Back in the stream of traffic, Richie continues, "Methadone is a synthetic drug, not a cure but a sanctioned substitute for addictions to heroin, morphine, pethidine, or codeine. It mimics some of the effects of these opiate-derived drugs, all important to the addict, but its most important practical effect is that a junkie withdrawing and switching to methadone does *not* get dope-sick."

"Mimics? You mean like getting high on heroin?" Katy asks.

Richie shakes his head. "Not exactly. When a person takes methadone there's no rush or getting high feeling, but there is a slight lingering sense of euphoria. The chemistry of the drug is similar to heroin, the *unfelt* physiological effects on the body about the same— that's why there are no withdrawal symptoms."

Richie crosses over Oak Street, which is one way going east toward the freeway, and swings the station wagon around a block to the west… finally finding a tight parking place on crowded Broderick Street, a half block off Oak.

They get out, Richie nodding toward the busy one-way street.

"There are two kinds of programs, long-term maintenance and short-term withdrawal," he explains to Katy, as they walk down and around the corner, approaching a small but well-maintained white Victorian with black and gold trim, on Oak Street. A line of twenty or so people extends up a flight of steps and waits single file at the closed front door of the building. For a moment Richie and Katy pause in front of the magnificent Victorian. A small gold and white sign at the foot of the stairs announces in black letters—

OAK STREET CLINIC (THE O)—Step back out into the sunshine, breathe the fresh air, listen to the birds, enjoy life.

Richie checks his watch and whispers, "These clients are waiting for the place to open in about three minutes. C'mon." He takes Katy's arm and hurries her up the stairs, explaining, "The O is a clinic program serving heroin addicts who are trying to kick using methadone-assisted, short-term withdrawal, except for a few, who have qualified for indefinite maintenance status. We'll talk about them later."

Richie rings the bell next to the locked entry door.

The folks in line remind Katy a little of the people waiting in line down at the pawn shops to hock stuff about this time of the morning. Similar appearance, mostly males dressed roughly, thin, restless, and nervous; but she doesn't read any high level of anxiety or see any distress on their faces.

She follows Richie in the front door.

Inside a big hallway, he nods at a guy holding a clipboard, wearing a black polo shirt with a plain gold letter over the heart: O. "Tim, I got permission over the phone last night from Dr. Nguyen to show a visitor around this morning. She said she would let you know. Okay?"

"No problem, Richie," the attendant at the door says, smiling politely at Katy. "She called me early this morning."

"Great," Richie says to Tim, then he directs his attention back to Katy.

"Tim, here, guards the door and will guide potential clients, if there are any today, into that room," Richie explains, pointing to a room right of the doorway with several school-like writing desk-chairs. "Potential clients fill out all the proper paperwork there. Usually, most of these clinics require four things to qualify: One, that you are an addict—they drop a bottle on you for immediate proof, and it is tested here on the premises. Two, some kind of proof of failure in an abstinence-only program, maybe something showing you attended meetings. Three, some degree of psychological screening—" Richie stops abruptly at this point and shrugs. "Usually a few standard questions, conducted by someone like Tim, a minimally trained counselor. Not a big deal. And, four, everyone requires clients to sign an agreement."

"An agreement about what?" Katy asks, watching Tim open the front door and begin talking to the first client.

"That you will participate in ongoing spot drug testing while a client, and normally something about jointly entering some kind of rehab program. Of course the clinics don't have the resources to do any follow-up of clients. So, signing the agreement about takes care of that last step. But here at the O, every client has to have a personal interview with Dr. Nguyen before starting treatment—she does the psych screening herself. That's why there probably won't be any potential clients filling out paperwork today. Can't see the director on a Sunday, so no methadone."

"This way," Richie says, taking Katy's arm and leading her down the hall past several closed office doors to an open doorway into a large room. "All of the prior-screened clients, on the roster of approved names on Tim's clipboard, will come down here for their daily dosage of methadone."

Standing at the door is another employee, wearing the black and gold polo shirt with the O over the heart. The registration clerk, also holding the day's approved roster on a clipboard. Richie says hello and begins explaining the authorization of the visit again—

Tim shouts from the front door, "Dr. Nguyen approved their visit, Olaf."

Olaf nods at them.

Richie directs Katy's attention to a large white sign next to the doorway, to specific client instructions lettered in red:

WARNING
Failure to observe these instructions exactly may result in cancellation of today's dosage

1 *All* clients must have a valid picture ID to show the registration clerk

2 *All* clients must sign-in on today's authorized list with the registration clerk

3 Clients *one* at a time will move into the dosage room and wait at the single yellow line

4 Clients will leave the single yellow line *only* when called forward by the medication clerk

5 Clients called forward will move to the dosage counter and *remain* on the yellow square until released by the medication clerk

6 Authorized dosages will be issued in a plastic cup and consumed by the client while *standing* on the yellow square

7 *After* medication clerk is satisfied that dosage has been fully consumed at the dosage counter, client is released to the double yellow line

8 Client *signs* receipt for today's dosage, and then is released to leave the room by the registration clerk

9 At *no* time will there ever be more than 3 clients in the dosage room.

—*DR. H. NGUYEN, M.D., DIRECTOR, OAK STREET CLINIC*

They watch the morning's first client step up to the registration clerk, show an ID, and then initial before her typed name on the list. After that, the registered client steps into the room and pauses at the single yellow line. Inside the room, the medication clerk waits behind a Dutch door, top half opened into an enclosed office. After calling up the client to stand on the yellow square and again checking her ID, the medication clerk looks over her clipboard which includes the amount of authorized dosage for each client; then she squeezes an eyedropper partially full of a red liquid, carefully measuring the authorized dosage into a plastic medicine cup.

"Usually a treatment program is thirty days, beginning with 60mg of methadone," Richie explains. "Initially the dosage stains the cup of juice bright red. But the dosage is tapered off as the days pass, and eventually, on the last day, a drop of methadone leaves only a faint pink streak of color in the juice."

The client drinks the cup of methadone-laced juice. She hands back the empty cup to the medication clerk. Then she opens her mouth to demonstrate the complete dosage has indeed been swallowed.

Richie whispers, "Of course methadone has street value and can be sold illegally. So, to maintain their licensing these clinics have to insure nothing is smuggled out of the clinic. Tight inventory control of a governmentally-controlled substance."

The medication clerk releases the client from the yellow square and she moves back toward the doorway, stopping on the double yellow line to wait for release by the registration clerk at the door, after she signs for her dose of methadone. In the meantime the next authorized client is called up from the single yellow line to the yellow square.

"Okay, I understand the reason for the strict set of rules now," Katy says, watching a couple more clients move through the rigidly regulated dosage process. At no time are there ever more than three clients in the room. Everyone follows the outlined procedure carefully. "Looks well controlled to me, Richie."

"They know the drill if they want their fix," he says as they walk back down the corridor, following clients out the main door and back down the steps.

The number of folks they pass in line waiting outside has now grown to maybe forty, several carrying or holding the hands of young children.

"How successful is this treatment?" Katy asks, as they head back toward the parked Volvo.

Making an eyebrow-arched expression that implies—*Who knows?* Richie replies, "Depends on the addict. If he actually is doing something as far as rehabilitation, you know, going to meetings, working the program and so forth, it can be successful. But some of the folks here today will start using again at the end of the thirty days, when the methadone is being tapered off. Some may be here for the sole purpose of dropping their tolerance for heroin, creating a smaller jones when they hit the street. But I think at least it does lower the crime rate during the period of time the poseurs are in clinic."

They get back to the Volvo and slide in the front seats.

"You mentioned long term maintenance—what's that?" Katy asks.

After starting the engine, Richie answers, "Hard core addicts can qualify for long term methadone maintenance. The screening is difficult, the qualifying steps more rigidly enforced. But long-term junkies can indeed qualify. And then it's just a question of taking their daily doses of methadone, going about a normal life. I know a number of people who lead crime-free lives, hold a job, and are raising a family on long-term methadone maintenance. The philosophy is that methadone is a medication for a disease, like insulin for diabetes. Of course this philosophy is about as popular in the straight community as being infected with a case of the clap. Law enforcement, politicians, most rehab professionals, probably the vast majority of the public, all believe that abstinence is really the goal in controlling drug addiction. The common belief is that the long term junkie on methadone maintenance is just trading one addiction for another."

They pull away from the curb, turn right, and head west on Oak Street.

"And how do you feel about it, Richie?"

He shrugs. "Well, I guess I feel that it is great if it works for someone, but *only* as a last resort. Methadone is just as hard to kick as heroin—some say it's even harder. The goal for the majority of addicts is complete abstinence. But I'm biased, you know, a product of one of the better abstinence programs at Walden House."

Richie glances over and grins thinly. "We're headed there now, my ol' hometown at 890 Hayes Street."

3

A couple of blocks on Oak, then they turn left, and then left again, moving back west on Hayes Street.

"There are generally two kinds of abstinence support programs," Richie says, as he slows the station wagon, looking for an empty parking spot somewhere along the 800 block.

Finding nothing, he turns right on Fillmore Street after passing 890 Hayes, squeezing into an empty spot a half block down the hill from Walden House on the corner.

"I know you're somewhat familiar with twelve-step programs," Richie says to Katy, cutting the wheels into the curb and setting the brake. "Spiritual programs, the religious angle built into the twelve steps. The key is probably how well a person bonds with their sponsor and works the steps, attending a lot of meetings during the process, which he has to take very seriously."

"Yeah, I've been to meetings with Johnny, not only here in the city, but back up in Sacramento, seen him working his steps faithfully, personally met two different sponsors. I know a little about the whole process."

"Okay, that's good, save me some breath," Richie says, sliding out of the Volvo.

"This place, 890, is a therapeutic community similar to Walden House's program at 815," he continues, as they walk up the hill and turn the corner at Hayes, approaching the stairs to the building. "But it has more beds, a stricter program, lasts longer, catering to a more hardcore population of adult addicts, many in residence as an alternative to prison or jail. A prime example of the second kind of abstinence program based on principles of behavior modification. Roughly all formal programs are either twelve-step or behavior modification, a few kind of a hybrid deal. Most of the behavior mod stuff harkens back to the days of Synanon."

Katy stares up at the building.

The facility at 890, like 815, is older construction, with a newer wood-framed addition around in the back. The main building fronting Hayes is four stories, stucco-finished, and painted a bluish-gray, with white and peach trim. Four white columns frame an impressive oaken entryway at the top of the stairs.

They pause for another moment at the foot of the steep stairs, giving Katy a chance to read something. To her right at the bottom of the stairs, inside a decorative black wrought iron fence, hangs a wooden sign, an optimistic announcement in carved letters:

TODAY IS THE FIRST DAY OF THE REST OF YOUR LIFE

"Pretty cool," Katy says, nodding to herself after reading the sign.

They climb the steep staircase leading up to the second-story entryway.

At the top, Richie presses a buzzer and speaks into an intercom, stating his name and staff position in Walden House administration.

After a moment, the oaken door whirrs and releases open.

They step into a long foyer, turning immediately left at an opened Dutch door and sign into the facility. "This is where everyone visiting is required to first get permission for entry, sign in, and pick up a guide if needed," Richie explains, indicating the tiny office. "Where residents sign out and back in on their return from work or wherever," he adds after scribbling their names on a clipboard. Then he guides Katy a few steps down a wide, carpeted hallway leading inside the building from the foyer, the well-lit, high-ceilinged corridor bustling with people moving about with purpose—

"Yo, Richie," a huge black guy says, offering his closed fist to Richie.

"Hey, Leon, what's happening, bro?" Richie replies, going through a ritualistic street handshake, his hard look easing slightly.

"Goin' good, man," Leon answers, grinning. "I'm healthy, you unnerstan'. You were right, man. Can't beat this place with an armload a' switches."

"Hey, that's cool, Leon, I'm glad for you," Richie says, slapping the big man's shoulder.

Leon leans over, and with a more serious expression, addresses Katy in a restrained voice, "You here with this dude?" He gestures dismissively with his thumb at Richie.

Katy nods, not sure exactly how to react to what feels like a confrontation.

Leon busts into a wide-toothed smile and announces, "Well alright. He's a *bad* man, lady, a real bad man."

"Hey, thanks, bro," Richie says with mock anger.

Laughing, Leon waves to both of them as he hustles off to the office by the front door.

"An old street acquaintance," Richie explains briefly, pointing out a large blackboard on the wall near a closed office door on the left. "Status board."

It appears to Katy to be similar to the one at 815, a public chalked announcement, listing people who have recently left the program early for the various reasons—splitee, banned, or spotted—perhaps a little longer list. To the right of the blackboard, on the other side of the closed door, is a beautiful, polished table under an ornate mirror. On it are a pair of cigarette rolling machines, papers, a sign-up board, and a large tin of tobacco... But Katy's attention is drawn to the huge glass bowl centered on the table and filled to the brim with a number of various brands of condoms. She points questioningly.

Richie smiles. "Among other things, we are taught safe sex here at Walden House. No glove, no love. That bowl is for use by folks signing out for the day or on an overnighter, you understand."

Katy nods.

"Let's check around," Richie says, leading them by another opened Dutch door on the right side of the hallway around a corner. "Central control, manned by a senior resident 24 hours a day," he explains, nodding at a young woman manning the desk and talking on a phone.

From deeper inside the office comes a hearty greeting, "Hey, Richie."

"Yo, how's it going, Elroy?"

A short, roly-poly guy with a big grin says, "Same old, same old, man."

Richie nods, turns back to Katy. "Elroy is the on-duty counselor, chief staff member in residence for this weekend. Sometimes a hotbox position. He's a good guy. He was my orientation counselor years ago, my first significant contact with Walden House."

"Really?" Katy says, following Richie a step or two down the corridor.

"Yeah, 890, as you probably have noticed, is like all of our four biggest facilities, a converted convent, and *The Family*, as the 230 or so residents here are called, maintain everything," Richie explains with a tiny hint of pride in his hard-edged voice. Katy glances around at the ornate oaken staircase to the left and the beautifully polished paneling along the hallway, the parquet floors, everything spotlessly clean, well maintained, the carpet freshly vacuumed.

They continue on to The Family meeting room, King's Hall, named for Martin Luther King. The room was obviously a chapel in the old convent days. And the religious splendor of the former use is still displayed in the huge, almost cathedral-like dimensions of the community room, the arched, stained glass windows with scenes depicting Biblical events, the religious stations between the windows, and everywhere in the room is ornate woodwork, including the beautiful, real paneling and parquet floor.

An impressive place, Katy thinks, looking around. A positive vibe here, too, just like over at 815.

Richie points out the Walden House Creed hanging at the front of the meeting room. "Family meets here at least every morning... Special meetings called over the intercom by central control whenever required."

He leads Katy out of King Hall and around the second story of the facility—mostly offices, smaller meeting rooms—occasionally speaking to someone, a few clients, mostly staff, and explaining to Katy about the 890 program as they tour the facility.

"This is a much stricter program here than 815. It's twelve months long now, used to be eighteen months when I went through. First thirty days are orientation, no visitors, no phone calls, complete restriction, getting your mind right. You begin getting acquainted with the Walden House Creed and all that means, earning your strength—"

"Strength?" Katy interrupts as they start up the stairwell to the third and fourth floors.

"Yeah, all along you need to earn strength," Richie explains. "At first, you don't have enough strength to... oh, open a window during the orientation phase. You must ask someone to open it for you. You work up strength to eventually go out after orientation, someone carrying your money. Then maybe a visit home, with someone along. Eventually you have enough strength to carry your own money. So forth. Earning strength by working on your addiction, demonstrating attitude changes. You have a main home group with a counselor, but you must face your other issues, too. Like a spirits group or a sex group—lots of sisters in that one. You learn to pack your own shit. When you screw up, someone is around to support you—points out your bad attitude or mistake. You own up to a counselor yourself when you screw up, or support goes a step further—someone owning up for you. You always react with a thank you for support, no hostility. Toughest part for the sisters and brothers in from one of the prisons—support. They see it as ratting someone out. But everyone comes around in The Family, eventually supporting and expecting support from the other brothers and sisters. In here, *complete* honesty is the rule, and rigidly enforced."

"You mentioned brothers and sisters. Is that a problem, doing a coeducational program?"

"You bet," Richie answers, "no sex inside here. Violation is a big bust, grounds for getting you spotted, if you don't own up. Of course it happens. But we are talking brothers and sisters, literally, okay?"

"I got it," she says.

Richie continues. "The program is well designed for you to eventually change and monitor all of your own behavior. Take responsibility for yourself. You must learn to live as a properly functioning member of society. Not an easy thing to learn in twelve months, after all the ripping and running, prison, whatever."

He leads them down a hallway on the fourth floor. "This is a male wing, all dorm-like rooms. As many as eight in the larger ones. Third floor has some three- and two-man rooms, for senior residents. All of the female rooms are in the addition out back."

They spot a guy coming out of his room and Richie asks permission to glance inside.

Two bunk beds, two closets, the room housing four residents, everything neat and tidy, awaiting a military inspection. On the wall, Katy notices four large corkboards with photos, newspaper clippings, and letters thumbtacked in place. "Everyone has their own bulletin board in here?"

"Yeah, everyone in the facility has their own personal board," Richie replies, his face taking on a darker expression. "One of my first roommates was this Chinese dude, came from a Hong Kong triad, learned English in San Quentin. When he got released from the joint to here, his gang sent him a message, not a note, nothing like that, just a photo he put up on his bulletin board. It was his girlfriend, hacked in pieces, dead. Message was clear—"

"Oh, my God," Katy murmurs, shocked.

Richie leads them out of the room. "Thanks, man."

They head back down the great stairwell. Richie continues describing the program as they descend.

"In the first months at 890 everyone works on his GED, eventually passing it before graduation from the program. At the same time you have a house job, in maintenance, at the mess hall, janitorial, whatever. Then around the fourth month, you get a job on the street, learning how to budget expenses, including paying a token portion of your room and board. The bulk is saved for first and last months' rent for an apartment when you graduate. The last few months of the program, you live in satellite, away from 890, an apartment owned by Walden House. You sign in and out of there, too, having occasional unannounced visits by your counselor, even bottle drops."

They reach the main corridor at the foot of the stairs, strolling leisurely back toward the entry.

"I lived in satellite out on the avenues by the Russian Orthodox Church," Richie says. "Worked in a small section that solicited outside businesses for donations, down in the administration offices on Townsend Street, where I work now in MIS. Been down there over eight years."

As they reach the entry office before signing out, Richie says, "Questions?"

Katy replies, "Yes, you mentioned a program here for prostitutes, when we were over on Capp Street the other day."

"Oh, yeah, SAGE," Richie says, snapping his fingers.

He turns and points back down the corridor. "They have an office here. Probably no one down there on Sunday. But I guess I can give you an overview…"

Richie pauses a moment, gathers his thoughts. "Let's see. SAGE is an acronym for Standing Against Global Exploitation. It was founded in 1993 by Norma Hotaling, a prostitute survivor of the street herself, a recovering heroin addict. SAGE received a city contract to provide residential treatment services for some of its women. Hotaling turned to Walden House. So we provide treatment for a number of women who also are members of the SAGE support group. In addition to helping woman become independent, SAGE provides employment opportunities for some of our Walden House graduates. SAGE staff are well qualified to reach out and help women off the street. It's a good program."

"Sounds like it's a *great* program," Katy says.

"It is," Richie agrees, smiling thinly.

They sign out, and as they walk down the steep stairs, Katy asks, "How successful is a program like Walden House?"

Richie stops and looks directly at Katy with his chilling Clint Eastwood glare bristling with attitude "It worked for me. If not for Walden House I would probably be dead or in prison. But statistics?" He shrugs, his expression again suggesting—*Who knows?*

"I mean, *if* a person finishes the whole year here at 890, follow-up stats indicate that 70% or so are drug-free a year later. But considering everyone who begins the program, I don't know. Probably not nearly so encouraging. You've seen the status board. People leave the program every day, and I'm sure they start using almost immediately. But I do know that the future of a Walden House resident is much better than Steven Okazaki's documentary film implies for his four young people. Even if a resident splits and uses again, Walden House has pissed in his beer. You know what I mean by that?"

Katy smiles at his crude expression, but nods.

Richie breaks off and checks his watch. "Guess we better get you back to dress for your basketball game."

4

Back at her Chestnut Street apartment, Katy slides out of the mustard Volvo, pausing at the opened window on her side.

"Well, I have some great stuff on heroin addiction, Richie. I've learned a lot, hope I can do the story justice. Thanks a lot. When I actually begin the article, I know I'll need to call you again, check out stuff that I forgot or just missed. Maybe talk some about the needed research that you mentioned during one of our earlier trips. Okay?"

"You bet, Katy," he says, his expression and tone more relaxed now. "I look forward to seeing what you come up with."

Katy stretches, and they shake hands.

"I'm going to hook up with Hap now, downtown at St. Anthony's," Richie says, "see if we can make any progress catching up with our friend Mr. Williams. Good luck at your championship game. I hate missing it. But duty calls, you know."

"Thanks."

Katy waves at him, as the station wagon pulls away from the curb.

TOURNAMENT - FINAL GAME

KINGSTON TRIO

LITTLE WOMEN

THE KINGSTON TRIO

Katy makes it easily on time to the Marina courts. Even though it's early there's a pretty good crowd forming. She checks out the facilities, which are about equivalent to the Panhandle courts except the nets are real cord nets, not metal, and there is more bleacher seating capacity, bigger permanent stands. She chuckles. Most shooters favor cord nets over metal, and indoor courts with plastic backboards. She is no exception. Part of the weird hoops mythology. Funny, because most players grow up on outdoor playgrounds, shooting at hoops with no nets at all, the wooden backboards often flaking paint and sometimes warped. But the better players, like Katy, go on to play in college with better indoor facilities and equipment. Only in recent times have 3-on-3 tournaments brought first class competition back outdoors to the old playground days.

"Yo, Katy," CeCe says, coming up to where Katy is sitting across from the bleachers at center courtside, pulling on her Converse sneakers. They tap fists. "Where's Sid?"

"Haven't seen her yet," Katy answers, looking up nonchalantly, keeping her tone neutral. Of course they both are very concerned about their teammate's health, the condition of her right Achilles tendon. Will Sid be okay to go this afternoon, or not? No substituting now. They've come so far, played so well. Be a shame if they can't compete for all the marbles.

"Hey, I see the Kingston Trio is here and ready," CeCe says, nodding at the basket to the right, the three red-and-white clad Kingston sisters already warming up and shooting around casually.

Katy glances right and nods. She read an article about them in the *Chronicle* sports section yesterday.

The sisters come from a basketball family. Their father played briefly in the NBA with Cincinnati and the Big O, Oscar Robertson. Their mother was a legendary all around high school athlete in the '70s in Indiana, excelling in basketball and track. A brother was a recent all Pac-10 basketball standout with USC, currently playing pro ball in Italy. The oldest sister, LeAnn, starred in basketball at SF City College seven years ago before crossing the Bay to play briefly at Cal. Lyn, the middle sister, was currently a junior on the basketball team at Tennessee on a full ride. Baby sister, Lennie, had just graduated from Lowell, the top scorer on that high school championship team, headed on to play basketball and run track at City College. A tough, hard-nosed team, winning all their games impressively. But all three members of the Trio are about the same size, 5'-8" or maybe 5'-9" at the most. They're quick, play tenacious defense, and can shoot, but they will be at an obvious disadvantage height-wise against Little Women. That's the conventional wisdom. Katy knows it's going to be a very hard fought game, close right up to the end.

The bleachers are almost full as CeCe and Katy begin warming up, first doing some stretching and flexibility exercises. But both keeping an eye out for their post player.

Still no Sidney.

"Hey, hey, where's my main hoopster, Swoop?" a falsetto voice shouts from half court in the middle of the stands. It is their number one fan, here early and fired up.

CeCe and Katy ignore the question and begin to shoot around, trying to relax, not look worried. No use. Katy is indeed tight, throwing up bricks, and CeCe is not doing much better. They both move in close, working around the basket, shooting high percentage shots with both hands... eventually relaxing a little, but still keeping a concerned eye out for Sid.

After bouncing a ball back to CeCe at the free-throw line, Katy hears the black dude clapping and making a big fuss in the stands, even before she spots Sid, fully dressed and jogging onto the center court.

"Hey, we were worried," Katy says quietly to Sidney, as CeCe bounces a pass to her tardy teammate.

"Yeah, girl, what's up?" CeCe says, a frown on her normally cheerful face.

"Woke up a little late, probably because of the drugs I took last night," Sid explains in a voice just loud enough for her teammates to hear. "Ankle was pretty stiff. But I worked on it, rubbed in some medicine, taped it up, and took some more anti-inflammatory stuff... It's okay now, I think." To demonstrate, she fakes right and drives left, shooting a lay-in off the heavily-taped right ankle, but going noticeably at only about three-quarter speed.

She appears okay to Katy, ready to play.

"Oh, yeah, oh, yeah, money in the bank." Little Women's number one fan is going off big time now. "Get 'em, Swoopster." He gives his partner a double high five. "Alright, my main *la-dy is red-dy, red-dy, red-dy...* time for Lil Wemmens to rock 'n' roll, y'all." He's bouncing up and down, pounding the stands with his feet, like a head cheerleader. Making a spectacle of himself.

The crowd around him, as if on cue, finally erupts with a loud round of applause for Sidney and Little Women.

Someone in the stands to the left starts a cheer for the Kingston Trio, as a neighbor turns up their boombox with a loud rendition of the old folk group's best known hit, "Tom Dooley."

Raucous, loud, excited, a palpable prestorm tension thickens the early afternoon air over the stands and center court.

Sidney nonchalantly goes about her pre-game routine, stretching, moving left and right, shooting, and passing back to her teammates... But Katy notices that Sid never really elevates very high off that taped right ankle, and never tries to tip any missed shots back in as she normally does in warm-ups. She's not a hundred percent.

Another couple of minutes of practice, and one of the referees blows his whistle. Time to get it on.

The crowd quiets down as The Kingston Trio wins the flip and takes the ball out, passing it around with a little flashy showboating, almost like a Globetrotters pre-game drill, everyone touching the ball, making fakes, getting loose. Then the younger sister tries to drive on CeCe, who easily blocks the lay-in attempt.

A loud round of applause. Then a falsetto voice over the clapping, "Oh, yeah, oh, yeah, *re-jek-shun!*"

But it's still the Trio's side out.

Katy is guarding Lyn, who moves all the time without the ball—constant motion. A pass is bounced to the Lady Volunteer, who fakes right, quickly drives to her left, pulls up abruptly, and cans a 12 foot jumper over Katy.

0-2.

Um, pretty quick to her left. Katy is steamed, knowing she reached when Lyn drove instead of moving her feet. Gerri, her old San Diego PAL coach, would've been pissed big time if she were here now. She stressed defense, using your feet, *never* reaching. Only tired or beaten players reached. And they were eventually losing players.

The ball goes into LeAnn, and then back out to Lyn who launches a long set and misses.

CeCe has boxed out perfectly, and pulls down the rebound.

Ball out to the top of the key.

Katy fakes a drive, goes up, and shoots from just inside the top of the key... A brick, no touch... But CeCe goes over the much smaller Lennie and tips the ball back in. She grins, making a semi-*yes* pumping move with her hand.

2-2.

The teams trade several possessions, no one scoring after taking long-range shots. Little Women never giving up an offensive rebound, easily pulling down everything over the smaller Kingston Trio.

But Lennie eludes CeCe off a nifty screen by LeAnn and makes an uncontested lay-in, Sid a step late providing offside help. Something she could've normally done easily.

2-4.

Ball out to the top of the key, and Lyn pushes up a long set over Katy's stretching fingertips. She knew she'd relaxed momentarily. *No more of that, girl,* she chastises herself sharply.

2-6.

Ball comes out again, then quickly back in to LeAnn, flashing into a low post.

CeCe slides over with backside help for Sid and gets a hand on the short jumper by LeAnn. Katy recovers the blocked shot, and takes the ball out to the top of the key.

"Okay, Lil Wemmens, le's make like a big wheel… an roll, y'all." Their number one fan stirs up the crowd again.

Little Women work the ball briskly around, each touching the ball and getting a good feel, the three finally loosening up. Then, Katy hits Sidney left of the key and cuts right away from the ball, picking off CeCe's man. Sid hits CeCe with a bounce pass as she rolls toward the basket for an uncontested shot.

"Way to go, girl," Katy says, slapping CeCe's shoulder, feeling excitement erase the last of her pregame tension.

4-6.

A moment later, Katy hits a short jumper off a CeCe-pick, but she knows she's not quite in the zone. No, not yet. Doesn't feel that special tingling in her shooting arm, that Eddie Felson touch. But she grins, because it's coming. Oh, yeah. The Fuller Brush guy is knocking.

6-6.

Katy misses a jumper, and the Trio get the long rebound.

But even without Katy hitting all her jumpers, Little Women hang tough, making the Trio earn everything, allowing nothing in close. But Katy is worried. Twice Sid has been inside of her man, and not been able to catch passes that would have led to easy lay-ups. The Achilles tendon has got to be hurting her, even if Sid won't admit it.

The game wears on, CeCe and Katy grinding it out, working hard for baskets in close, playing tough D, boxing out, rebounding, calling on their experience. Every effort is applauded vigorously by their number one fan and the crowd.

But the Kingston Trio team are all tough and quick, LeAnn actually outplaying Sid, who is always a fraction of a second late defending her shorter opponent.

After a hectic twenty minutes of back-and-forth play, the score is 10-16, the Trio comfortably in the lead.

The Trio takes the ball to the top of the key, and Lennie bounce passes back across court toward her sister.

Katy anticipates and leans into the passing lane, tipping the ball away from Lyn and right into Sid's hands.

Out, and back in to Sid, who spins left and tries to elevate over LeAnn for a short five footer—

Her right ankle gives way partially and she stumbles to the court, the ball sliding out of bounds.

Kingston Trio's ball. Out to the top of the key, back down to LeAnn, who spins by the limping Sid for an easy layup.

10-18.

Not looking good, Katy thinks, sucking it up.

Lennie is at the top of the key, bounce passes right to a momentarily open Lyn.

But Katy gets a slight piece of her opponent's fifteen-foot jumper, and CeCe snags the short shot.

Out to Katy at the top of the key.

She fakes a jumper, gets Lennie off her feet, drives right, bringing CeCe's defensive player over to her, then a nifty bounce pass back to CeCe for an uncontested lay-in.

12-18.

Back out to Katy.

Lennie drops back a step, and Katy takes an eighteen-foot jumper, the ball arcing gracefully and swishing.

Sweet.

I feel it coming now, Katy thinks, bouncing the ball at the top of the key. The touch, in the flow.

Lennie shadows her close now, so Katy drops the ball in to Sidney, who has slid out to a high post. CeCe comes over and sets a rugged pick on Lennie. Katy breaks loose, Sid drops the ball to her as she slides by for a ten-footer that arcs up, spinning smoothly… and swishing.

16-18.

The fans are standing and hollering in the stands, the black dude drowned out by the loud noise around him.

Katy takes the ball to the top of the key, feeling it big time now.

But Lennie hounds her closely.

So, Katy fakes a jump shot, and then drives left toward the bucket, a half step ahead of Lennie who has gone for the fake. LeAnn releases from Sidney to block Katy's path to the goal. Katy pulls up but can't shoot because LeAnn is in perfect defensive position; so she lobs the ball over LeAnn to Sid who has rolled low, a piece of cake—

But Sidney seems to be moving in slow motion, a step late, and Katy's pass is an inch long, trickling off Sid's fingertips and out of bounds.

Oh, no.

"My fault," Katy says, as the Trio takes the ball out and to the top of the key.

Sid just shakes her head, pointing at her chest. "No way, my bad."

Lennie tries to drop a lob into her sister, LeAnn, who is down low behind Sid. But CeCe releases from her opponent with weak side help, just barely flicking the ball away at the last second.

"Way to go, girl!" Katy shouts, thinking—*It isn't over yet.*

The Trio work the basketball around after taking it out, moving it quickly around the court.

And Katy is picked from her blind side.

Unguarded now, Lennie drives in to the basket and elevates over a game but hobbled Sid for an acrobatic, twisting lay-in… the ball going up against the backboard and angling softly for a slick bucket.

And just like that it is over. The tournament.

Game time.

They have lost.

The far stands empty out quickly, the Trio fans smothering their team with congratulations.

Dumbfounded by the suddenness of it all, Katy, CeCe, and Sid can do nothing but stand and watch from their court positions.

Then, Sid limps over to the bench and her gear, a painful expression on her face. No question, she's hurting.

Katy hustles over to her friend's side. "Hey, Sid, you did your best. I'm so proud of you, know you are hurting. Great effort!"

Sid looks and nods with a thin smile. "Yeah, thanks."

CeCe comes over after congratulating the winning team. "Hey, wait until next year. We'll get them then. They'll be lucky to score ten points on us. You hear me?"

Katy nods, and can't help grinning at her friend's never-say-die attitude, despite just losing the city championship minutes ago.

Yes, indeed, there is always next year, Katy agrees silently. She sucks in a deep breath, as Johnny comes up and hugs her.

"Too bad, girls, a great game."

TWENTY-SIX

Then shall the dust return to the earth as it was; and its spirit shall return into God who gave it.

Ecclesiastes 12:7

The crowd in the stands to the far left rise around you as if one person, hooting, cheering, stamping their feet at the end of the game. Inwardly, you feel sheepish for worrying needlessly. Even without your disguise—a Giants cap pulled down, sun glasses, your black windbreaker collar pulled up high around your neck—no one would even notice you here in this excited mob. John Cato is sitting two stands away out of sight, and the woman, Katy Green, is much too busy out on the court. Neither is even vaguely aware of your presence.

You have taken advantage of your opportunity and been watching the team, Little Women, very carefully.

Of course you know very little about basketball, especially women's basketball; but despite that fact you realize Katy Green is an excellent player. Graceful and elegant for a woman her size. You also realize that her team was destined to lose; her friend, the tall black woman, obviously played hurt, favoring her right foot, unable to jump and move quickly, and do her share as a team member—a fatal flaw on a three member team. A pity, because Katy Green's team is very impressive physically, and have apparently played well during the tournament, drawing a sizeable section of rooters, including a very loud and boisterous head cheerleader, standing in the middle of the three sets of portable stands.

Watching the stands completely empty after the brief awards ceremony, you do not see any of the others from the private investigator agency, only John Cato, who has joined the team of Little Women across the court. The husky Hispanic team member has handed him the 2nd place trophy to admire. They are all too busy to even look your way.

Your interest is drawn back to Katy Green, as she kindly comforts her injured teammate.

Thoughtfully, you watch as Katy Green picks up their two sports bags, and John Cato assists the tall, black woman as she hobbles along toward the parking lot beyond the basketball courts.

Katy Green must personally care a lot about her teammate's welfare.

And that is good, you think, smiling to yourself. Yes, indeed, very good... *for you.*

Time for you to go, too.

TLACHTLI?

Back in their Marina apartment after the tournament, Katy takes a long bath, letting the hot water leach away some of the soreness from her aching muscles. This last game has definitely exposed her, because she feels every one of her thirty-four years. But only time will help heal her ego. No question it has taken a hit. So close… Little Women had come so far, only to lose the championship. But close doesn't count, Katy reminds herself with a wry smile. Nope, they weren't throwing hand grenades. And poor Sidney, she must be a wreck even now, blaming herself.

Perking up a little, Katy decides to call her friend as soon as she finishes her physically revitalizing bath.

"Hey, kiddo," Johnny says from the bathroom door. He's holding the phone. "A call for you, from Sid," he adds.

"Thanks," Katy says, taking the phone.

"Hello, Sidney, how's it going?"

She is on the phone for a minute or so, a major frown developing, as she mostly just listens to her friend.

"Yeah, sure," she replies. "I can probably be there in twenty minutes, give or take a few minutes. Okay?"

Then, "See you soon."

Katy nods to herself, staring at the phone.

"What's the matter?" Johnny asks, still standing in the doorway. "Sid's Achilles tendon barking, swelling up... what?"

Katy shakes her head. "No, she claims her ankle is fine now. She's been icing it, rubbing on some prescription stuff she has, taking painkillers and anti-inflammatories. It isn't her Achilles... Hand me the blue towel, will you?"

Johnny hands her the towel as Katy stands up from the tub.

"What then? Why the big frown?"

"It's something funny she said," Katy replies, absently drying herself off, the frown still a deep crease between her eyes. "And her general tone wasn't right either."

Johnny hands Katy a clean bra and panties sitting on the toilet, waiting for her to continue the explanation.

Katy slips into her undergarments and a pair of Levis. Then she slips on a Giants, black and orange T-shirt. "Yeah, really strange," she begins to explain, absently combing her hair in front of the wide-angle bathroom mirror. "Sid wants me to come over to talk about a project of hers. Some artwork regarding a Meso-American game, Tlachtli, and some writing she says I agreed to do for it..." She pauses, staring directly at Johnny.

"And," he says impatiently. "What's so odd about that?"

"There is no project."

"What do you mean?"

"I mean Sid and I are *not* working on a project, nor do we have anything planned in the future," Katy says thoughtfully. "But we did talk about the game of Tlachtli last Wednesday after practice." She nods, as if something were beginning to come clear. "You know, I think Sid was sending me a coded message here. As if someone was listening closely to what she was saying over the phone. Obviously the eavesdropper wants me to come to Sid's place."

"You mean you think someone is there with her now at her apartment?"

Katy nods, absently running her fingers through her hair. "Tlachtli was an early kind of basketball game played in Central America. Maya and Aztec, and maybe others too, I'm not really sure. Anyhow—this is the kicker, pal—the losing teams were murdered by the priests right after the game."

"So?" he says after a moment's thought, looking puzzled. "I guess I'm not tracking here."

"We just *lost* a basketball game."

Johnny stares blankly for a few more moments... Then he frowns. "You think she's being threatened by someone at her apartment?" he asks tentatively. Then adds in a more confident voice, "Someone with bad intentions, who wants *you* to come over to Sid's?"

"Bingo," Katy says.

"Who could it be? Someone from over at the tournament—?"

She shrugs, then says hoarsely, "It just may be our boy, and he forced Sidney to make the call." After a second or two, she adds, "I'm getting that tingling in my gut here."

Johnny nods thoughtfully. "And Sid figured out a way to alert you in on the danger by mentioning the Tlachtli?"

"You got it, pal."

They both were quiet for a minute or so, thinking over the bizarre situation.

"Before we do anything else, let me call Hap and Richie," Johnny suggests. "They can meet us over there. Hap still has a permit to carry his old .38."

"Okay," Katy says, still frowning. "But no cops yet," she adds with a thin smile. "If it is our boy, we don't want to scare him off with sirens and all that stuff."

Johnny tries Hap's cell phone number.

He shakes his head. "No answer," he says to Katy, then back into the phone, "Hap this is Johnny. We think our boy is holding Sidney, Katy's teammate, over at Sid's apartment. Call me. And meet us over there as soon as you get this..."

Johnny gives the big guy specific driving instructions to Sid's place in Pacific Heights.

"C'mon," Katy says, leading Johnny out of the apartment. "We can't wait for help."

2

Johnny parks his Mustang down the street a block or so from Sid's apartment in Pacific Heights. They cross the street and come through the park, stopping near the basketball court where Katy practiced on Wednesday night. They hesitate, wishing it were dark. But it's only 6:30, twilight a good hour and a half away. They creep out to the street behind a large SUV, hoping they are out of view from Sid's apartment across the street.

"Now what?" Katy asks in a hushed tone.

Johnny frowns. "I think I should work my way around the back of her apartment. It's on the left, ground floor, right? If our boy is in there, maybe I can surprise him from behind."

Katy nods, remembering that she is not armed. She reaches out and touches Johnny's sweater, where it covers just above his right rear pocket. Feeling his holster and .357, she sighs and smiles with relief.

He looks back at her with his game face on now. "That's right, kiddo," he whispers, "I'm holding."

Brinnng. Johnny's cell phone startles both of them.

"Yes... Hey, Hap."

Johnny grins broadly, nodding and listening.

"That's great," he says, after listening for several moments.

Then, he gives Hap the address again.

Johnny explains to Katy. "They caught Jackson Williams a few minutes ago, downtown at some other residential hotel—"

"They did?" Katy interrupts. Puzzled, she glances across the street in the direction of Sid's apartment. *Who's in there with Sid?*

"Yeah. He sent some numbnuts to collect his money at Hotel Majestic. Hap and Richie just followed the dummy straight back to Jackson. They'll be here with him in about ten minutes. But—get this, kiddo—Hap and Richie don't think Jackson is our guy; they don't think he has been murdering anyone."

"Really?" Katy says. She is even more surprised by this revelation. She was sure he was the one, the guy in the old photo, probably the guy holding Sid. But Jackson obviously wasn't inside Sid's apartment, if Hap had him in custody.

"They will explain everything when they get here."

Katy nods, a kind of mixed expression on her face—intrigued confusion; then after a moment or two, she looks back across the street and asks in a more than curious tone, "And what do you suppose is going on with Sid? Is there really someone in there with her now? Maybe she isn't even being held hostage after all?"

Johnny shrugs. "Too many pain pills you think… ? Or maybe something else related to her ankle?"

"Hmm, well, maybe," Katy says, but not totally buying that explanation. She knows Sid is pretty tough, strong-willed, and she doesn't think a few pain pills would send her into la-la land, acting goofy, making crazy-ass phone calls. No, that didn't feel right.

"Let's walk over and check it out," she suggests to Johnny, stepping out around the SUV sheltering them from view.

3

You've been watching them out the front window in your ski mask, careful not to give away your position, just opening the pulled shade a crack. John Cato has just had a conversation on his cell phone. He appears relieved. You hope he has not called the authorities. That would ruin your plans for Katy Green.

You glance back over your shoulder, down the long hallway. The tall, black woman, still wearing her basketball sweats, is tied securely to the chair in the kitchen, her gag tightly in place. Good.

You peek back out through the crack in the shade again.

They are standing up in clear view now, easing around the dark SUV… But for some reason they hesitate at the edge of the street.

"Come on, come on," you say under your breath, as if coaxing a spooked dog to come to you. To no avail. They remain in place, in plain view, not moving into your trap.

4

"No, let's wait a few minutes," Johnny says, reaching out and taking a hold of Katy's arm, preventing her from crossing the street. "Let's wait, see what's going on with the rest of our team."

So, they wait, standing in front of the parked SUV, both looking across the street at Sid's apartment building.

5

Annoyed now, you storm down the hallway, and roughly drag the black woman tied to the chair back up to the front of the house. You pull on the Hand of God. Then you throw open the front door, pushing the gagged woman bound to the chair into the doorway, in plain view of the two across the street.

"Hey, Cato and Green," you shout, your voice muffled slightly by the ski mask. You hold up the Hand of God, and rest the tip of the talon against the black woman's throat.

6

Katy spots him as soon as he opens Sid's front door… and sees her friend tied to the chair, gagged.

"Oh, my God," she whispers to herself, realizing the guy is wearing the white glove with the poisoned talon at its fingertip, and threatening to scratch Sid. Jackson Williams is *not* their boy for sure. Who the hell is this guy?

"Hold it, man!" Johnny shouts at the guy. "Wait. Don't hurt her."

"Send the woman over," the guy in the ski mask demands across the street. "Only she can save her friend from dying in this chair. Send her over now."

He wants to do his number on me, Katy thinks, her heart pounding, her pulse racing now.

No one moves, either up on the porch or across the street by the SUV.

Stop frame.

<u>7</u>

Suddenly, a mustard-colored Volvo station wagon brakes right in the middle of the street, beside the parked SUV.

Doors fly open.

Richie jumps out of the driver's side.

Hap piles out of the back seat, dragging a man beside him.

It's Jackson Williams.

At that point, they all look at Katy and Johnny, then across the street at the scene on the front porch. Obviously having sized up the situation as they drove up the street.

<u>8</u>

The car startles you, makes you hesitate in place, the Hand of God hovering over the gagged woman's neck.

Three men spill out of the vehicle parked in the middle of the street.

One of them looks in your direction and shouts, "No, no, Billy!"

Then everyone is advancing across the street.

You tighten your hand, ready to scratch the bound woman—

But you freeze.

You're paralyzed by the sudden but familiar onset of your seizure: the tunneling of vision, the smell of eucalyptus, the sense of the old man admonishing you... And the sliver of pain exploding into your sinus cavity, absolute agony... blackness quickly closing down.

<u>9</u>

"No, no, Billy!" Jackson shouts across the street at the masked figure. "It is *over*. No more. You have disobeyed, turned from your calling, and killed innocent people."

He starts across the street, Hap and the others following closely. They all stop as the figure on the porch, threatening Sidney with the poisoned talon, hesitates, then stiffens like a statue... and eventually slumps over, his gloved arm dropping away harmlessly, as if caught in the grasp of an invisible grip.

Silence.

Everyone stands in place.

Finally, Jackson says, "Don't you recognize me, Billy?"

10

You groan, a familiar voice shocking you back to consciousness.

"Don't you recognize me, Billy?"

You blink, looking at the man standing halfway across the street.

It's J.J., your brother! All grown up.

"Please, Billy, surrender," he says, pleading. "It's over. You have done too much harm. You're not doing the Lord's work."

"W-w-why…" you stammer, the truth of J.J.'s statement ringing in your ears, *You're not doing the Lord's work.*

Of course what he's saying is true. You haven't been doing the Lord's work for a long time. You've just been meeting your own sick, dark need. *Addicted to the Deathflash.*

An abomination.

These people are going to put you away, put you in prison…

No. You can't let that happen.

No, indeed.

11

As they all watch helplessly, the man in the mask pulls up his sleeve and rakes his own arm with the deadly talon—

"No, Billy!" Jackson shouts out, breaking loose from Hap's grip, darting across the street and up the steps. He kneels and takes his brother's hand in his, crying.

Confusion reigns, as everyone finally rushes across the street. All trying to go up the narrow steps at once.

Katy manages to reach Sid first and tear the gag from her mouth.

"Sid, are you—"

"I'm okay," the bound woman says in a dry, throaty whisper.

Katy unties her.

Hap and Johnny try to administer to the masked man lying on the porch, now in his brother's arms, convulsing violently.

Johnny shakes his head, glancing at Katy. Too late.

Everyone tries to talk at once, except for Jackson who is staring entranced at his brother's chest:

"What—?"

"Why—?"

"When—?"

"But I thought—"

Then they all turn to Sidney, concerned about her welfare. After they are all assured by her protestations that she is indeed all right, Katy moves over and touches Jackson's shoulder.

"I'm sorry," she says.

He looks up with tears in his eyes and nods. "I have to take him back home," he says hoarsely. "Back to the Flock."

"We need to call this in," Hap says, pulling out his cell phone.

Everyone gathers closely, as Johnny kneels and carefully removes the ski mask.

Katy gasps with recognition, looking down into the man's sky-blue eyes staring off into eternity.

It is the orientation counselor from over at 815.

"Jeff Walters," Richie whispers in a disbelieving tone. "A pseudonym?"

Katy nods. "He was Billy Williams, Jackson's brother."

Then, Johnny shakes Richie's hand. "You were right, man, from the get-go. Maybe your brother and all the others can rest in peace, now."

Richie nods. "Thanks."

"Okay, my boys from Homicide are coming out," Hap says. "As best we can, we need to preserve the scene for them." He takes a half stub of a cigar from his pocket and smiles his John Goodman smile. He lights up the stogie, and puffs with delight.

Case closed, Katy thinks.

EPILOGUE

Jackson Williams does eventually take his brother's remains back to the Ouachita Mountains after an official inquest. He writes back that he is now the Shepherd of the Flock, to no one's surprise. Although Katy can't help occasionally wondering if he inherited the Gift of Sight—no one remembers if he was holding his brother's hand when Billy died.

Six months after she publishes a two-article series in the *San Francisco Bay Guardian* entitled, "Rippin' 'n' Runnin'," Katy wins the first place award for feature story in the annual contest by The California Newspaper Publishers Association. She begins another novel, autobiographical fiction concerning her last case in Sacramento, when they caught Red Chief, calling it *Shadow of the Dark Angel*.

From the publicity surrounding the closing of the Underclass Murders, as they are dubbed, Johnny and Hap's P.I. business is overwhelmed with new work. They expand, eventually taking on Damon Dupree's brother, David, as an associate.

Richie continues on the straight and narrow, doing college work in Nonprofit Administration, his work responsibilities increasing as Walden House continues to grow within the CDC prison system. He hooks up with a counselor from 815, Julie Engleman, and they are frequent dinner guests at the apartment in the Marina. But success doesn't spoil Richie; he continues to drive his beat-up old mustard-colored Volvo station wagon.

The End

… and don't miss out on the other thrilling books in this series:

The Crime Files of Katy Green #1: Double Jack
The Crime Files of Katy Green #2: Shadow of the Dark Angel
The Crime Files of Katy Green #3: Deathflash
The Crime Files of Katy Green #4: A Stick of Doublemint

ALSO FROM DARK MOON BOOKS:

A WORLD OF HORROR

Every nation of the globe has unique tales to tell, whispers that settle in through the land, creatures or superstitions that enliven the night, but rarely do readers get to experience such a diversity of these voices in one place as in *A WORLD OF HORROR*, the latest anthology book created by award-winning editor Eric J. Guignard, and beautifully illustrated by artist Steve Lines.

Enclosed within its pages are twenty-two all-new dark and speculative fiction stories written by authors from around the world that explore the myths and monsters, fables and fears of their homelands.

Encounter the haunting things that stalk those radioactive forests outside Chernobyl in Ukraine; sample the curious dishes one may eat in Canada; beware the veldt monster that mirrors yourself in Uganda; or simply battle mountain trolls alongside Alfred Nobel in Sweden. These stories and more are found within *A World of Horror*. Enter and discover, truly, there's no place on the planet devoid of frights, thrills, and wondrous imagination.

"This breath of fresh air for horror readers shows the limitless possibilities of the genre."

—*Publishers Weekly* (starred review)

"This is the book we need right now!"
—*Becky Spratford; librarian, reviewer,* RA for All: Horror

"A fresh collection of horror authors exploring monsters and myths from their homelands."

—*Library Journal*

Order your copy at www.darkmoonbooks.com or www.amazon.com
ISBN-13: 978-0-9885569-2-8

ALSO FROM DARK MOON BOOKS:

THE FIVE SENSES OF HORROR

Hearing, sight, touch, smell, and taste: Our impressions of the world are formed by our five senses, and so too are our fears, our imaginations, and our captivation in reading fiction stories that embrace these senses.

Whether hearing the song of infernal caverns, tasting the erotic kiss of treachery, or smelling the lush fragrance of a fiend, enclosed within this anthology are fifteen horror and dark fantasy tales that will quicken the beat of fear, sweeten the flavor of wonder, sharpen the spike of thrills, and otherwise brighten the marvel of storytelling that is found resonant!

Editor Eric J. Guignard and psychologist Jessica Bayliss, PhD also include companion discourse throughout, offering academic and literary insight as well as psychological commentary examining the physiology of our senses, why each of our senses are engaged by dark fiction stories, and how it all inspires writers to continually churn out ideas in uncommon and invigorating ways.

Featuring stunning interior illustrations by Nils Bross, and including fiction short stories by such world-renowned authors as John Farris, Ramsey Campbell, Poppy Z. Brite, Darrell Schweitzer, and Richard Christian Matheson, amongst others.

Intended for readers, writers, and students alike, explore *THE FIVE SENSES OF HORROR!*

Order your copy at www.darkmoonbooks.com or www.amazon.com
ISBN-13: 978-0-9988275-0-6

ALSO FROM DARK MOON BOOKS:

POP THE CLUTCH: THRILLING TALES OF ROCKABILLY, MONSTERS, AND HOT ROD HORROR

Welcome to the cool side of the 1950s, where the fast cars and revved-up movie monsters peel out in the night. Where outlaw vixens and jukebox tramps square off with razorblades and lead pipes. Where rockers rock, cool cats strut, and hot rods roar. Where you howl to the moon as the tiki drums pound and the electric guitar shrieks and that spit-and-holler jamboree ain't gonna stop for a long, long time . . . maybe never.

This is the '50s where ghost shows still travel the back roads of the south, and rockabilly has a hold on the nation's youth; where lucky hearts tell the tale, and maybe that fella in the Shriners' fez ain't so square after all. Where exist noir detectives of the supernatural, tattoo artists of another kind, Hollywood fix-it men, and a punk kid with grasshopper arms under his chain-studded jacket and an icy stare on his face.

This is the '50s of *Pop the Clutch: Thrilling Tales of Rockabilly, Monsters, and Hot Rod Horror*. This is your ticket to the dark side of American kitsch . . . the fun and frightful side!

"A fitting tribute to the 1950s with this 18-story compendium of hot rods, rock 'n' roll, and creature features come to life."

—*Publishers Weekly*

Order your copy at www.darkmoonbooks.com or www.amazon.com
ISBN-13: 978-0-9834335-9-0

ALSO FROM DARK MOON BOOKS:

Death. Who has not considered their own mortality and wondered at what awaits, once our frail human shell expires? What occurs after the heart stops beating, after the last breath is drawn, after life as we know it terminates?

Does our spirit remain on Earth while the body rots? Do the remnants of our soul transcend to a celestial Heaven or sink to Hell's torment? Can we choose our own afterlife? Can we die again in the hereafter? Are we given the opportunity to reincarnate and do it all over? Is life merely a cosmic joke or is it an experiment for something greater? Enclosed in this Bram Stoker-award winning anthology are thirty-four all-new dark and speculative fiction stories exploring the possibilities *AFTER DEATH . . .*

Illustrated by Audra Phillips and including stories by: **Steve Rasnic Tem**, **Bentley Little**, **John Langan**, **Simon Clark**, **Lisa Morton**, **Joe McKinney**, **Ray Cluley**, **David Tallerman**, and exceptional others.

"Though the majority of the pieces come from the darker side of the genre, a solid minority are playful, clever, or full of wonder. This strong anthology is sure to make readers contemplative even while it creates nightmares."

—*Publishers Weekly*

"In Eric J. Guignard's latest anthology he gathers some of the biggest and most talented authors on the planet to give us their take on this entertaining and perplexing subject matter . . . highly recommended."

—*Famous Monsters of Filmland*

"An excellent collection of imaginative tales of what waits beyond the veil."

—*Amazing Stories Magazine*

Order your copy at www.darkmoonbooks.com or www.amazon.com
ISBN-13: 978-0-9885569-2-8

ALSO FROM DARK MOON BOOKS:

Darkness exists everywhere, and in no place greater than those where spirits and curses still reside. Tread not lightly on ancient lands that have been discovered by this collection of intrepid authors.

In **DARK TALES OF LOST CIVILIZATIONS**, you will unearth an anthology of twenty-five previously unpublished horror and speculative fiction stories, relating to aspects of civilizations that are crumbling, forgotten, rediscovered, or perhaps merely spoken about in great and fearful whispers.

What is it that lures explorers to distant lands where none have returned? Where is Genghis Khan buried? What happened to Atlantis? Who will displace mankind on Earth? What laments have the Witches of Oz? Answers to these mysteries and other tales are presented within this critically acclaimed anthology.

Including stories by: **Joe R. Lansdale, David Tallerman, Jonathan Vos Post, Jamie Lackey, Aaron J. French**, and twenty exceptional others.

"The stories range from mildly disturbing to downright terrifying . . . Most are written in a conservative, suggestive style, relying on the reader's own imagination to take the plunge from speculation to horror."
—*Monster Librarian Reviews*

"Several of these stories made it on to my best of the year shortlist, and the book itself is now on the best anthologies of the year shortlist."
—*British Fantasy Society*

"Almost any story in this anthology is worth the price of purchase. The entire collection is a delight."
—*Black Gate Magazine*

**Order your copy at www.darkmoonbooks.com or www.amazon.com
ISBN-13: 978-0-9834335-9-0**

ALSO FROM DARK MOON BOOKS:

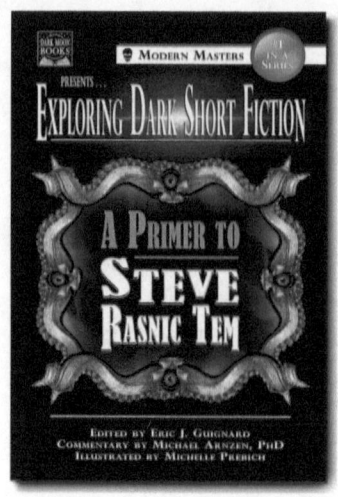

EXPLORING DARK SHORT FICTION #1: A PRIMER TO STEVE RASNIC TEM

For over four decades, Steve Rasnic Tem has been an acclaimed author of horror, weird, and sentimental fiction. Hailed by *Publishers Weekly* as "A perfect balance between the bizarre and the straight-forward" and *Library Journal* as "One of the most distinctive voices in imaginative literature," Steve Rasnic Tem has been read and cherished the world over for his affecting, genre-crossing tales.

Dark Moon Books and editor Eric J. Guignard bring you this introduction to his work, the first in a series of primers exploring modern masters of literary dark short fiction. Herein is a chance to discover—or learn more of—the rich voice of Steve Rasnic Tem, as beautifully illustrated by artist Michelle Prebich.

Included within these pages are:
- Six short stories, one written exclusively for this book
- Author interview
- Complete bibliography
- Academic commentary by Michael Arnzen, PhD (former humanities chair and professor of the year, Seton Hill University)
- . . . and more!

Enter this doorway to the vast and fantastic: Get to know Steve Rasnic Tem.

Order your copy at www.darkmoonbooks.com or www.amazon.com
ISBN-13: 978-0-9988275-2-0

ALSO FROM DARK MOON BOOKS:

EXPLORING DARK SHORT FICTION #2: A PRIMER TO KAARON WARREN

Australian author Kaaron Warren is widely recognized as one of the leading writers today of speculative and dark short fiction. She's published four novels, multiple novellas, and well over one hundred heart-rending tales of horror, science fiction, and beautiful fantasy, and is the first author ever to simultaneously win all three of Australia's top speculative fiction writing awards (Ditmar, Shadows, and Aurealis awards for *The Grief Hole*).

Dark Moon Books and editor Eric J. Guignard bring you this introduction to her work, the second in a series of primers exploring modern masters of literary dark short fiction. Herein is a chance to discover—or learn more of—the distinct voice of Kaaron Warren, as beautifully illustrated by artist Michelle Prebich.

Included within these pages are:
- Six short stories, one written exclusively for this book
- Author interview
- Complete bibliography
- Academic commentary by Michael Arnzen, PhD (former humanities chair and professor of the year, Seton Hill University)
- . . . and more!

Enter this doorway to the vast and fantastic: Get to know Kaaron Warren.

Order your copy at www.darkmoonbooks.com or www.amazon.com
ISBN-13: 978-0-9989383-0-1

ALSO FROM DARK MOON BOOKS:

EXPLORING DARK SHORT FICTION #3:
A PRIMER TO NISI SHAWL

Praised by both literary journals and leading fiction magazines, Nisi Shawl is celebrated as an author whose works are lyrical and philosophical, speculative and far-ranging; "...broad in ambition and deep in accomplishment" (*The Seattle Times*). Besides nearly three decades of creating fantasy and science fiction, fairy tales, and indigenous stories, Nisi has also been lauded as editor, journalist, and proponent of feminism, African-American fiction, and other pedagogical issues of diversity.

Dark Moon Books and editor Eric J. Guignard bring you this introduction to her work, the third in a series of primers exploring modern masters of literary dark short fiction. Herein is a chance to discover—or learn more of—the vibrant voice of Nisi Shawl, as beautifully illustrated by artist Michelle Prebich.

Included within these pages are:
- Six short stories, one written exclusively for this book
- Author interview
- Complete bibliography
- Academic commentary by Michael Arnzen, PhD (former humanities chair and professor of the year, Seton Hill University)
- ...and more!

Enter this doorway to the vast and fantastic: Get to know Nisi Shawl.

Order your copy at www.darkmoonbooks.com or www.amazon.com
ISBN-13: 978-0-9989383-4-9

ALSO FROM DARK MOON BOOKS:

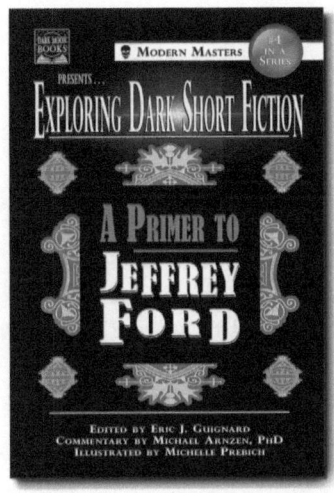

EXPLORING DARK SHORT FICTION #4: A PRIMER TO JEFFREY FORD

Author of the fantastic and the bizarre, Jeffrey Ford's work has won awards and acclaim across the globe for his stories of humor, horror, and unconventional beauty. "Powerful and disturbing in the best possible way" (*Gawker*) and "Intensely engaging" (*Publishers Weekly*), Ford crosses speculative genres with literary ideals, which has earned him the World Fantasy Award (seven times), the Shirley Jackson Award (four times), the Edgar Allan Poe Award, and France's vaunted *Grand Prix de l'Imaginaire*.

Dark Moon Books and editor Eric J. Guignard bring you this introduction to his work, the fourth in a series of primers exploring modern masters of literary dark short fiction. Herein is a chance to discover—or learn more of—the extraordinary voice of Jeffrey Ford, as beautifully illustrated by artist Michelle Prebich.

Included within these pages are:
- Six short stories, one written exclusively for this book
- Author interview
- Complete bibliography
- Academic commentary by Michael Arnzen, PhD (former humanities chair and professor of the year, Seton Hill University)
- . . . and more!

Enter this doorway to the vast and fantastic: Get to know Jeffrey Ford.

Order your copy at www.darkmoonbooks.com or www.amazon.com
ISBN-13: 978-0-9989383-8-7

ALSO FROM GENE O'NEILL AND DARK MOON BOOKS:

DOUBLE JACK

—Book #1 in the series, *THE CRIME FILES OF KATY GREEN*

The novella that started it all!

It's night, Sacramento, and single female drivers who break down on the side of Interstate-5 are relieved to see the highway safety CalTrans truck arrive to give assistance... until they realize that's not what the 400-pound ex-boxer who gets out has in mind...

Such is the M.O. of serial killer, Jack Malenko, who preys on women in distress in full sight of passing traffic. Assigned to the notorious case are homicide detectives Katy Green and Johnny Cato, dubbed by the press as Sacramento's "Green Hornet and Cato." However, from the beginning of this case, the two detectives seem to continually be one step behind their huge killer... and each day that passes brings worse news and fresh victims.

How fast can they track down the predatory monster to save further lives, and if they do find him, can they save their own lives in the violent encounter?

Discover why readers have been applauding this stark, fast-paced noir series by multiple-award-winning author, Gene O'Neill! Read *DOUBLE JACK* and then continue the shocking case files of Sacramento's "Green Hornet and Cato":

- **THE CRIME FILES OF KATY GREEN #2: SHADOW OF THE DARK ANGEL**

- **THE CRIME FILES OF KATY GREEN #3: DEATHFLASH**

- **THE CRIME FILES OF KATY GREEN #4: A STICK OF DOUBLEMINT**

Order your copy at www.darkmoonbooks.com or www.amazon.com
ISBN-13: 978-0-9988275-6-8

ALSO FROM GENE O'NEILL AND DARK MOON BOOKS:

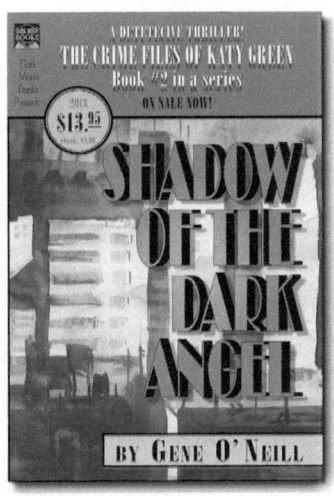

SHADOW OF THE DARK ANGEL

—Book #2 in the series, *THE CRIME FILES OF KATY GREEN*

Samuel Kubiak has severe issues. A distraught survivor of the California Foster Care System, he suffers from a condition of alopecia, incessant bullying, and a bizarre sexual frustration... But just as life seems its worst, he's visited by a dark guardian angel: One who whispers into his ear that by walking in His shadow, Samuel can avenge himself on all who have wronged him.

And so do a string of grisly murders begin to emerge across Sacramento, victims whose killer seems to have emerged from nowhere and left without leaving any clue.

Assigned to the gruesome case are homicide detectives Katy Green and Johnny Cato, dubbed by the press as Sacramento's "Green Hornet and Cato." There hasn't been a case yet they haven't solved, but now how can they track down a psychopathic suspect that comes and goes in the shadows?

Discover why readers have been applauding this stark, fast-paced noir series by multiple-award-winning author, Gene O'Neill! Read *SHADOW OF THE DARK ANGEL* and then continue the shocking case files of Sacramento's "Green Hornet and Cato":

- **THE CRIME FILES OF KATY GREEN #1: DOUBLE JACK (a novella)**

- **THE CRIME FILES OF KATY GREEN #3: DEATHFLASH**

- **THE CRIME FILES OF KATY GREEN #4: A STICK OF DOUBLEMINT**

Order your copy at www.darkmoonbooks.com or www.amazon.com
ISBN-13: 978-0-9988275-8-2

ALSO FROM GENE O'NEILL AND DARK MOON BOOKS:

A STICK OF DOUBLEMINT

—Book #4 in the series, ***THE CRIME FILES OF KATY GREEN***

On a warm San Francisco night, an innocent young woman is gunned down during a gang-related drive-by shooting. The overworked police department have no leads and no suspects, and seemingly little interest in pursuing yet another case involving ongoing gang violence. Then those involved in the shooting start turning up dead, with a stick of Doublemint gum in hand. What does it mean, and who's responsible?

A new detective is assigned to the case, and he quickly realizes he's going to need help to solve it, so turns to old friends, Katy Green and Johnny Cato, now part of a successful private investigation firm!

So begins a race against the clock to stop further murders and to discover the perpetrator. Can the investigating duo, dubbed by newspapers as "Green Hornet and Cato" solve this latest case of the vigilante killings, or will the culprit continue to bloody the city?

Discover why readers have been applauding this stark, fast-paced noir series by multiple-award-winning author, Gene O'Neill! Read ***DOUBLE JACK*** and then continue the shocking case files of Sacramento's "Green Hornet and Cato":

- **THE CRIME FILES OF KATY GREEN #1: DOUBLE JACK (a novella)**
- **THE CRIME FILES OF KATY GREEN #2: SHADOW OF THE DARK ANGEL**
- **THE CRIME FILES OF KATY GREEN #3: DEATHFLASH**

Order your copy at www.darkmoonbooks.com or www.amazon.com
ISBN-13: 978-1-949491-18-0

ABOUT THE AUTHOR

Photograph by Jason V Brock

Gene O'Neill has seen over 175 of his stories and novellas published, several also reprinted in France, Spain, and Russia. Some of these stories have been collected in *Ghost Spirits, Computers & World Machines*; *The Grand Struggle*; *In Dark Corners*; *Dance of the Blue Lady*; *The Hitchhiking Effect*; and *Lethal Birds*. In addition, he's published six novels.

Gene has been a Bram Stoker Award® finalist twelve times. In 2010 *Taste of Tenderloin* won the haunted house for collection, and in 2012 *The Blue Heron* won for Long Fiction. Upcoming in 2017 are the four trade paperback versions of the *Cal Wild Chronicles* from Written Backwards Press, a number of short stories, and a novelette. A long novel, *The White Plague Chronicles*, is a work in progress, parts to an interested publisher.

Gene lives in the Napa Valley with his wife, Kay. He has two grown children, Gavin, who lives in Oakland, and Kaydee who lives in Carlsbad and rides herd on his two grandchildren, Fiona and TJ.

When he isn't writing or visiting grandchildren, Gene likes to read good fiction or watch sports—all of them, especially boxing.

www.ingramcontent.com/pod-product-compliance
Lightning Source LLC
Chambersburg PA
CBHW021005120726
47905CB00009B/2863